Courting Scandal

MOST IMPRUDENT MATCHES
BOOK ONE

ALLY HUDSON

Busy
Nothings
Books

Digital Edition ISBN: 979-8-9882181-0-4

Print Edition ISBN: 979-8-9882181-1-1

Cover design by Holly Perret, The Swoonies Romance Art

Copy and Line Editing by Rebecca Sanchez, Once Upon an Editor

Freelance Developmental Editing by Ann Leslie Tuttle

FIRST EDITION

To mom.
Confession: I used to read your Regency romance novels instead of doing my homework.

A fondness for reading, properly directed, must be an education in itself.

— JANE AUSTEN, *MANSFIELD PARK*

Courting Scandal

One

WAYLAND'S, LONDON - JANUARY 12, 1814

MICHAEL

DAMN IT ALL! Bleeding again. It was a wonder I had fingers left at this rate. I loathed this part of my work; spending hours buried under financial documents and transactions.

Opening a gaming hell. It had seemed so glamorous four years ago. The prospect had been full of amusement, riches, and a guaranteed disinheritance from certain, less than congenial, family members. I had precisely nothing to lose. And, over the last several years, reality mirrored my expectations precisely. Except for the ledgers; the ledgers had always been unbearable. And, as of this morning—the invitation—the invitation signified the end of all peace.

The heavy oak door flew open, banging against the opposite wall—nothing like a knock preceding the thunk and bits of plaster crumbling to the green carpet below. There was already a hole in the wall from the handle; Augie just made it larger. I could ignore the rudeness, and I could even be convinced to overlook the property damage. What I could not forgive were the two thick stacks of documents, tenuously balanced, one in each of his hands. "Augie, no..."

"Augie, yes. You requested these, remember?" As my second, Augie loved to actually fulfill the requests I made. It was his greatest flaw.

"I'm certain I didn't."

"I'm certain you did," he said, lifting the larger of the stacks above my desk. He dropped it from an unreasonable height with a resounding thunk that drowned out my pathetic whine.

"I'll never see the sunlight again."

"Likely not." He flopped the second stack with slightly less fanfare. "You didn't request these, but you will when I explain the situation, so I brought them anyway."

"I very much doubt I'd ask for yet more paperwork. What is the concern?"

"Johnson and Samuels, on Saturday." The boxing match. Shillings and pounds have been pouring in for a fortnight. The ton was eager for blood and a good wager.

"What of it?"

"Johnson is heavily favored."

"I am aware...."

"So why is Westfield betting some £3,000 on Samuels?"

"Westfield?" The name was familiar, but I could not recall which degenerate *gentleman* responded to that title.

"Richard Dalton, Earl of Westfield." Dalton... sweaty, portly man with few funds and even less luck.

"Dalton has £3,000 to wager?"

"I very much doubt it." Augie flipped through the pages in front of me before pointing at an entry. "See here, that's nearly what he owes us. He's quite cleaned out."

"And these are his records?" I peered over the stack below, thumbing through pages warily.

"Had a Dunner bribe his solicitor personally."

"Which one?"

"Baldwin." That's good. He was competent. Wouldn't have bribed the wrong solicitor or drawn unwanted attention. I flipped through the pages halfheartedly, searching for something I knew wasn't there. Augie wouldn't have brought this to me if there was evidence that Dalton had the funds.

"Who let him place it?"

"Potter." I couldn't hold back a sigh at the name. I liked the man, and he had a family to feed. But he has been gulled by everyone who walks past. At least I was confident he wasn't part of any havey-cavey business with Dalton. He wasn't smart enough to have made this mess intentionally.

"Alright, I'll deal with that later. I assume you've already located Johnson?"

"Of course."

"Why is my name on the building and not yours, Augie?"

"I've no idea, but the carriage is ready for you." I gathered my hat and great coat to ward against the winter chill before leading him out.

"Humble as always, Augie. Are you coming?"

"Of course. Someone will need to call for a surgeon after Johnson is through with you if you're wrong."

"If I'm wrong? You're the one who caught it!"

"I have no idea what you're talking about, sir. I'm just a lowly superintendent." He added that just before settling in the carriage, leaving me to clamber in after. Lowly my arse.

"Wonderful. After Johnson is finished physically beating me within an inch of my life, I'm to dine at Grayson House tonight. Agatha can handle the emotional torture."

"Why on earth are you dining there?"

"I received an invitation this morning. Apparently, Hugh's new wife comes from some sort of happy family. Whatever that is. Seems to think forced proximity is sufficient to encourage familial congeniality."

3

"And you're sure she meant to invite you? Not Tom?"

"Tom will be there also."

"At least you'll have one ally."

"I was hoping for two." I drew the last word out, waiting for him to make the connection.

"No, absolutely not."

"Augie..."

"No. Besides, if you're dining out, someone needs to watch the play."

"I'm given to understand that Anna has taken over as lady's maid for the new viscountess... I'm certain her hair is still pretty, and she retains that scent of pastry you find so alluring."

"I told you that in confidence." His tone was sharp, reproachful, but there was always an undercurrent of fondness whenever Anna was mentioned.

"You were soused when you told me that."

"Soused is a kind of confidence. What time?" An exasperated sigh accompanied the reply. I hid my smile; he wouldn't appreciate it.

"Seven." Before he could question me further about Anna's situation, we shuddered to a stop outside Johnson's training ground.

Once inside the training room, Augie was content to linger in the shadows forged by the roped-off ring. I left him to approach Johnson at the heavy bag alone.

The man was an intimidating three hands taller than me and nearly five stone heavier. His appearance was slightly worse for his profession; his ears resembled cruciferous vegetables, and more than a few teeth were long gone. Still, we'd enjoyed a drink and each other's company in the past. There was every possibility that Augie's offer for a surgeon would be unnecessary.

Unfortunately, I miscalculated how much the repeated

blows had impacted Johnson's hearing. My approach startled the man. The last thing I saw was a massive fist aimed right at my eye.

~

I WAS ALIVE. That much was obvious. Whether it was a good thing remained to be seen.

Hot, thick, agony burned along the right side of my face and jaw. The pain radiated just below my eye, throbbing in time to my heartbeat. Nausea swept over me in waves. Indistinct muttering swirled around me, indistinguishable amid the roar of my angry blood as it rushed through my ears.

A hiss escaped me when someone pressed a wet cloth to the laceration. A sharp, astringent stinging released into the wound, running up into my eye for added insult. It was brandy judging by the smell. They could at least sit me up before burning my eye out.

I gave words a try. "What the devil are you putting that in my eye for? Drinking it's the only thing that will help."

My speech must have been somewhat comprehensible because I heard Augie say, "He'll live. Help him up."

Too many hands worried over me, sliding under my shoulder to wrench me from my place on the floor. The nausea that had dissipated in my distraction returned with a tidal wave. My innards threatened to make themselves my outtards. Outtards—probably not a word. The sour, sick taste filled my mouth, mixing with the copper tang of blood, distract from my musings.

A cool glass found its way into my right hand. Smart glass. I took a grateful sip, choking when brandy found the ragged cut inside my cheek and stung it. "You were right, Augie."

"I think we need to call a surgeon. He's concussed."

"Hilarious, Augie. Help me stand?" It was likely a poor

idea, but the floor was cold, damp, and smelled of sweat, blood, and other various fluids I didn't care to consider just now.

Several pairs of hands assisted me, and finally I was righted. I took another sip of the brandy, ignoring the immediate bite in hopes of future relief. They deposited me in a nearby chair before Johnson crowded over me—all apologies.

"It's my fault, Johnson. There's no reason to apologize. I shouldn't have startled you."

"I'm still sorry, Mr. Wayland. I should have stopped quicker."

"I think if you could stop quicker, you would be pulling your punches. We certainly don't want that happening Saturday, do we?" He froze. It was unnerving, unnatural, seeing someone that large so still, particularly out of just one eye.

He jerked into motion just as suddenly, settling into the seat across from me. "Who told you?"

Now I was grateful for my wound. He would be less forthcoming were he not already wrestling guilt for the punch. Not so grateful, that I rejected the refill of brandy from Augie's outstretched hand.

"The numbers told me. Westfield isn't bright enough to spread his bookings out across multiple purses."

"Damn."

"What did he offer you?"

"£350."

"You're undervaluing your honor. He wagered £3,000 against you."

He shifted his gaze to his feet, shuffling them uneasily.

"How's £1,500 for a fair fight?" His head shot up at my offer. He stared at me in disbelief. "That and an agreement that you come to me if someone tries to fix one of your matches again. I guarantee I can beat their offer."

His agreement was almost comical in its enthusiasm.

"Alright then, we're agreed. And not a word of this to Dalton, yes?" His nod was solemn. Agreement in place, I swallowed the last of my brandy before heading off to ready for supper, wishing the man luck as I departed. I considered bringing the bottle. After all, it could only improve the evening.

Two

MICHAEL

TRAFFIC WAS FAR TOO light for my taste. The carriage rattled down South Street with ease. Where was a carriage accident when you needed one?

Faced with the promise of seeing the lovely Anna, Augie put more care into his dress than usual. As far as I knew, he hadn't seen her since his father died some time ago. He was unusually reticent in the carriage. It was a slight inconvenience; I was counting on his insubordination and back talk to soothe my own unease. Four years' absence from the Park Street residence had not been nearly long enough.

I hadn't missed the place. I hadn't particularly missed my middle brother either. Every day without my spiteful shrew of a stepmother, Agatha, was a precious gift to be cherished. My youngest brother, Tom, was the exception to my general familial disdain.

As the eldest, the London house and the Kent estate should have fallen to me after the viscount's death more than a decade ago. Unfortunately, my... slightly dubious parentage ensured that the properties, fortune, and title all fell to the oldest *legitimate* son, Hugh. Recently married Hugh.

I was about to make a fine first impression on his wife too. "Darling wife, please meet my degenerate elder brother. He's a gambling magnate. He's bankrupted half of the ton. I swear both his eyes opened when we last spoke."

And then there was *Agatha*. Although I would be quite happy never to set eyes—or eye. as the case may be—on the woman again, a small part of me was looking forward to the fit of apoplexy she'd display at the sight of me. With any luck, it would actually kill her.

All too soon, the carriage clattered to a stop. I scrambled out with Augie close behind. He stared at the house with slightly less antipathy than I did. The imposing black-painted, double doors, framed by the harsh archway, stared back at me, taunting me. Centered beneath the redbrick and Grecian-style columns of the rooms above, the house was every bit as ostentatious as I remembered.

"Are you going in the front or the back?" Augie asked. That was the question. I *should* enter through the front as an invited guest, even if I'd rather dine below with Augie, Anna, and the others.

With a sigh, I replied, "I suppose I should knock. Did we determine a distress signal?"

"We did not, and I won't be rescuing you. I will be wooing Anna with my handsome countenance and vast wealth. You're not to interrupt. You might distract her with your wealth and countenance."

"That seems unlikely, but I wish you the best of luck. Two quick rings of the bell followed by two slow then?"

"I'll leave you to rot."

"Good luck with your wooing. Don't forget to invite me to the wedding."

Augie scampered off eagerly down the side alley to the

servants' entrance, leaving me with the chafing prospect of knocking on the door to the home I'd funded for seven years. Eventually, I managed the several steps to the door, suddenly regretting my decision to limit myself to two glasses of brandy with Johnson. I knocked before I lost my nerve.

Weston, the butler, opened the door with all due cere-mony—until he saw me. His polite greeting was cut abruptly with the recognition, and he hauled me in the house with one hand, embracing me with the other. The uncharacteristic affection soothed the last of my nerves, and I returned it freely.

I was about to ask after his family when I heard a throaty, feminine "Oh," from off to the side. "You must be Michael... Mr. Wayland, I mean. I'm Kate, I mean, Lady Katherine."

I turned from Weston to face her. The woman before me was nothing like what I expected from my brother. The first surprise was her size. She was quite short, but what she lacked in height, she made up for in curves. With skin too pale and eyes and lips too big for her face, she was the exact opposite of the ton's ideal. And her introduction, far easier of manner and less demure than I expected from Hugh's choice. I offered her a respectful bow before the man himself stepped into the entry, presumably in search of his wife.

My brother and I had communicated solely through letters and solicitors in recent years. I wasn't prepared for the sight of him. He was a gangly lad of eighteen when I handed the estate and ledgers over to him. He had filled out in the interim, grown into his height. He had several inches on me now and likely a full stone. It was all muscle. His hair was as dark as mine but straighter and cropped closer to his head. Of my brothers, my complexion was the darkest, a golden tone. Hugh's eyes were a dark gray in sharp contrast to my brown. He had always *fit* in the ton in a way I'd never managed. Still, the resemblance between Hugh, Tom, and myself was unmistakable. Despite my father's best efforts to label me as a ward, there was no question of our relation.

Hugh towered over his diminutive wife, hand resting possessively on the small of her back as he outstretched the other toward me.

"Hugh, good to see you," I said.

Instead of a greeting, I was met with a flustered response. "What on earth happened to your eye?" I had honestly forgotten the dull throbbing until Hugh's outburst.

It was a stupid question given my profession. But faced with Hugh's disapproving face, I couldn't help myself. "Do you know, it was the strangest thing. I was promenading in Hyde Park, as I like to do. Out of nowhere, this enormous swan dove straight from the sky at me. Beak first! Went right for my eye. Honestly, it's a miracle I wasn't killed."

His stern slash of a mouth was evidence of his irritation, but his viscountess's giggle reminded him of her presence and somewhat endeared her to me.

"Kate, this is my brother Michael. Michael, this is Lady Katherine Grayson, my wife."

"Pleasure to meet you, Lady Katherine."

"Oh, do call me Kate! I've always wanted more brothers, and now I have two to add to Kit."

I barely managed to cover my derisive snort with a cough. Still, I detected no lie in her countenance. She genuinely seemed to believe this farce of a meal was all that was needed to bring us together. If her efforts were directed toward anyone else, I would find them charming. Toward me, they were just an annoyance.

Weston gave a pointed cough, and Kate finally remembered to invite me into the drawing room for drinks before supper.

Even in the hall, I could hear the shrill protestations of the dowager viscountess. I pitied whichever servant was receiving her wrath. Pausing for a fortifying breath at the threshold of the drawing room, I considered my escape options. Weston, sensing my hesitation, gave me a sharp thunk on the back with his fist. I collapsed into the room in an ungainly pile of limbs. Righting myself, I closed the double doors and shot the man a glare for his efforts. He merely grinned in return with a cheeky wave.

Resolutely, I turned to face Agatha for the first time in four years. Distracted as she was by her abuse of the footman, I had a moment to take in my surroundings. The drawing room had been redone; likely the new viscountess's doing. The wall coverings and carpetings were now a soft pink color with beige accents. Far more tasteful than in Agatha's day. I believe she also added wall sconces, resulting in a brighter and more welcoming room.

The footman Agatha was berating from her position on the settee was new. She screeched at the poor lad, something about a failure to provide plates in lieu of napkins for the nuts placed on the center table.

She caught sight of her daughter-in-law, and her ire shifted. I watched the poor girl actually shrink under the weight of Agatha's displeased gaze. She was much too short to lose any further height.

"I suppose in the backwater county you hail from, they eat out of their hands like rodents?" Agatha's sardonic tone was more subtle than the one she reserved for me, but I could see the girl flinch as the barb landed. The answering silence stretched a moment too long. It became clear that Hugh had no intention of checking his mother. I was left to rescue his bride myself.

Fortunately, it took only my presence to thoroughly distract Agatha from her replacement's inferior hosting efforts. With a bow, I addressed her in my most deferential tone. "Good evening. It's a pleasure to see you again. I hope you're in fine health."

Agatha's indignant attention swung to me, and Kate offered a grateful smile in return. The smile was soon wiped away, replaced with horror as the full extent of my stepmother's hatred became apparent.

Agatha's address was filled with all the venom she possessed. "What are you doing here?" Ah, so no one told her to expect me. Even better.

"I was invited."

She turned back to Kate. "Who would do that? Katherine? Did you invite this knave into my home?"

The girl moved to answer, but I discouraged her with a surreptitious shake of the head.

"I was led to believe this was a family gathering, your ladyship. I am family, am I not?"

"You are not! You're nothing but a street urchin my husband took pity on. And look how that turned out. A villain, stealing the fortunes of respectable gentlemen, preying on their good natures!" Her pitch grew higher in anger, each word more shrill than the last. "I should have had you thrown from the house when I first arrived, sent back to the sewers with the rats where you belong."

Kate's eyes had gotten impossibly wider, as though they'd filled with tears. It was difficult to discern from the distance with only one working eye.

Hugh had just sighed, turning to the drink tray when I first addressed his mother. He drained a glass of something expensive in a single gulp before refilling it, pouring a second, and passing it to me. I swallowed it down—scotch. This time I relished the burn in my cheek. There was a second where I hoped that maybe, just this once, Hugh would curb his mother's tirade. As usual, I was left disappointed.

When no help from his quarter appeared forthcoming, I

replied with forced casualness. "But they're so easy to steal from. I'll do my best not to spread fleas over the furnishings while I'm here, Agatha." She hated few things more than when I addressed her so casually, and her wordless huff satisfied something sick inside me.

From the corner of my eye, Kate made a motion to intervene. Luckily for all involved, Tom chose that moment to make an appearance.

My youngest brother was blessed with the kind of jovial manners and open countenance that are universally beloved. While he was still at Eton and Cambridge, I visited him often. He was the only member of my family who took pains to visit my establishment, once he reached an appropriate age, of course.

He was only seven when the viscount died, and I sometimes felt he was more son than brother. Fortunately or unfortunately, depending on the moment, his conviviality often meant he was forced to act as buffer between Agatha and me. Hugh and I could usually maintain a polite, if stilted, discourse on our own.

Everyone in the room, at least those who held a title other than dowager viscountess, was desperate for a cease-fire. We mutually seized on Tom's presence to diffuse the tension. Used to this, Tom greeted everyone affably. It seemed he had grown more in the month or so since I last saw him. He was several inches taller than even Hugh. Unlike Hugh, he hadn't managed to grow into his limbs yet. His hair was lighter than ours, and he left it in too-long curls. This, combined with his enthusiastic manner, often reminded me of an overeager spaniel puppy. My fondness for him was the sole reason I retained any contact with my family.

"What happened to your eye, brother?" Unlike Hugh, Tom's question seemed to be born of genuine concern. Tom never hesitated to refer to me by our relation. Hugh steadfastly refused to refer to me as anything other than "Michael," denying me the distinction of family.

"Satin shortage at the modiste."

Tom's agreeable laughter was infectious. His easy manner lessened some of the tension brought by Agatha's displeasure.

"Lucky you survived the fray then," he added.

"I even avoided bleeding on the white lace."

Before he could retort, the poor footman, so recently escaped and still weary from his recent abuse, was thrust back into the lion's den to inform us that supper was served. The dining room, had been redecorated in my absence. Agatha's ostentatious crimson and gold had been replaced with an airy cream and sage. Kate must have ordered the leaves removed from the table. The intimidating sixteen-person place setting on which her predecessor insisted, was shortened to seat just six. Her efforts were a substantial improvement.

What followed our entry into the dining room could only be described as the most beautifully choreographed dance I ever had the pleasure to witness. Footmen, both new, waited at the seats reserved for the viscountess at the foot and dowager in the middle. Agatha approached the foot of the table to the left of the man and made a sound that was half grunt, half pointed hacking cough to remind him to pull the chair for her. At the same moment, Kate approached the footman's other side. The man, clearly used to this display, pulled out the chair and simultaneously shifted it to the side that Kate occupied. She slipped in elegantly, leaving Agatha to scoff and stomp toward her designated seat in the middle of the table, across from Tom.

I grabbed the glass of wine at my place and toasted in Kate's direction while Agatha fussed in her spot. She bit her lip to hold back a laugh. It was then that I determined that she was quite too good for my brother.

With my first sip of Mrs. Hudson's winter squash soup,

my cold heart warmed slightly. That woman was the finest cook in all of England, I was quite certain of it. Even Agatha could find nothing in the meal about which to complain. Instead, she reserved her barbs for Kate and me. Tom was in fine form, though, ready with a new subject at every opportunity; the weather, the upcoming ball, the latest gossip, the play showing at Drury Lane.

Rather than separating after supper, leaving poor Kate to Agatha's clutches undefended, I chose to beg off. Partially in hopes that Agatha's desire for Tom's company would outweigh her desire to harass her new daughter. But mainly in a desperate need for escape. Instead of seeing myself out as I indicated, I slipped down to the kitchens.

There I found Augie, entirely in his cups, performing some act that *might* be construed as wooing—if one tilted his head and squinted. Whatever it was, Anna seemed to be enjoying it as she giggled at his antics.

They were surrounded by a few familiar faces. Weston and Mrs. Hudson remained, Mary, too, now an upstairs maid, survived from my tenure. All the other maids and footmen were new.

With little warning, Mrs. Hudson wrapped me in her arms, squeezing tight. I had missed her desperately, and her embrace soothed the tension that Agatha's presence had wrought. Anna's subsequent hug was as welcome as her mother's. Always a beautiful girl, she was now a stunning woman with long red hair and a figure to be envied. Though I felt nothing more than brotherly affection for her, I understood Augie's fascination on an intellectual level.

The kitchen was the same as ever. Large counters for meal preparation and a massive cooking fireplace overtook the room's front half. The back was centered with a long wooden table, with matching benches alongside it for staff to eat.

I made myself comfortable at the worn table of my child-hood, and a small ale appeared in my hand, courtesy of Mrs. Hudson. "What happened to your eye, young man?" No matter my age, I remained "young man" to her. She fussed over my injury, placing a cool rag over my eye and tutting in a motherly tone. Her ministrations and the drink went a long way toward improving my foul temper after supper.

"I was knocked out by Johnson." My tone was slightly boastful, but frankly, I was hit by Daniel Johnson and lived to tell it. Anna rolled her eyes, but the new footmen were suitably impressed. Arguably the best of bare-knuckle boxers, a punch from Johnson could knock out a seasoned opponent. Surviving an undefended fist from the man was a feat to be celebrated.

Augie produced a deck of cards from somewhere, and I began to teach the younger footmen and maids to play crib-bage. All the while, Mrs. Hudson plied me with more apple tarts than were likely safe to consume. Clearly made by her and not her daughter, they were good but not the exceptional quality of Anna's. She was the natural baker.

"I should see to Lady Kate. Tom will be gone by now, and she'll want to escape." Anna seemed genuinely concerned for her employer.

"Does Hugh never check Agatha?"

"Never. She has made the poor girl cry more than once, and they only returned from their honeymoon a month ago. I could throttle him for his disinterest. I understand no one wants to scold his own mother, but he married Kate. His alle-giance should be to her. Especially since she's been nothing but sweet to that woman."

With Anna's retreat, Augie was more inclined to let the evening close. The crush would be starting at Wayland's for the after-dinner hour, and I should be there to supervise. Since my superintendent was in no shape to work this evening, it would undoubtedly fall to me. I heaved him up and out the back, down to the waiting carriage. Accompanied by Augie's drunken snores, I watched through the window as the house faded away into the distance.

Three

JULIET

WAS THAT A HOLE? Had I actually worn a hole in the carpet? I bent down, inspecting further—no it was father's cigar burn from a few years ago. Still, the pacing must stop, the formerly crimson rug was threadbare as it was; it did not require my assistance.

It was a wonder I had not worn the carpet down to strings these last days. Pacing, tapping, fluttering about; I did it all. With my stomach flipping, sinking, tossing every which way, and my heart stopping, pounding, and rushing, I was all but useless. If only I had a name for the pangs of guilt and unease, a cause. But there was nothing.

Three days ago, I blamed the jitters on the anticipation of my entry into society. But that was still weeks away, and there was no reason to expect it would be an eventful presentation. I would attract some notice as the daughter of an earl, of course. There were always title hunters. But I was just short of the label of spinster at two and twenty, which would certainly give some members of the ton pause. I was pretty enough. I would even go so far as to say my eyes were a striking shade of blue, but nothing particularly out of the ordinary. My dowry was certain to attract no notice at all. And, of course, there was the other concern... No, I mustn't think on that.

Worse still, whatever inexplicable disquiet had overcome me seemed to have spread to the entire household. Our footmen perpetually hovered just out of sight, straightening uniforms. Hannah, our maid, scrubbed the unused silver twice in a week. It was as though we were circus performers on one of those tight ropes, desperate to maintain the balance. My unease, my restless dread, was contagious—I was one misstep away from sending us all plummeting to our doom.

I was not a stranger to the feeling, but it had rarely been this extreme. The unnamed sense of dread, a twisted combination of sourceless guilt and uncertainty, called my periphery home. It may have been my oldest companion. I could not recall a time when I was without it. But this, this was beyond reason or convention. Something was coming. Soon.

My father made himself scarce throughout my turmoil. The only evidence of his existence were the missing tumblers each morning, presumably locked in his office. An ungenerous part of me laid the blame at his feet. But his presence was usually required to extract a price this high.

Day and night, I fought for some useful occupation. For months, I spent hours each day updating my late stepmother's gowns to fit and suit. When father balked at my request for a line of credit at the modiste, I took matters into my own hands. I began letting out hems and pulling in busts. It was a substantial undertaking as Sophie's gowns were suited to a married woman. They were darker in color and heavier in fabric than is appropriate for a debutant. Also, her lengthy confinement and subsequent illness meant they had all seen several seasons. But with this never-ending agitation, even the simplest of hems resulted in frustration, blood, and an uneven line. For every stitch I made, I had to rip two out and begin again. I was actively losing ground.

Even with all my fretting and vigilance, I was unprepared when the inevitable happened. A tentative knock at my sitting room door startled me, and I pricked my finger with the needle. Hannah poked her head around the open entry. "Your father is looking for you. He's in the study, my lady."

And I knew.

Blood ripped from my extremities, leaving them chilled and tremulous. My heart stopped before resuming its pounding with a vengeance. Air trapped in my lungs as they hitched, and my chest tightened with the pressure. I couldn't breathe! My vision blackened to a pinhole. Sound drowned in the rushing of my ears. Desperately, I fought to remember Sophie's words. Sophie. Remember....

Count! Sophie said to count breaths. One, two, three, four, five on inhale. Five, four, three, two, one on exhale. It took two attempts before my vision cleared. The rushing in my ears shifted to a more manageable ringing. Five, four, three, two—exhale. Three more counts before my lungs obeyed of their own volition. My chest was still hot and tight but leaving father waiting would do more harm than good.

HOW MANY HOURS had passed staring at this door over the course of my life? Carved and chipping slightly at the edges, it remained perpetually closed and typically locked. It served as one final opportunity to count my breaths before knocking. Hands still unsteady, I managed to gather the will to knock.

"Enter," Father said. His tone was lighter than I anticipated. It was incongruous with the turmoil inside me and, if possible, made my agitation worse.

With a final, fortifying breath, I turned the cool metal

handle and stepped inside the study as he commanded. "You asked for me, Father?"

The room was familiar, though I spent little time here. It was heavy with deep midnight purple fabrics, dark woods with ostentatious golden accents, and an overwrought fireplace. As usual, father was flipping distractedly through the day's paper, feet propped on the clean desk—he must have had Hannah remove the glasses before summoning me. His workspace was always clear. For a study, there were always remarkably few documents, ledgers, or books. What father lacked in paperwork, he more than compensated for in liquor. The shelf behind him to the left of the fireplace was well stocked with all the drink a gentleman of leisure might require (and quite a bit more).

The racing results clearly held more interest than whatever he had summoned me to discuss. Without permission to sit, I was left to hover in silence between the door and the desk.

Drat! Must not pick at fingernails. I never knew what to do with my hands when he left me to stand. The perfectly ordinary limbs suddenly became ungainly and unruly in his presence. They developed a mind of their own, battling against one another, drawing blood.

Father found such displays of unease unladylike, and torn and bitten cuticles were repulsive and symptomatic of ill-breeding. Agh! They had moved together once more, nails catching on the callus of my ring finger where my embroidery needle always landed, digging, scraping.

I moved to clasp both hands behind my back, striving to keep the movement slow and purposeful to avoid unwanted attention. His paper lowered slowly with a rustle—not as subtle as I had hoped then.

He eyed me warily, as though searching for whatever misdeed he had sensed. Finding nothing obvious from his slow appraisal, he set the pages aside. "We are to dine with a friend of mine tonight."

I kept my face carefully blank, determined that my eyes would betray none of my shock. I had never been invited to a dinner with him. He continued, "His Grace, Alexander Hasket, the Duke of Rosehill."

Oh. The puzzle pieces clicked into place with a sickening snap. My chest tightened once more, and I fought to keep my expression unchanged.

I mulled over my words for several seconds, but a weak "I see..." was all I could summon. I was, however, able to get a significant grip on the callous, tugging with more force.

Dark eyes, yellowed at the edges, squinted beneath wire-rimmed glasses, scrutinizing me once more, "Do you see?"

"I believe so, sir." As I picked at a bit of skin, I laced my fingers together behind me, trapping them against one another.

"He is seeking a wife this season. This dinner is to see if you suit his needs."

Silently, I counted to five on inhale and back down on exhale, trying to suppress the noticeable rise and fall of my chest.

"I understand."

"You are to show yourself to the greatest advantage. I expect you to be poised, agreeable, graceful, and affable." I nodded in understanding, but it was insufficient. "If you blunder this evening, I will never forgive you. There is no world in which you could aspire to a greater match. It is a miracle I was able to convince him to see you."

My gaze slipped just over his right shoulder during this speech. It was no less hurtful for its familiarity, and I knew from experience that if I listened to the words, the placid, closed-mouthed smile painted on my face would slip.

However, if I was paying insufficient attention, the speech

would quadruple in length. I wished with all my heart that the words would stop stinging every time I heard them. Awareness of my own failings did not lessen the pain my father's acknowledgment caused.

Fingers behind my back fought for freedom but I laced them tighter. I forced a quick count before responding, fearing tears if I forsook the effort. "I understand. I am so grateful for your efforts on my behalf. I will do my best to make you proud." His answering snort was derisive and somehow more hurtful than any words he could have offered.

I made a quick curtsy and turned to escape before he could add anything else devastating, fleeing to the safety of my room.

I COLLAPSED ON THE BED, desperately counting breaths in and out until the emotion dissipated.

It took several minutes before I was sufficiently calm. I approached my closet with trepidation. What did one wear to dine with a duke, a future husband?

My hard-won composure lasted only long enough to recognize there were only three options that could possibly suit such an engagement, one of which wasn't nearly finished. I pulled out my favorite piece first, a floaty periwinkle gown to which I had added delicate gold embroidery to the under-bodice and hem.

No! There were small tucks and snags where I pulled the threads too tight. Had my hoop been loose? It was unnotice-able, perhaps, to the untrained eye, but unacceptable for a duke.

The only remaining alternative was a sage silk gown. I struggled to don it without the help of Hannah. The fasten-ings tangled, knotting in my hair. I had not rung for her earlier, wishing to spare her my hysteria. Her duties were that of three maids anyway; she did not need to add soothing a panicked employer to the list. I managed to drag the gown over layers of petticoat, corset, and chemise. Once on, I could see that the hem was slightly uneven. It could conceivably be excused as a fold of the dress.

In my earlier distress, my pale skin had adopted a horribly unfashionable flush. It was not limited to my cheeks but had spread all the way down my chest, below the edge of my gown. My hair seemed to be making a sincere effort to embody the chaos inside. The dark curls had slipped their coiffure and were plotting an escape from my head entirely. With no effort to keep my hair attached to my head, I yanked the trapped pins out roughly before forcefully ripping a brush through the tangles. Hannah was better at this. I, on the other hand, had little patience for their misbehavior.

A quarter of an hour passed in a similar fashion before Hannah found me and took the brush from me. She refused to return it and began to work through the snarls more gently. Eventually, she managed to gather it into some sort of order and pinned it into a passable chignon. The style was out of date, but my hair was keener to obey the coil than the high tight ringlets that were so popular now.

Distracted by my hair, the flush receded and remained only in my cheeks. It was a passably pretty effect. When Hannah pointed out the hour, I was forced to make do with passable.

There was a small scuff on my slipper, but no time to correct it. All my efforts and I was about to dine with a duke. Apparently, "good enough" was the best showing I could make. The effort was less than promising.

And so it was, uneven hem, out-of-date coiffure, reddened face, and scuffed slipper, I was bundled into my father's carriage. Fortunately, the drive was short. My father used the time to comment on, not only these defects within my power to amend, but also those of my countenance, accomplishments, and general behavior.

He could not be constrained to recent faults and foibles either, instead sampling from my two and twenty years for available options. Though his efforts did little to curb my apprehensive nausea, they did much to ensure my gratitude on arrival. Peering up at the foreboding mansion, I felt all my earlier trepidation return. Unfortunately, my father felt none of it and did not hesitate to drag me to the door. Though I could not recall for certain, I suspected this behavior was the result of the aforementioned scuff. It was certainly responsible for the new one.

A WELL-DRESSED butler ushered us into the drawing room. There, I found myself faced with three of the most glamorous people I had ever seen. Until that moment, I had not realized I feared a gentleman older than my father; perhaps one who smelled of moldy cheese. Physically, this man—presumably His Grace—was quite ordinary. Average in height and weight. His dark hair swept high off his forehead in an unusual style and his brow was dark and heavy across his forehead, drawing attention to equally dark eyes. But the way he carried himself, it was unlike anything I had ever seen. He had long limbs which unfurled when he stood, greeting my father with a graceful nod. His apparel was unique, straight off the ship from Paris. Something I had never seen before; he wore all black, even his shirt, except for his white cravat and black-and-white brocade waistcoat. The effect was equal parts intimidating, fascinating, and intriguing.

He was accompanied by an older woman in the most unusual dress. It was made of vibrant white satin. Every inch below the bust was covered in black feathers of varying densities, lighter at the top before reaching peak thickness at the hem. Her powdered wig, which added nearly a foot in height, was topped with a solitary black feather, extending it yet another several inches. On anyone else, the gown and wig would have been the subject of ridicule, but she carried them well.

There was also a younger woman, barely more than a girl. Only she had chosen a color, a rich satin of ice blue. Her gown was simpler, though clearly still straight from Paris and therefore several seasons ahead of what the modistes of London were creating. She wore a matching jeweled band low across her forehead. The rest of her hair was styled into an elaborate bow shape on the top of her head. I had no idea how the style was achieved, but I was certain my curls would never allow for it. She was tall with a delicate frame and had the same dark brow of His Grace. On him, it was severe; on her it was arched, feminine. It drew the gaze to her dark eyes and long lashes. Her complexion was pale and clear. Of the three, her elegance was the most approachable.

Never in my life had I felt so shabby. I had deluded myself into hoping these people would not notice my crooked hem and scuffed slipper. They spotted my out-of-date gown the second I stepped into the room, likely down to the season it was made. Had I commissioned a brand-new gown delivered just this morning, it would still be unfashionable by their standards. Oddly, instead of increasing my nerves, this knowledge soothed. I had been doomed from the onset, and nothing within my power could have changed it.

With the kind of confidence that arose from certain failure, I allowed His Grace to press a kiss to my gloved hand before introducing me to his mother, Lady Clementia, and sister, Lady Davina. He encouraged my father and I to take a seat on a settee across from the family.

Finally, I was able to observe the drawing room—white walls, white furnishings, white curtains, white marble floors, and the occasional black accent. The only color in the room was the enormous dark, rich, crimson rug beneath our feet. I had the irrational fear I would start my monthly courses in the minutes between taking a seat and rising for supper. How could his sister bear the daily uncertainty?

The silence stretched for an uncomfortable few minutes, and I struggled for a topic. Finally, I settled on the obvious. "Your home is so lovely. I certainly have never seen its like."

The most fascinating thing happened with my statement. The Duke's face cycled through a myriad of expressions and emotions. A furrowed brow of skepticism, a thoughtful mouth twitch, a studious squint; each was plain on his visage. At last, his face relaxed, accepting my comment as a compliment. He gave an exaggerated gesture with lithe hands and long fingers toward his mother, marking her as the decorator.

"Yes dear, I am a most enamored scholar of the latest interior design fashions. Is that a topic that piques your interest?" Her Grace asked.

Out of the corner of my eye, my father shot a look that clearly meant I was to lie. I had quite forgotten his presence in the face of all this novelty. I wavered for less than a second before determining that deceit would backfire spectacularly. This woman was clearly well versed in the subject and would spot my falsehood instantly.

"I have not had the opportunity to study the latest trends, Your Grace. Your efforts here are most inspiring though, I shall have to research further." She seemed appeased with that compliment.

"What interests do you have, Lady Juliet?" His Grace questioned.

I opened my mouth to answer, but my father interjected. "She's quite proficient on the pianoforte, Your Grace."

My mouth dropped, hanging open a beat longer than appropriate, before I remembered myself and closed it with a tentative nod. I was fond of the pianoforte. Until he informed me that my efforts, when combined with my inferior singing voice, were in vain. From that moment, I only played when he was away from home. I had not exhibited in company since. Finally, some three years ago he sold our instrument entirely. I prayed his comment would not result in a request to play; I was quite out of practice, and it would surely end in disaster.

"That's a wonderful talent my dear. Lady Davina was sure to become a master in her youth but the instrument was ill suited to her talents," the Dowager Duchess added.

Lady Davina scoffed out an embarrassed, "Mother!" in response.

"Well, if you'd ever practiced you wouldn't have to be ashamed of your failings," His Grace shot at his sister.

I watched in horrified fascination as she let out an angry, "Ugh, Xander!"

He merely raised a sardonic brow in response. The girl actually crossed her arms and, pouting, turned back to us. My chest tightened, as I awaited his answering ire at her poor manners, but he turned back to us, unaffected by her display.

Equally unruffled, his mother questioned, "Do you have an interest in art Lady Juliet? My son is an impeccable curator of the most fashionable painters." She gestured toward an exquisite landscape framed in a recess above the fireplace. I was saved from having to offer any substantive comment about the piece by the announcement that supper was ready.

What followed was the most excruciating dinner of my entire existence. His Grace, though kind to me, continued to snipe at his sister and vice versa. The entire evening I waited for his patience to end, prepared for second-hand shame at the inevitable check on her behavior, which never came. His mother continued to use five words where one would suffice.

My father was no help, speaking only to offer up accomplishments I did not possess. The food was more plentiful than flavorful. The dining room decor was no less intimidating and impractical than that of the drawing room.

I waited, anticipating the inevitable distress. My utter failure to secure a suitor should vex me. It was not forthcoming. It was so evident that His Grace and I were ill-suited. I could not think even my father would be disappointed when no courtship was formed.

I thought wrong. The dressing down I received in the carriage had no equal. I thought I had seen my father angry before, but this, this was something else entirely. His fists beat the carriage walls, he screamed himself hoarse, his face turned a purplish red color for which I had no name, and the vein in his neck made a valiant attempt at escaping his flesh.

Instead of the usual combination of guilt, nausea, and terror I felt at his rages, I was numb. There was absolutely no situation in which His Grace could have found me an appropriate match. Perhaps if I had weeks to study current trends in interior decorating, learn the latest London gossip, research fashionable painters; then I could have proved an acceptable conversationalist. Maybe if I had hundreds of pounds to order the finest gowns from Paris I could have impressed. But I had only a few hours' notice and no warning.

Absolutely nothing I could have done with the resources I had available could have salvaged the evening. The absurdity of the situation left me indifferent and exhausted to his ravings for the first time in my life.

When we arrived home, my father remained in the carriage, breathing heavily. The footman was more gentle and attentive than usual as he escorted me to the door. I realized with shame that everyone within half a mile of the carriage had heard my father's every word. The footman handed me over to Hannah at the door, and she guided me, still dazed, through the house to my room, where she undressed me and readied me for bed without a word. At some point I must have fallen asleep, but I don't remember falling nor waking.

In the morning, the numbness remained, right up until I was summoned to my father's study once more.

Four

JULIET

"I'm to be *what*?" The numbness was gone now, as if it had never been there at all.

"Honestly, Juliet, it is a wonder anyone wants anything to do with you with manners such as those." My father followed that statement with a nonchalant sip of wine and a turn of the page. Apparently, this conversation was unworthy of eye contact. As if the subject at hand was no more interesting than the weather. As though he had not just offhandedly informed me of my impending nuptials.

My chest tightened as the air trapped in my lungs. There was a paralysis spreading to my fingers. *Not now. Please, not now.* I beat back the rising panic with everything I had. I fought to bring the numbers forth in my mind. One, I tried to inhale only for my chest to hitch on intake. I tried the reverse, one... two... three... four... five... on the exhale. Again on inhale. Exhale. My lungs reluctantly obeyed my commands again. Not without thought, that would take time, but they responded once more. Now, I was glad of my father's inattention; he had not noticed my distress.

"Apologies, father, my mouth ran away from me again." My voice was raised and raspy with panic, and I prayed he would not hear it. He detested conversing with hysterical women. "It's just... I had not thought to find a match so quickly, with so little effort—"

"So little effort?" *Oh no!* My heart sank, and blood froze in my veins. Practice ensured my expression kept my terror in confidence. One... two... "So little effort? Do you think it was a simple matter to bring about? That unmarried dukes wander aimlessly around London looking for insipid, ill-mannered, ungrateful, dull-witted women to wed?" Here he paused, face reddening with ire.

"No, Father, of—"

"I'm not finished." The pause had been a trap. "So little effort! Ungrateful, spoiled, selfish girl. So little effort! Can't even let a man finish his thought before interrupting. You'll be married less than a fortnight before His Grace sends you back to me. Ashamed of your manners and countenance, to be sure. Mark my words, I won't have you then. Once I've rid myself of your burden, I won't take it back." The blood vessel under his starched collar was straining the confines of his shirt. I stared at it while I counted.

It would be some time before he tired himself out. I struggled to keep my countenance suitably contrite. The tears that burned could come later, when I was alone. Few things incurred my father's fury the way that being interrupted did. Tears were one of them. My blood was rushing through my ears, and it made hearing him difficult. I desperately hoped I didn't miss a comment that required acknowledgment.

"...worked tirelessly to find a man who would have you. Odds are good you have the same condition your mother had, and you'll never provide a man with an heir. Still, I managed to find a gentleman who would accept you. A duke, no less! And you're nothing but ungrateful." He paused for breath again here; I would not fall for it this time. "You have nothing to say? Of course, you're not even the slightest bit remorseful for the shameful way you've treated me..." I guessed wrong, then. The vein was making itself even more noticeable. What would happen if it ever gave way?

Married. To a man I met only the night before. I had not been out in society, not truly. But I could not imagine a pair less suited than His Grace and myself. The rest of my life... My breath hitched again at that thought, one... two.... three...

He paused for breath again; this time, I was ready. "I am sorry, Father. I know my conduct is not what it ought to be, and I will endeavor to do better in the future. I am, of course, incredibly grateful for the efforts you have undertaken on my behalf. I am the most fortunate of daughters." With that, I slipped on the placid, slightly vacant smile I had perfected over the years. Mouth closed, lips turned up at just the corners. I tipped them just slightly higher than usual while delivering the compliment before settling to their resting place. He has complained before that my expression at rest is gloomy and discontent. He hated to see me wandering around the house looking so sour. I had worked to adopt a more serene countenance. In moments like these, it was a delicate balancing act. My expression should be contrite and grateful without veering toward smugness or mocking.

"Quite right." The urgency of his anger had departed, but it remained, humming under the surface.

"I do have a few questions. If you can spare a moment?" I strived to keep the trepidation from my voice, and was mostly successful.

With a put-upon sigh, he delivered a sharp, "Does it need to be now?" For one hysterical moment, I almost asked why his question was less ill-mannered than mine. Fortunately, I remember myself.

I had thousands of questions; I settled on the few that were absolutely essential. "Do you know, is His Grace planning on calling to pay his addresses today? I should like to have Mrs. Elliot prepare her best sandwiches for the occasion and have the silver polished."

This was dangerous ground. In my question was the implication that I was not managing the household as well as I ought. That it was not fit for royalty at all times. That I would take pains for a visitor that I would not exert for him. That he was not deserving of polished silver and exceptional sandwiches. Still, he had been tighter with the household funds in the last months. I already let a footman and a maid go, and Cook has been forced to take the less savory cuts of meat. If His Grace was to call, there was work to be done.

"Is the household not prepared for visitors?"

"No, Father, it is. I just thought to ensure the staff are all prepared for his visit." I resisted the impulse to keep talking, to further explain myself, to offer excuses. No good would come of more words.

He eyed me warily, weighing whether to take offense. Under his scrutiny, it was more difficult to keep my calming breaths from becoming apparent. There was a danger here, of them becoming too shallow and undoing my efforts. Through it all, my serene smile never faltered, but I hoped desperately that there were no self-satisfied undertones in it.

"I see no reason Rosehill should call to pay his addresses to you. He and I have discussed it, and I have informed you. There's no need for you to be involved in the matter; it does not concern you." The smile slipped just a fraction before I righted it. I rather thought the matter concerned me a great deal. Still, it was a relief not to upset the entire household. "I imagine he will call at some time or other. It hardly signifies when. The household and your person are fit for a visitor of any station at any time, yes?"

"Yes, Father. Did you and His Grace have the opportunity to discuss when the wedding might take place? I will need to prepare a trousseau."

"We agreed the end of the season would be best. His Grace would like you to fully enter society before you wed. You will need to make connections that will serve you as a duchess. Regarding your trousseau, I hope that wasn't a request for funds. You have plenty of pin money for such things." I did not, actually; he had not given me pin money in nearly a year.

He had always been odd about money. One day, he complained that Sophie and I were spending every coin he had; the next, he was gifting me a horse I neither requested nor wanted. I learned not to ask and to appreciate the windfalls as they came.

He turned back to his paper dismissively, and I was forced to forgo further questions.

The relief I felt when I pressed the study door closed behind me was immense. My breath came back to me in great lungfuls without permission. Dizzy with the excess of air, I was forced to pause in the hall; one hand to the wall and the other to my chest. My inhales were great raspy gasps, my exhales, barely restrained sobs. Both were impossibly loud in the empty hall. I could not remain here; he would hear.

I rushed to my room, striving to keep my footsteps light so as not to draw attention. By the time I arrived, I was somewhat more composed. Unfortunately, I was immediately beset by the gowns I had considered and rejected last evening. They served as a forceful reminder of how ill-prepared I was for my future role. I grabbed the one nearest and threw myself in the chair by the window with my embroidery supplies. Small shears in hand, an eerie calm settled over me as I snipped the threads forming the flowers on the bodice. The ones I painstaking stitched on the dusky blue-lavender silk over the course of a fortnight. Until last evening, I had been pleased with my results. But every flaw was apparent when I pressed the gown to my chest. The flowers were uneven, the stitches were loose, and the ones in the middle pulled the delicate fabric. Now, one by one, I removed the offending threads until I was left with bare material.

It was not until I went to my thread basket that I remembered I had used the last of the beautiful gold thread on the dress. It accented the shadowy bluish purple so well, and now it was gone. I snipped every single piece.

And that was it.

The dam holding back my tears gave way to shuddering, silent sobs. I frantically grabbed the pillow at my side, pressing it tightly to my face. As soon as it was in place, my throat took that as permission to release every anguished gasp I was suppressing. There was no counting my way out of this. The pillow made breathing difficult, but I didn't dare remove it, certain it was the only thing between me and an even worse fate.

I did not even know what, precisely, I was crying about. My father's harsh words? Those were nothing new. My engagement? I always knew I would marry eventually. The last of the beautiful thread my friend, Kate, gifted me with? My stepmother's beautiful gown that I had just mangled? Sophie herself, my mother in all but blood, leaving me to navigate this alone? All of it? None of it?

"HE TOOK one look at you and was determined to have you for his own. It's so romantic!" My dearest friend had a flair for dramatics. My stepmother was Kate's aunt through her mother. Her friendship sustained me through the long months of Sophie's illness. I generally found her enthusiasm charming; in this circumstance, it was exhausting. A few days was not nearly enough time to recover from the shock of my betrothal. Still, she was the closest thing I had to a sister and I appreciated her excitement on my behalf.

She had gained an incredible library with her marriage to Viscount Grayson. A room I was far more fond of than she was. It was stunning with floor-to-ceiling shelves filled with innumerable tomes. Additional shelves were added once the walls were filled to bursting. The room was decorated an airy blue color with floral prints. Two arched mahogany doors, carved with elaborate vines and scrolls, served as the primary entrance. A second entrance with a single, more simplistic, door that I assumed led to a study sat along the side wall. There were large windows for light with an oversized, comfortable chair in front of each that served as a repose for the reader. Between the chairs, abutting a wall, was a moderately-sized rectangular table covered in a fine white cloth. It was intended to rest books, but Kate and I had adapted it for tea.

Once she showed me the room, I claimed it for my own, and she now did me the kindness of receiving me there. And sent me home with all the books my heart could desire. Most days, I never wished to leave.

"Kate, on the whole, I've spent no more than five hours in his presence! I don't even know how he takes his tea." I gestured with my cup for emphasis. "He never stays long enough for it to arrive. How am I to succeed as his wife?"

His Grace had visited twice since our disastrous supper. The first time, alone to propose and provide me with the ostentatious ruby ring now adorning my finger. The second, with his sister. Both appeared mildly uncomfortable when presented with the prospect of resting their fine clothing on our shabby furnishings.

His Grace and Lady Davina expressed some admiration for my embroidery on their joint visit. I appreciated their compliments. I also appreciated their tact in choosing not to mention the lack of a pianoforte anywhere in the home.

"You will learn, and I'm sure he's more interested in other activities than tea preparation." Kate never met a topic of conversation she considered improper. For a vicar's daughter, she was unusually comfortable with more scandalous subjects. Her fondness for causing me discomfort had not lessened with her new title.

"Kate!"

"Well, it's true. The servants prepare Hugh's tea. The only use he seems to have for me is in the bedroom." Her tone was less upbeat than I expected of her, almost guarded. I was about to interrupt her to ask more when she continued. "But Rosehill, he's so handsome! I'm sure you're looking forward to such attentions."

"I had not given it much thought." That was a lie. I thought of little else but my impending nuptials since that horrid day in father's study. The wedding night included. The prospect of such... *activities* filled me with more dread than anticipation. Kate never understood my perspective on such things.

She was not yet sixteen the first time she fancied herself in love. In the five years since, she found no less than two dozen men to be the handsomest of her acquaintance, and she never went more than a month without rhapsodizing about one pair of fine eyes or another. Her marriage to the viscount had been something of a surprise to me. Instead of months of admiration, I heard almost nothing of him.

I understood their first meeting to be something of a disaster. An incident with a glass of lemonade had me both laughing at her expense and embarrassed on her behalf. He must have found the incident charming; after all, he chose her for his bride.

I had been a poor friend during her debut. Sophie had mere months left when Kate was presented, and the following year was spent in mourning. While circumstances, not desire, kept me from her, I now lamented my lack of support.

Her husband was something of a mystery to me. Though I called often, he seemed to take little notice, looking to his wife for introductions on more than one occasion. I was not overly fond of the man, but I had never met a woman more determined to marry for love than Kate. If the viscount met her approval, my opinion did not signify. She was a romantic sort, my friend.

I never felt such things when I looked upon gentlemen— the girlish flutterings and hopeful longings of first love. Even those generally thought handsome by the ton held little appeal. I could observe what was handsome in each part, but I felt none of the butterflies or pounding pulses Kate described when the whole was put together. I had always supposed that my husband, whoever he may be, would be the exception. Now, that seemed unlikely.

"Oh, but you must have! It's because you haven't yet danced together. Dancing is just the thing to induce all sorts of romantic notions!"

"I am sure you are right. Is that what happened with you and the viscount?"

She carried on without mentioning her husband. "He's turned down the invitation to my ball Friday night. You must press him to change his mind. Then you will see, it's just the thing."

"I am sure he has pressing plans that cannot be changed, Kate. His Grace is a very busy man. Besides, I am not certain I will be able to attend." I had not yet managed to finish repairing the gown I had ruined in a fit of pique, and none of the others were suited to such an occasion.

"Oh, but you must come! I need you there, Jules! I won't be able to manage it without a friendly face. And all that besides, His Grace wanted you to have a season, to make connections. How can you do that when you never leave this settee?"

In addition to a lack of tact, she had the infuriating habit of always being right.

"I will discuss it with Father."

"That's all I ask."

Five

MICHAEL

RICHARD DALTON WAS DODGING ME.

A month ago, it was rare that he missed a night in my club. Now I had neither seen nor heard from him in more than a fortnight. The man had never possessed a coin he wasn't desperate to wager; he had to be gaming somewhere.

At first, I was confident he'd make his way back to my club after a few days without a game of dice. After a week with no sighting, I had to admit I had underestimated him. I was forced to exert some effort to locate him, sending men to his town house and his known associates' estates. I even directed them down to my old gaming hells in Piccadilly. It was unlikely an earl would be seen there; those hells are reserved for second and third sons with too many coins and too few responsibilities. Titled gentlemen preferred my establishment.

Avoiding me may have been the smartest thing the man had ever done. Attempting to have the match thrown was certainly not.

It was unlikely I would see my money. One couldn't get

blood out of a stone, after all. Still, I had a reputation to maintain. I couldn't be seen to be forgiving debts, and I certainly could not allow cheating to go unpunished. If he got away without penalty, there was no telling what advantages the rest would try to press.

Intelligence finally came from an unlikely source. Once again, I found myself attending the now weekly supper at my brother's house. Kate insisted on the effort. I suspected she appreciated my talent for directing her mother-in-law's ire away from herself. It was unclear whether Agatha's barbs were losing their sharpness or whether familiarity was toughening my skin, dulling impact.

The more time I spent with Kate, the more I was certain my brother had done far too well for himself. She was thoughtful, attentive, funny, and all-around delightful. Her husband watched his wife ill-used by his mother with nary a reproachful comment. I would have checked him if I had even the slightest belief that my efforts would not have the opposite effect. Our precarious relationship, held together entirely with manners, ensured that any attempt to correct the man would be met with ire.

As was the usual pace for these suppers, Kate chattered on about the ton gossip while I dodged well-placed insults from Agatha. All the while attempting to shield the new viscountess from her predecessor's censure.

I began to suspect Kate had matchmaking efforts in mind with her gossip. Married women adored matchmaking. In my experience, well-settled women were always trying to create more women well-settled in matrimony. Try as I might, I could not convince her to focus her efforts on Tom. True, he was barely out of the school room and more than determined to ingratiate himself with every actress in the country, but he had the name.

For all her wonderful qualities, Kate had an unfortunate

tendency to forget my parentage. Or, not so much forget, as fail to understand why such a thing would signify. She may have been willing to overlook the situation, but the peerage certainly wasn't about to wed their daughters off to a degenerate, gambling bastard.

"—and so I was telling Jules that she simply must attend the ball I'm hosting on Friday next."

"Jules?" Hugh interrupted; I would soon bless my brother for his inattentiveness.

"Lady Juliet Dalton. You've met her several times now." Kate's face was pinched with bit-back irritation. It was an expression usually reserved for Agatha.

The name, though, caught my attention instantly. Careful to modulate my interest, I strived to keep my intrigue subtle lest Kate develop matrimonial inclinations.

"She informed me that she is attending with her father as chaperone. I will have to keep that odious man from the young ladies. He's on the hunt for a third wife to torment, you know."

"You're hosting a ball?" The question slipped free unbidden, and it was the wrong thing to ask. The hurt registered on Kate's face, sent from my corner this time. I regretted my lack of attention now. From the other side of her, I saw Tom's face meet his palm in a familiar reaction. I had thought the dowager viscountess had it lectured out of him.

"I am hosting a ball, Michael Wayland. As you well know because you've promised to attend. Twice now. You've promised twice."

"I thought that was a dinner."

"It is a ball; you'll be here on Friday next, properly attired and on time. What dances are you familiar with? I've got several young ladies I'd like you to meet." There it was—the damn matchmaking.

"I don't dance."

"You will at my ball."

"Kate..." The look she shot Hugh stopped his interruption in its tracks. Now I was responsible for yet more marital discord. One of the many reasons I was ill-suited to matrimony; I need not be wed to the lady to upset her.

Tom, my favorite brother, skillfully changed the subject. Within moments Kate was distracted from her romantic notions and back on ton gossip. I shot him a grateful look before returning to contemplate my soup. Prior to drinks, I feigned an exit before joining Augie in the kitchens. He joined me every week now. Each time I entered the kitchens at the end of supper, he was pressed even closer to Anna's side, heart in his eyes. As happy as I was for him, I couldn't help but worry I was about to lose my superintendent.

Six

GRAYSON HOUSE, LONDON - MARCH 4, 1814

MICHAEL

I was well beyond fashionably late. Kate would have my bollocks, and Hugh would take no pains to prevent it. I doubted "unavoidably delayed by fisticuffs" would appease her.

Fights breaking out at my club weren't so unusual. As a general rule, the combination of money and drink tended to result in violence.

Kate wouldn't appreciate my blackened eye, but there was nothing to be done for it. My only hope was that it would dampen her matchmaking endeavors.

I signaled my driver to pull off early. If I could sneak in through the servants' entry, perhaps I could avoid a scowl from Kate and a glare from her groom.

Once inside, I hurried along the corridor to the servants' entrance of the ballroom. I hadn't anticipated the decor, though. Opening the door, I was smacked in the face with heavy velvet fabric, dusty with age. I could hear the orchestra somewhere off to my left. They were completing the final strains of a quadrille. Pressed close to the wall, I slid in the opposite direction, hoping desperately for a break in the fabric. For the life of me, I couldn't recall where they might split.

Finally, my hand broke free from my velveteen prison. Extricating myself with as much grace as I could muster given the circumstances, I breathed the fresh air of the back corner of the ballroom. I'd escaped near the trays of sandwiches, teacakes, and glasses of lemonade and punch.

A gaggle of wallflowers and mammas was occupying the seats nearest the food. I would need to flee quickly; if Kate found me too near the spinsters, the matchmaking would begin. Though ill-bred, I would prefer to avoid disappointing my new sister by refusing a dance with her friends. Distance was the safest course.

Running my hand through mussed hair in an effort to straighten it, I dodged more than one lady stepping into my path. It was almost certainly a ploy for attention. I didn't play the games of the ton, but I knew them all.

Across the way, I caught sight of a dream in indigo satin. Petite, with an elegant blonde coiffure and bright green eyes, Celine was a vision as always.

Though my paramour of several years, I wasn't entirely sure of her title. She was the daughter of a marquis who lost his head in the revolution. She'd wed the eldest son of the Duke of Rosehill, but he passed before inheriting the title. Duchess? Or dowager? Countess? Lady? Fortunately, the title did not signify in her boudoir.

She was accompanied by her feather-clad mother, brother and sister by marriage. I believed the brother was now Duke of Rosehill.

Meeting my hungry gaze, she raised her glass in silent acknowledgment, running her eyes over my form with an approving raised brow. I offered her an appreciative nod in return, maintaining a discreet distance. Searching for an unoccupied area of the wall, I found a spot to prop up my person while I scanned the crowd for Dalton.

I was quite comfortable on my patch of brick, appreciating the floral arches and twinkling candles Kate had added to the room. Throughout the entire dance, a cotillion, there was no sign of Dalton. I understood from Kate he was in want of a wife, but he certainly hadn't found anyone willing to join him on the floor. Given his appetites in the club, I thought to look for him at the food tables, but there was nothing of interest over there but spinsters.

It was a mild irritation when a pair of gossips chose my corner for their mongering, blocking my view of the room. I recognized Lady Charmaine James on reputation alone. She was infamous at my club. Her paramours were less than flattering in their descriptions of her, remarking that she had more bust than brain. Though the reverence with which they whispered marked it as more feature than defect. Her husband, on the other hand, thought only of losing his annual income in my club.

Her present companion, Mr. Wesley Parker, was a frequent patron of my establishment and a regular solicitor of her affections.

"Did you see her gown? It has seen three seasons at least and is certainly borrowed for all that it suits her," Lady James feigned in a whisper behind her glass.

The nearby members of the ton straightened and inclined their heads with little subtlety. From my vantage against the wall, I couldn't see around them to the lady they mocked.

"It hardly signifies what she wears. She is the future Duchess of Rosehill," Parker said.

That was intriguing. I hadn't thought the Duke's interests lay that way.

I had half a mind to interrupt the gossipmongers, if only

to clear my view, when I felt a pointed jab to my shoulder. I turned to find Kate in her most dignified fury.

"Hours late and eye blackened! I look forward to the explanation I shall receive on the morrow," she hissed while searching for further damage to my person.

"Would you believe I was attacked by a rabid swan?"

"No," she replied with a roll of her eyes as she brushed unseen dust from my lapel. Probably left from the curtains. "I expect you'll be wanting something stronger than lemonade. Hugh and Tom are in the study with the good scotch." With that, I was dismissed, and she turned to greet other guests.

I'd managed to avoid the study in all my visits to Grayson House in recent weeks. The room I found was much the same as it was under the late viscount's reign. Dark cherry wood adorned every available surface. Hugh seemed content to allow the stacks of ledgers to overtake the shelves behind him, much like his father. Father's desk appeared smaller than it had during his life, less imposing. Featured prominently behind the desk, the man's portrait remained. Stern of jaw and dark of hair, he was prepared to judge every decision I made at that desk.

The desk that was never mine. I had merely borrowed it for a time. Still, it stung to see Hugh with his feet propped casually on the surface. The one on which I toiled for years. I forced myself to bite back a comment regarding the mistreatment of furnishings. After all, Hugh was a grown man, and the desk was his to abuse.

I could see almost nothing of the small, skinny, red-faced boy who had returned from Eton, angry, hurting, and utterly unprepared for the duties of viscount at one and ten. He blamed me for his father's death. He never said as much, but he was less than subtle. I knew better, though. I knew the gift I had given him. Blissful ignorance.

Tom was making liberal use of the liquor at the sideboard

between the two carved doors, one to the hall, the other to the library. He poured a glass for me without a word. The boy was not yet eight when his father passed, and I still found it strange to see a young man, making free with the scotch, in his place.

In his youth, Tom held none of the bitterness of Hugh, merely sadness. He, too, knew only that our father had fallen in the lake that bitter morning in January. He understood that I had been too late to save him. That was all he would ever know. It was better that way.

I took a seat across from Hugh. Tom chose a seat on the desk rather than the perfectly serviceable chair beside it. Hugh said nothing about it, and I was left to hold my tongue. I was not his father.

Hugh broke the companionable silence. "What the devil did you do to your eye this time?"

"Swan."

"Really? Again?"

"I've used that one before? I need to start keeping a list. Kate will suspect I've been less than truthful with her."

"I hate to be the bearer of bad tidings, but Kate knows all."

"You almost sound as though you admire your wife, Hugh."

I knew better than to comment on a man's marriage, but the temptation was too strong. Tom shot a reproachful look in my direction. I ought to avoid antagonizing Hugh if only to save Tom the effort of maintaining the peace.

Hugh's brow furrowed. His expression shifted slowly as he tried to determine whether my comment was a compliment or insult. Before he could settle on the right of it, I changed the subject. "What do you know of Richard Dalton?"

"Is he a guest?"

"The one Kate wanted to keep from the ladies," Tom added.

A spark of recollection dawned on Hugh's face. "What do you want with him?"

"A simple conversation."

"The man is a loose screw. How much does he owe you?" For all his talents, Tom hadn't yet mastered the art of subtlety.

"Enough."

"If I get him to the library, you'll talk to him. Nothing else." Hugh was grave, and it stung a bit coming from him. "You'll not have a row with him during Kate's ball."

"Certainly not!" I cried, offended by the notion. My business may be unscrupulous, but I would never dream of insulting my sister in such a manner. I lived outside the watchful eyes of the ton; but I knew how to comport myself, a fact Hugh well knew.

"You can wait in the library; I'll try to lure him away from the debutantes. At least Kate will thank me for that effort." Hugh was off with Tom trailing behind. I was left alone in the study I had once occupied, now a guest.

I tipped the last of my scotch in a toast toward the late viscount's portrait before swallowing it back. "Cheers, my lord." His disquieting presence dismissed; I made use of the second door into the library.

Seven

GRAYSON HOUSE, LONDON - MARCH 4, 1814

JULIET

I WAS DETERMINED to pay them no notice. Lady Charlotte and her admirers would not ruin my enjoyment of the evening. Kate had decorated the ballroom so beautifully, it was a turnout to be proud of, and all remarked on the food. My dance with His Grace, while not the magical moment Kate had predicted, was very nice.

I thought I had done well with the dress. It was one of the last ones my stepmother ever had created—a dark rose pink chiffon with gathering on the bust and rosettes on the hem, neckline, and sleeves. Sophie was smaller than me, and I had difficulty finding the right lace to add to lengthen the hem. There had not been enough excess to let it down, and the rosettes had made the process more difficult. True, I could not locate the jewels she typically paired it with, but the effect was more than passible.

Still, I should have known Charlotte would find fault with my work. She found fault in my every move since my betrothal was announced. She had set her cap at His Grace several seasons prior. Kate told me their courtship was abruptly dropped. She had not been able to discern the reason. But Charlotte was left to wed a plain baron of no notable means in lieu of a handsome duke of considerable fortune.

Eventually, the rumormongers abandoned me in search of other victims. My pride finally allowed a retreat. I slipped into the corridor, down the long halls toward the library. Kate would not mind my escape; she all but offered it as a refuge when I first arrived tonight. She would not begrudge me a novel.

The hall grew quiet the farther I journeyed from the ballroom. I pulled open one of the double doors to the library—my second home. Scents of vanilla, dust, parchment, and aged paste welcomed me. I left the door ajar for light rather than secure a candle. I knew my way around.

I set my evening gloves on the cloth-covered table between the windows. Thumbing titles quietly in the slip of light from the hall, I explored, more than one novel sparking interest.

Distracted as I was, the jangle of the secondary door opening startled me. In the months I had been calling here, no one had ever been in the library but Kate.

I could not explain the panic that flooded me. My perusal could hardly be offensive to anyone. Without conscious decision, I threw myself under the table. Crouching beneath the delicate draping, I pressed my hands tight to my mouth, covering my harsh breaths.

Now that I had made the undignified choice to hide like a thief, I was trapped until the intruder left. I could only hope their visit was a short one. I flopped indecorously to my rear, silent in my endeavor.

My breathing was harsh in my ears. Over the top of it, I could hear heavy masculine footsteps. The panic was rising, one... two... three... inhale. Exhale. I had to pull my hand away to quiet the sound, it was harsh against my skin.

There was an indiscriminate tap, tap, tap of a finger dragging against the spines of hardbound tomes. Each step, each tap, brought him closer to my table. No more than a foot from me, he made a selection, the whisper of leather against leather severe in the silence. The spine cracked open, tight from disuse. Pages sighed, brushing against one another as he flipped through them with disinterest. The book sang with his perusal.

The peace was interrupted by a new cacophony coming from the direction of the hall. The jarring sound of muffled voices, discordant in the quiet, joined the melody. My heart dropped with understanding, blood frozen in my extremities.

I was alone.

With a man.

In a darkened library.

Soon to be full of witnesses.

I was ruined. His Grace would never have me. No one would have me. I would be a burden to my father forever. He would turn me out, and I would wander the streets as a beggar. Or worse still, live in that house, wraithlike, until his temper consumed me the way it had Sophie.

Just when I was convinced this situation could not be more disastrous, my captor leaned back against the table. It was not such a large table that I could move away. One misstep, and he would kick me. I pressed both hands tightly to my mouth to suppress the terrified squeak that fought to escape.

Through the gauzy fabric, I made out a pair of fine boots, imposing in their size. The quality was excellent, leather soft as butter. They were clearly well-maintained, polished, and shined to a mirror finish. But care could not hide the worn soles; these were well-loved. Thick, masculine calves peeked out just at the top into satin breeches, black. It was difficult to discern the quality of the fabric through the haze of tablecloth, but the fit was exceptional.

The hall entry clanged open farther, banging against the opposite wall. I winced, reminded of my ever worsening, ever more scandalous, completely ruinous position. There was a stumble, feet tripping across the carpet. Feet that were attached to a gentleman; heavier than a lady's, by the sound of it. He stumbled to a halt before my unknowing captor.

"Just talk, remember." A sturdy, honeyed voice warned from the hall. Terror found a home inside me once more. Some poor man had been thrown to my jailor for threats?

The hall doors clattered closed, shrouding the room in darkness. We were alone. My captor, his victim, and myself. The only remaining light streamed from the open study door, wavering in the low-burning fire. It left a masculine silhouette through my cloth—the prisoner.

"Dalton," a silvery voice drawled above me, filled with barely checked distaste.

My breathing ceased entirely. Caught. My joints, frozen in terror, ceased to obey commands as I tried to control my panicked breathing.

"Wayland."

My stomach sank through the floor with that single word, that familiar voice. I bit back a hysterical sob. I would recognize that venomous hiss anywhere—my father. The man was threatening my father. I had not been caught out. But this monster had my father. For better or worse, the only family I had in the world.

"You've been dodging me."

"I would never; I've merely been busy, you see. It is my daughter's first season, and without a wife, much of the responsibility has fallen to me."

Sniveling, his tone was one I had never heard. It was obsequious and nasal. Subservient, almost. It was entirely new to me and utterly horrid. Underneath my shock, a touch of indignation burned. His characterization of the efforts he undertook on my behalf was an overstatement at best.

"So, I've heard. I'm confident I'll have the £6,000 you owe me in hand on the morrow. I've been assured that you and your daughter have no pending engagements."

The sum caught in my mind, circling there. A missing puzzle piece I had not yet manipulated to fit.

"Now, Wayland, you must be reasonable—"

"I've been reasonable for weeks, Richard. You've yet to see me in an unreasonable state."

He did not deny it. My father did not deny the debt. £6,000. It was an insurmountable sum: my entire dowry and more. And he made not the slightest effort to refute it.

"—So, you see, if you just wait until Rosehill weds the chit in five months' time, he'll give me the funds for you—"

My father's sycophantic pleading was abruptly cut off with a choking sound. Shelves at my side shuddered under sudden weight and motion. From what little I could discern through the cloth, the man had shoved my father against the shelf. His forearm pressed against Father's neck.

"You're selling your only daughter to pay your debts?" The man's voice was a penetrating growl; my hair rose on end in the face of such intensity.

"Oh, come off it. He needs an heir out of her, and he hasn't any other takers," my father's voice was only a wheeze. The shelves rattled again as the man adjusted his grip.

"I won't accept funds at your daughter's expense. Find another source." The words were bit out between clenched teeth.

He was defending me? There was no sense in it. A man so unscrupulous as to confront a gentleman during a ball, so determined to collect his funds, he had all but thrown a man against a shelf. *This* man was scrupulous enough to care about the source of his payment?

"Papers have already been signed. And he added another £2,000 on top of the six. He will have my head if I back out now."

"You should be afraid of me," he said, voice taut with anger. "If you sell that girl, I'll have your head, but that will be the last piece of you I receive. Do we have an understanding?"

The bile rose in my throat as truth finally dawned.

"Yes," my father bit out with no small amount of venom.

The man released him abruptly. My father dropped to his knees with the weight of his sudden freedom. Meanwhile, the man stalked to the hall door; his motion oddly graceful in opposition to the brutality I had just witnessed. He yanked it open, light streaming in from the hall once more, silhouetting the position of both men. My father straightened from the floor, righting his clothing in an absurd display of pride before he strode out with the remnants of his dignity.

"Have a lovely evening," the man threw the words down the hall after him. There was no small amount of sarcasm in the phrase. The door clicked gently closed, a contrast to the violence of the last minutes.

For the briefest moment, I was free to grapple with all I had learned—privacy abundant under my cloth. Then, heavy footsteps revealed that, instead of abandoning me, the man had enclosed us both in the darkened library once more. He crossed back to the table, leaning against it. The slap of palms landed on the wood, accompanied by a fatigued sigh. I was still trapped, then.

I released a near-silent, shaky breath; one, two, three.

The cloth was unexpectedly ripped up. I startled and tried to shuffle away in the non-existent space. Instead, I banged my head against the leg of the table. The knock upset a vase on the top and flowers spilled and water dripped to the floor beside me.

The man leaned down, his head peering sideways under the table. He was all dark hair, fiery eyes, and sharp cheekbones.

"Learn anything interesting, little eavesdropper?" he asked, his eyes smoky, tone unreadable. Annoyed perhaps. It was slightly preferable to the barely suppressed rage he had offered my father.

I nodded mutely, mouth gaping. I could not seem to command my eyes to blink. He brought a hand down and held it out to me. He was... helping me up? Should he not be raging at me? I couldn't bring myself to take his hand. Instead, I scooted awkwardly on my bottom, freeing myself from my table prison, before pressing myself up to stand beside him. I misjudged the distance between us though. Once I rose, I was pressed, too close, against him—bare inches between us.

He took a dignified step back and reached past me to the table. He pulled back, presenting me with my own gloves. I closed my eyes against the humiliation rushing through me. The entire time...

"Care to tell me what you were doing down there?" His tone was... amused? His grin was crooked, and his earlier rage seemed to have evaporated.

"I was searching for a book."

"Under the table?"

"Yes."

"And did you find the book? Under the table?" His eyes crinkled a bit at the corners, matching the grin. It gave him a boyish look, it was much less threatening.

Involuntarily, my muscles relaxed, one by one. I had not realized they were tight.

"Obviously not."

"Obviously... Miss?"

58

"Lady Juliet Dalton."

I saw the exact moment he made the connection, eyes widening and brows raising.

"Oh." He brushed a wayward lock of hair behind his ear sheepishly. "I apologize most sincerely, Lady Juliet. That was not for your ears."

"Undoubtedly. I believe I should return to the ballroom. Someone will have noticed my absence."

"Let me escort you."

"Thank you, but no. I believe I know my own way."

With that, I made my way out of the library with all the quiet dignity I could muster.

Eight

JULIET

I COULD NOT SLEEP last night, instead replaying the events of the prior evening in my mind again and again. He had not denied it. Not once. My father had all but admitted he had lost everything.

Hundreds of little moments that had given me pause over the last few months now made horrifying sense. The unease shrouding the household. The endless tirade about my ungrateful nature when I asked after overdue pin money. My stepmother's missing jewelry. Servants leaving, one after another. Smaller portions at meals. We were surely ruined. Destitute.

Odder still was the notion that His Grace would pay my father's debts. Surely that was not the usual order of things. But even that, despite all logic to the contrary, felt... right. From the start, I questioned his interest in me. A pair so ill-suited we were destined for disaster, headed to the altar. His apparent disinterest in getting to know me still gave me a slight pause. I resigned myself to further investigation. I certainly could not throw over a man of His Grace's consequence. Not without a great deal more evidence than vague implications gleaned from eavesdropping.

If I were to call off the engagement, I would be ruined. In the eyes of the ton, we were as good as married. I would never marry. I would be forced to stay with my father forever, if he would even have me. Such an odious thought. More likely, I would be thrown to the streets. It was too much to consider!

The lack of sleep and distressing thoughts had me aching with exhaustion. It was no difficulty to feign a headache when Hannah arrived to assist me with my toilette. If my illness cleared as soon as I was sure my father would be out for the day, it was mere coincidence.

It was well past noon before I ventured from my room.

I had just reached the bottom of the staircase when our butler informed me of a visitor. Nerves rushed through me at the thought of facing His Grace without further explanation. But instead of the black-clad figure I had come to expect, I was presented with a silhouette in front of the windows. All too familiar from the night before, I would recognize it anywhere —my captor.

~

MICHAEL

I ABSOLUTELY SHOULD NOT have been there. On the list of worst decisions I'd ever made, this was near the top. She could not possibly wish to see anyone less than myself. It was just... I was unable to sleep last night for thinking of her.

The moment she'd uncurled from the floor, I was finished. She was tall, statuesque even. In the candlelight, her mahogany curls shone with a hint of golden red. Her pale complexion was offset by the dusky rose gown, cut low enough to reveal the tantalizing suggestion of décolleté. It was her eyes that haunted me, though. Wide and blue as the sky and full of heartbreak. Hot, sharp, and instantaneous, the guilt at being the cause of such heartache was immense.

All night I mentally—occasionally audibly—raged at her father for putting her in this situation. In rare introspective moments, I berated myself. I shouldn't have let her run out like that. I should have ensured the room was empty. I shouldn't have approached Dalton at Kate's ball. I never should have allowed my man to place his wager knowing his financial status. I ought not make my living robbing gullible, arrogant men of their fortunes. I'd found any number of reasons for self-flagellation.

The truth was, I had never considered the families of the men in my club—night after night, placing wagers beyond their means. Someone was suffering for their choices, and it certainly wasn't them.

I had already called at Grayson House ostensibly to apologize for my appearance and late arrival at the ball. I pressed Kate for as much information as I could glean without giving rise to expectations. It wasn't much. Kate's knowing brow indicated her suspicions, and I ceased questioning.

Now, I was standing awkwardly in the drawing room of Westfield's home. I had also forgotten what to do with my arms while standing. I could not recall ever giving the practice so much thought. Each position was more ungainly than the last. My coat pockets seemed to have shrunk as well. They were always large enough for my hands before.

I had no business here, calling on the daughter of the man I'd threatened last evening. I had been left to wait an inordinate amount of time. At least she didn't have me thrown bodily from the house. Yet.

The butler directed me to the drawing room. It was decorated in cheerful yellows and spring greens. The furnishings and carpets were well cared for but had seen some age. The rug was matted down in places, a map of the most frequently traversed paths. The settee beneath the wall-length windows was fine but well-loved. It had faded to a cream color, corners indicating that it, too, was once a pale yellow. One side was more threadbare than the other, marking what must be a favored spot.

On the floor beside it was a basket of sewing notions, bits and bobs I didn't know the use for and a rainbow of threads. A side table was next to it, topped with a small stack of novels, each bookmarked with strands of multicolored thread.

At first, I had hoped to avoid the appearance of snooping, but after a quarter of an hour with little else to do, I flipped through the titles with interest. *Virtue Rewarded*, *The History of Sir Charles Grandison*, *Udopho*, *The Sylph*. The reader, presumably Lady Juliet, had diverse tastes. The last two, placed on the bottom of the stack, appeared to be from Grayson House library. She had said she was searching for a book last evening.

I itched to crack open one of the titles, boredom and unease chafing in equal measure. Instead, I peered out the window at the street below. The view was nothing spectacular, an alley between two great houses. Servants coming and going through the corridor. Arms laden with purchases.

My disinterested observations were interrupted by a feminine gasp behind me. There she was, eyes even more shockingly blue and brighter in the sunlight. I couldn't name the color: sky too light, cornflower too dull, gunmetal too icy. Perhaps sapphire was the closest, but it, too, was lacking. They were wide with shock, likely at my audacity and my presumptive presence here. It was certainly unwelcome after the events of last night.

Dark, shadowy, purple circles made a home under her eyes. She had not slept either. Her fair skin was flushed. It was an intriguing peachy shade. Embarrassment? Irritation? Something in between? I'd hoped my visceral reaction to her last night had been a singular event. Clearly, it was not.

Her face was remarkably expressive. Shock, irritation, and determination crossed the lines of her mouth and brow. Decision made, her posture shifted, her shoulders back, her spine long, and her eyes steely.

She gestured toward the worn settee, manners impeccable. "Please, do be seated. Shall I call for some tea? Mr.?"

She was to stand on ceremony then. She glided into the room, steps delicate and poised, and perched at the edge of the nearby chair. I took my indicated place, settling lazily on the settee. Her mouth twitched slightly, indignation perhaps, at the sight of my sprawled posture. I crossed an ankle on my knee, hoping I could manage an eye twitch out of her with the effort.

"Michael Wayland. There's no need for tea. It's a pleasure to formally make your acquaintance, Lady Juliet."

"Of course. May I inquire as to the occasion for your visit? I was not expecting callers this afternoon." Her reply was prim, directed just to the left of my ear.

"Lady Juliet." I paused until her eyes met mine, questioning. "I wish to apologize for the events of last evening. Surely, you know I would not have said such things had I known of your presence."

Her eyes narrowed in fierce irritation. An unexpected reaction to an apology, to be sure.

"If I'm to understand you correctly, sir, you're apologizing, not for the content of your words or actions. But instead, because I happened to overhear those words," she said, fire barely constrained beneath impeccable civility.

Oh, she was furious with me. Though not entirely unwarranted, it was adorable. I suppressed the smirk lurking within me. While I managed to keep it from my lips, I suspect my eyes gave it away if the flash of irritation was any indication. My effort hadn't appeased the angry kitten before me.

"You comprehend me perfectly."

It may have been my imagination, but I think I detected a nearly silent growl from her.

She rose more quickly and with less delicacy than she'd previously displayed, gesturing toward the door. "Right, well, if that's all, I bid you adieu."

I was a truly horrible man, taking no small pleasure in her barely suppressed rage.

"I think I will take that tea, actually. It sounds lovely just now."

"But... I thought... You said you had come to make an apology. You have done so, and now you're free to go on with your day. I am sure you have other gentlemen to accuse and assault."

"Nothing of the sort planned until after supper."

I saw it again, the barely restrained rage. It was taking absolutely every one of her gently bred manners to refrain from throttling me. It was, perhaps, the funniest thing I had ever seen. She was breathing heavily, and her chest rose and fell, enticing me with every breath.

She closed her eyes before gritting her teeth and biting out, "I will return shortly. I need to ring for it."

She stalked from the room, none of the delicate grace from earlier. She was a well-trained one. Kate would have thrown the nearest object at my head long before now, and Anna would have verbally castrated me. She would make an excellent duchess. Too bad Rosehill would make her a poor husband.

Before that thought could sour my mirth, she returned. Instead of burning embers, I was met with a placid smile and an empty gaze. Her eyes were dull now, elsewhere. The smile was shallow and insipid, far from her eyes. The look was all wrong for her, and I couldn't help but want the rage back.

That was the only explanation I could offer for the words that followed. "Earlier, you seemed upset. Is something the matter, Lady Juliet?"

"No, nothing at all, Mr. Wayland." There was no fire in the reply, no irritation, not even mild annoyance. It was as if her body was present, but her mind had escaped elsewhere.

"Perhaps you feel I should apologize for more than the misfortune of you overhearing my words?"

I was needling her; I knew I should stop. She'd heard things about her father last night that no one should have to learn. And from my lips. She didn't deserve to be mocked in her own home on top of the other insults.

"If you feel you have more apologies to give, by all means."

"I don't." The serene smile wouldn't budge, even at the sight of my crooked grin. Her face, moments ago so expressive, was all but motionless. There was nothing behind her eyes. I hated this. I was about to say so when a servant interrupted with the tea tray.

Lady Juliet busied herself with pouring. That was when I caught it, the slightest tremble in her hand. She was affected. I couldn't explain why that knowledge relieved me.

Unfortunately, it was that exact moment, that very tremble, that caused it—the disaster that followed. The cup caught on the edge of the saucer as she replaced it. The whole lot went flying, landing at my feet with a crash. Tea all over me. All over the carpet. I would have assumed she did it on purpose if it weren't for her reaction. No one could blame her for wanting to scald me; I'd been badgering her on purpose and retribution was only fair.

The way her eyes widened with horror instantly dispelled that notion. Before I could move, she was on the floor before me gathering shards of teacup with bare hands. All the while apologizing with alarming veracity. Now I wanted the placid smile back—anything but this panicked, frantic shell of a woman.

As soon as my thoughts caught up with her movements, I knelt to help her. When I finally managed to wrest her hands from the teacup remnants, she was bleeding on both palms. I bit out a curse at the sight, but she flinched in response and started to beg forgiveness once more for bleeding.

The realization lapped over me in waves like a tide coming in. The bile rose in my throat, anticipating the understanding before it actually dawned. *Richard Dalton, what have you done to this girl?* I should have hit him last night.

I was shaken from my reverie by her distressed cry. A small amount of her blood dripped onto the carpet. I pulled her hand into mine, the one with the worst injuries, trapping it there with my thumb. If I let her go, I didn't doubt she would cause more damage to herself in her desperation to clean. Her hand was so tiny in mine, delicate and soft. She still trembled, but her apologies ceased, and she stared up at me, wide-eyed and unreadable. Gently, I pressed my handkerchief into the largest of the cuts. She winced, the pain finally cutting through her panic. Only then did I notice the soft, soothing sounds that escape me unbidden.

"It's alright, Duchess, you're alright." My voice was low, hoarse.

She swallowed harshly before replying, "I am no duchess."

I couldn't restrain the small, ironic chuckle. "You're a duchess in all but title. I've never met anyone with such infallible manners. I'm sorry for vexing you. I shouldn't have done that."

"You were doing it on purpose?"

"You're beautiful when you're angry." I didn't give my mouth permission to utter that sentence. I regretted it almost instantly when she tried to pull her hand free from my grasp. I liked her hand there. It was tiny and warm and graceful with underlying strength.

Over the nearly imperceptible copper tang of her blood, I caught her scent for the first time. Apples, citrus, and something woodsy but fresh. It was intoxicating. She finally succeeded in wresting her hand from my grasp just as the maid returned to refresh the tea.

I assumed the maid's panicked cry was due to our improper proximity. Instead, she, too, fell to her knees beside us, frantically blotting the carpet with the edge of her apron. My earlier nausea returned with a vengeance. A startled gasp ripped free from Juliet. My hand tightened on hers without permission. Reluctantly I released her, forcing myself to take a calming breath. I needed to remain in control. She was frightened. I didn't want her to be frightened of me. We would likely never meet again after I left. She had no cause to fear me.

Juliet rose to her feet to call another servant. It was an awkward movement, given the limited use of her hands. She returned with a footman on her heels. He was equipped with a stiff brush and some cleaning solution that smelled strongly of vinegar. He joined the maid on the floor, moving with a slightly more covert terror.

I peeled myself off the floor, only then noticing the discomfort of my wet clothing and raw skin. Juliet was still fussing nearby, her hands clasped worriedly in front of her. A few of her curls had escaped her coiffure in the chaos. They framed her face, catching the light of the late-afternoon sun. Her skin was flushed with her recent agitation, and her lips were bitten with an enticing red.

I stepped toward her without conscious thought. She pulled back, reminding me of my place. I pushed down the sting of the rejection. After all, she wasn't mine. Not to comfort. Not to admire. Not to tease. She would never be mine. Even if she weren't promised to Rosehill, she wasn't for me. Daughters of earls didn't belong with bastards.

"I'm sorry," she whispered with a gesture at my person and the chaos around us.

"You have no reason to be, Duchess." I embedded the sentiment with as much sincerity as I was capable. Willing her to believe it, even for a moment.

My heart ached a little at her dismissive shake. It was clear she did it without conscious thought, as if she knew without question that she was at fault. I stifled the sigh of frustration that brought.

"I'd best be off. I doubt your father would approve of my being here." I couldn't help but add, "For what little it's worth, I am sorry you found out that way. I shouldn't have let him place the wager in the first place; my men knew he wasn't good for it."

"Thank you. If it eases your conscience at all, I am glad to know... Even if I wish it weren't true."

"Good day, Lady Juliet."

"Good day, Mr. Wayland."

With those final words, I stepped past her into the hall. The butler handed me my hat and overcoat, shutting the door firmly behind me.

Nine

MICHAEL

THE ROUND, bronze door handle of the Brook Street house may have actually inserted itself into my arse. Apparently, I hadn't found my way into the Dalton family butler's good graces. There were any number of reasons for his distaste. If one were capable of communicating distaste solely by the manner in which one handles a door, that man was an artist.

For early March, it was unseasonably warm, and the beau monde was taking full advantage. The rapidly melting snow mixed with the remains of the carriages and was forming a hazardous slush. The ladies and gentlemen were content to ignore both the smell and sight in favor of a promenade.

Even in my cynicism, I could not resist the allure of the sun's rays. With no particular hurry, I decided against hiring a hack, instead contenting myself with a lengthy walk. In a backward glance through the drawing-room window, I caught a glimpse of wild curls, a flash of skirts, and nothing more.

East on Brook Street, south on Davies Street, east on Grosvenor's Street, and then I found myself outside a familiar house with white pillars hidden behind a black ironwork fence. Two vibrant purple wisteria vines framed the door perfuming the air. The petals had already begun to fall creating violet piles beside the trunks. Celine.

She maintained a residence apart from her late husband's family. It was convenient for our liaisons and allowed her the freedom she was due as a widow of means. Though I saw her briefly last night, it had been more than a fortnight since we had enjoyed each other's companionship. With little thought and even less effort, I decided to inquire if she was home to see me.

The butler directed me to her boudoir, as was our usual practice. My journey through the halls of Cadieux House caused little fanfare from the servants. They were accustomed to my comings and goings. Decorated in silvers, grays, and taupes, her rooms were elegant yet tasteful, much like the lady herself. Moneyed by both inheritance and marriage, her home and apparel were always the height of fashion.

I sank into the settee by the window, noting absently that the blood-covered handkerchief was still clenched in my fist. The crimson stain was extensive. Lady Juliet bled through all four folds of the fabric. Absently, I noted the floral shape of the discoloration. She would bleed prettily.

Celine's arrival pulled me from my musings. Even at the late hour, she was still clad in her deep purple dressing gown. Ever the socialite, she returned late and woke late. Her long, golden hair was still unbound, cascading down one shoulder in large waves. Green eyes assessed me critically beneath dark, full lashes. Historically, my visits began with more ardor and less anxious contemplation of ruined fabric.

"Oh," her usual elegant prose escaped her at the sight of me. My eye must be in a worse state than I thought. It was a surprise her butler allowed me through the door. "Who is she?"

Well, I hadn't expected that.

"Who is whom?" I asked, feigning ignorance.

"You've met someone."

"Cee," I sighed, more exasperated than I intended. "I have no notion of whom you speak of."

"You've met a woman. Someone special."

She was poised beside me, hand on my knee. It was a greater comfort than I would have expected. Usually, her touches served to arouse rather than soothe. I missed the tension in my shoulders and brow, noting it only in its absence.

"I haven't met a woman, Celine. There's only you."

"Oh, Michael. Tell me the truth. We are friends, are we not?"

She turned my face towards hers with one sun-kissed hand on my jaw. There was nothing but earnest sympathy in her expression.

"She's no one."

"Michael, I always knew this day would come. You are a romantic at heart, even if you will never admit it. I want you to know love, real love. I know you think you are unworthy of such things, but you're mistaken."

I shook my head, disagreeing before she was half finished with her speech.

"Cee..."

"No, Michael. We've always been able to discuss all things. If this is to be your last visit, I want to know you will be going to good, kind hands."

"This isn't my last visit, Celine. Nothing needs to change."

It was the truth when the words left my lips, but they rang false once spoken.

"It is *mon amour*, much as I have loved our time together. I will not be a second choice for anyone. I became one the moment you met her."

"Celine..." I was pleading now. I had never needed to plead with her, at least not in this context.

"Michael, you have helped me in ways I cannot begin to express. In the months and years after my Gabriel's death, I was lost. You brought me back to myself with your friendship and your kindness. You made me feel, not only like a person again, but like a woman." Her voice was thick with emotion in a way I had never heard. "But you were never mine. She was always out there, waiting for you. What we had was wonderful, but I want for you what I had with Gabriel. You have so much love to give."

I buried my face in the curve between her neck and shoulder. My eyes were pressed tight against the tears. Her hands found the back of my neck and tangled soothingly in my hair. "Now, tell me about her."

I hesitated, fearing to give voice to what I had yet to acknowledge. "I found her last night, hiding under a table in the library at Grayson House after I had interrogated her father. I didn't notice her until her father was already gone. Her eyes, Cee. They were so devastated."

By the time I laid all my misdeeds at her feet, Celine enjoyed a good laugh at my expense. She had some choice words for Richard Dalton as well.

"You never like to make things simple for yourself. She needs someone to love her the way she deserves to be loved. You are a man more than equal to such a task."

"Celine, even if she wanted someone to love her, surely she wouldn't want me. She's set to become a duchess; she was born to be a duchess. I'm a bastard, running a gaming hell, extorting her father."

"It is not extortion if he brought it on himself."

"I think your English is lacking in this case."

"My English is always perfect, as is everything else I undertake."

"You're right. What was I thinking?"

"I have no idea. And you must stop speaking of yourself like that. You are the smartest man I've ever met. You are fiercely loyal to an unappreciative family. And now that I have taught you, you are not an unfortunate lover. She would be lucky to have a man such as you."

"Wait... I was an excellent lover before we met, and I've only improved from there."

"If you say so." She sounded less than sincere, and if we weren't having such a profound discussion, I might have pressed her on that further.

"None of that changes the fact that I can't give her what she deserves. I have no title to offer her, no name that anyone would want."

"You insist she is a duchess in all but the title. Have you asked her if she wants the title?"

"Of course, she wants the title. Everyone wants the title." The most fundamental truth of my life.

"But, you said yourself, she is not like anyone you've ever met." She paused, "What did you say her name was again?"

"Lady Juliet Dalton."

"And she is engaged to?"

"Rose— Oh, damnation." Her late husband's brother was the very same Alexander Hasket, Duke of Rosehill. "Cee, I am so sorry. I should not have involved you in this. Would you believe I forgot?"

"I would be more shocked if you remembered. For a man who makes his living off the gentry, you have a terrible time remembering the titles."

"Celine..."

"Well, that does answer some questions."

"What?"

"The necessity of payment, of course. In the business of marriage, the money typically travels to the bridegroom, not the other way around." That confirmed the needling thought I had when Dalton mentioned the name.

"So, the rumors are true then?" Her response was little more than a noncommittal shrug.

"There are men who would make worse husbands. If the match goes through, he will be kind and treat her well. Likely better than her father, at least."

"I wanted to ask you for advice. That seems wrong now."

Her eyes narrowed at me, contemplating. "That is for the best, I suppose."

"Regardless, thank you, Celine. Truly. I'm going to miss you terribly."

"I will miss you as well. I hope you will come to me if you need anything or if your Lady Juliet needs anything."

"Celine, that is too much to ask."

"You are not asking; I am offering. You would do the same for me without hesitation, and you know it. Besides, I believe you've inspired me to try to find love again. It will be different from what I had with Gabriel, but why should that mean it is not worth finding?"

My throat was thick with emotion. I had no words to offer anyway. I wanted that for her desperately. I pressed my lips to her forehead in lieu of empty promises. She, in turn, pressed a final kiss to my cheek in turn with a bittersweet smile. I bowed my head to her one final time before I crossed the threshold of the chambers.

Ten

JULIET

THE DAYS after Mr. Wayland's visit were quieter than I anticipated. I saw little of my father, which suited me just fine. We successfully removed the stain from the rug, which was a relief.

I had taken to trying Father's study door whenever he left the house. He was fastidious about locking the room. That was the extent of my search for proof of Mr. Wayland's accusations. I had no idea how to go about learning anything further. Regardless, did I really need evidence? He never denied the accusations.

His Grace called only once in the days since. We went for a stroll through Hyde Park on a particularly fine day. He brought his late brother's wife as chaperone. Lady Celine was unspeakably beautiful. Petite, blonde, and displaying an elegant blue-green walking dress to great advantage, she greeted me warmly with genuine enthusiasm through an easy French accent. It was evident she had been in this country for quite some time. Though intense, she was an enthusiastic conversationalist, unlike His Grace.

Outside of that one day, I had little to occupy my time beyond preparing my trousseau. I now had every reason to suspect there would be no pin money forthcoming. There were days I did nothing but refresh gowns. Through it all, I steadfastly refused to consider their purpose.

My only other outlet was visits to Kate. Given her status as a newlywed, I tried to limit my visits to weekly and to keep them somewhat brief. We continued to meet in the library, a room which certainly did not remind me of Mr. Wayland in the slightest. Even with the humiliation I suffered there, I could not bring myself to abandon it as a meeting place.

Someone had been shuffling books about in the library lately. Perhaps one of the servants or the viscount. They had taken to abandoning small stacks on my table, the one I had hid under, presumably to be returned later. Often, one or two would travel to Dalton Place with me instead, only to be replaced on my next visit. Whoever my curator was, they had exceptional taste.

Kate's lady's maid, a pretty redhead, often dropped off the tea treats. Though it was not strictly in her duties as a lady's maid, she seemed to take no issue in performing other tasks.

"Thank you, Anna."

Though her copper hair and freckles were not strictly fashionable, she was a singularly striking woman. I could not help but wonder at her choice of profession; surely, a woman of her looks and countenance would have no difficulty marrying well above her station.

"Of course. Is there anything else I can bring you?"

"No, thank you, we're quite alright for now."

She offered a curtsy and made her escape, the very picture of grace.

Kate turned her attention back to me. "How is your

engagement progressing? You were saying you went for a promenade in Hyde Park?"

"Yes, though his brother's widow was more interested in interrogating me than he was in furthering our acquaintance."

"Oh, Lady Celine?"

"You know of her?"

"Yes, she is very kind. She assisted me after the lemonade incident in my first season. I should have made an effort to introduce you at the ball the other night."

"I had nearly forgotten about the lemonade."

"I wish I could do the same. I'm certain she had nothing but the best intentions. She really is a treasure." That was something of a comfort. Her questioning had been rather one-sided, which was unnerving in retrospect.

"I have seen little of His Grace since. It is likely for the better, I will learn his foibles at some point, and he will do the same. Better to postpone it as long as possible."

"You're such a romantic. Has anyone ever told you that?"

"You, but always with a touch of sarcasm."

"If your fiancé has no plans to woo you, how would you feel about joining me in the country? Hugh and I were planning to visit the estate. Tom will bring their mother a few weeks after we arrive to take in the country air."

"So, you wish for an ally while you face the dragon."

"Something to that effect. Please, Jules? You could bring your mending and tailoring works, and perhaps have some time left for reading."

That was a tempting thought. Weeks without my father. Weeks with nothing pressing on me. A few weeks to be just Juliet, before I became the Duchess of Rosehill with everything that entailed.

"I will ask my father."

"Thank you." She returned to her tea, and I took the opportunity to eye the current stack of novels eagerly.

I left some hours later with one in hand, *Sense and Sensibility*.

The following day, I approached my father with the request. Years of practice had taught me the best method for achieving the desired result when asking something of my father. Between the second and third drink was ideal. Explaining the request so the answer one wanted was apparent but still requesting his input worked well. My father was confident that he was the smartest in any given room. With a minimal expenditure of effort on my part, I secured permission to join Kate and made my escape just as he was pouring the third glass of Port.

MICHAEL

"I FORGOT TO TELL YOU, Juliet will be joining us in the country," Kate said, casually informing my brother while passing the potatoes.

In one sentence, she destroyed the work of weeks.

I'd tried to excise Lady Juliet from my mind. To think of something else. To focus on my work. My efforts were ineffective at best, at times actually detrimental. Were it not for Augie's attention, my ledger mistakes would be enough to bankrupt a tiny principality. My personal coffers were feeling the effects of my distraction at the gaming tables.

I did, however, pay more attention during the last three dinners—hoping for brief mentions of Kate's friend—than I had in all previous dinners combined. Today was especially fortunate as Agatha was dining out with a friend. It was surprising to me that she had any friends, quite honestly. Her absence meant the distraction of dodging well-placed barbs and deflecting them from Kate was lifted from my shoulders.

Kate was truly kind to mention her without prompting. Thus far, I had been preoccupied the entire evening, desperately searching for an opportunity to turn the conversation in Lady Juliet's direction. I had not thought they would head back to the country so soon after their honeymoon as well.

"Who?" Hugh asked.

Tom's face met his palm in exasperation across from me. Even with no particular interest in the girl, Tom knew she was a regular dinner subject. That Hugh could not remember his wife's dearest friend was an insult to the lady.

"Lady Juliet." Kate's tone was clipped, irritation barely restrained.

Hugh moved his peas around his plate absently, not glancing at his wife. "Have I met her?"

The question was followed by the scratch of wooden chair legs on a matching floor. Silverware clattered with the motion, the table shuttering slightly at Kate's sudden rise. The movement seemed to draw Hugh from his plate, confused at the jarring shudder. She offered no explanation before her hasty retreat, only a thick, emotional, "Excuse me, gentlemen."

Tom and I were left staring and gaping as burnt-orange skirts swishing around the corner, trailing in her wake. We turned our attention toward our nitwit of a brother, and he gawked back at us.

Shrugging his shoulders, he concluded, "Must be feeling poorly."

Words escaped me, and Tom, ever the sociable brother, was left with nothing more than an exasperated, "Hugh!"

"What?"

Tom and I exchanged a significant glance. Given a choice between Hugh and Kate, I much preferred the latter. And frankly, given the same choice, Tom was far more likely to have success with the former.

I nodded my head toward Hugh before rising. "I'll be back in a moment," I said before following Kate's path.

Hugh's question followed me out, "Do you suppose it's the roast?"

I had never been more confident in a choice than I was just then, leaving Hugh to Tom's care.

Now alone in the hall, I had no idea where Kate might go to collect herself. No plan appeared forthcoming, so I was left to peer into various rooms along the corridor. Drawing room —empty. Billiard room—empty. Nearing the end of the hall, there was a stream of light under the library's double doors.

With a fortifying breath, I knocked and entered simultaneously. Though rude, I didn't wish for her to have the opportunity to refuse me entry. She whirled around from the novel she was paging through. It belonged to the stack, the ones I set out on my visits.

"Oh, Michael, can I help you with something?"

Her voice was small and tight, and her blue-gray doe eyes were glossy, an avalanche of tears clinging to the edge of her lashes. Her always pale skin was flushed with upset. I hadn't wanted to punch Hugh in his smug face this badly in ages. Perhaps not since the time, years ago, when I actually had.

"I came to see if you're alright."

"Of course, it was nothing. I'm perfectly alright. Fine really. Nothing to worry about."

"Right. Because if you were, perhaps, less than fine, irritated with my inconsiderate brother even, I would be available to listen if you weren't fine... which you are."

Her answering sigh was long. "Am I to spend the rest of my life reminding my husband that he's met my dearest friend? Numerous times, in fact. Frequently multiple times in a week."

"It seems likely. Which is most unfortunate; she is a lovely girl."

"Honestly, *she* is the kind of woman Hugh should have wed. He would have been happy with her. She's everything a lady ought to be. I am constitutionally incapable of pleasing my husband."

"I'm certain that's not the case. He married you, after all."

"That's not..." She stuttered, continuing, "I hoped by taking a visit to the country, away from the ton, we might be able to connect. Now that we're more accustomed to each other than we were on the honeymoon."

"...and away from Agatha."

"Yes, but he is insisting Tom bring her when he joins us later in spring when she might get some fresh air to help with her megrims."

"The only thing that helps with her megrims is constant, fawning attention from her sons." That earned me a bright burst of laughter.

"Once it was decided she would join, I thought to invite Jules to have a friendly face. But I will be humiliated, and she will be insulted daily."

"Certainly, once you're in the country, Hugh will remember the girl staying in his home."

Her answer was nothing but a skeptical look. "Alright, perhaps not."

Her gaze shifted, moving over me thoughtfully, a calculating gleam in her eyes.

I eyed her back and warned her, "Whatever you're considering, absolutely not."

"You don't even know what I'm about to say."

"I've seen that look in a woman's eyes before; it never ends well for the gentleman she's eyeing."

"Please, Michael?"

I ran a tired hand along my face. "What is it?"

"Join us in the country."

"Absolutely not."

"Please, I just need you to distract Jules from my husband's poor manners."

"And provide another target for Agatha."

She shrugged in answer, not denying my accusation.

"If you're so inclined, I won't reject help from any quarter."

I should have said no outright. I should not even have considered this. I had no business flitting about the country with an engaged debutant. My foolish brother would not be pleased with my presence. Not to mention the neglect my own business would suffer in my absence. But... It was Lady Juliet.

Eleven

JULIET

HE ORCHESTRATED THIS ENTIRE EVENT. I had not the slightest idea how or why, but I knew it was him.

Somehow, I was sitting across from Mr. Wayland and Viscount Grayson in the family carriage with Kate at my side. Mr. Wayland was wearing a feigned look of innocence. Kate as well. All was well when Kate and the viscount arrived to collect me. Then they informed me of another stop before we set off to Thornton Hall. Without a word of warning, the carriage turned down Curzon Street and pulled to a halt outside a gambling hell. A gambling hell called Wayland's.

My stomach sank with realization and horror and had not yet recovered. Before I had even a moment to prepare, the door opened, and Mr. Wayland took a seat across from me.

"Lady..." the viscount began.

"Juliet," Kate interjected coolly.

"Juliet, have you met my brother?"

The viscount's brother? That only served to confuse me

further. Now that I could see them next to each other, they did share a resemblance. But Mr. Wayland was clearly several years the viscount's senior. I sat there gaping like a fish, the answer just beyond my grasp.

"Half brother," Mr. Wayland corrected.

Suddenly the pieces slipped into place. I remembered myself and gave a quick bow in his direction.

"Yes, briefly," I said, tossing the comment in the viscount's direction.

Mr. Wayland removed his hat and adjusted his hair. I averted my gaze; it would not do to be found staring.

"It's good to see you again, Lady Juliet. I trust you've been well?"

"Yes, quite," I forced out, panic rising in my chest.

Two months. Eight weeks. Sixty days in his presence. Under the same roof. The disconcerting man who single handedly shattered the pretty illusions under which I had been living my life.

I threw a dismayed look to Kate, whose innocent smile had not faltered in several minutes. Kate never smiled like that. Every thought that passed through her head shone on her face for all to see. She had never seen the purpose in hiding her emotions as I had. It was all the confirmation I required.

He set this up on purpose. Whether merely a carriage ride, my invitation, or the entire house party, I could not be certain. But this was a plan, and Kate was involved. White, hot betrayal burned through my veins.

Surely, she could not be aware of it all. Kate would never put me in this situation if she understood Mr. Wayland's relationship with my father. Nor the humiliation I suffered when he called. She could not. I refused to believe that of my dearest friend.

I bit back the angry tears, staring at my hand. There was a

small hole in the thumb of my white leather glove. The tiniest bit of my nail peeked through the hole. I studied it with more attention than I had devoted to any previous lesson. It would need to be repaired shortly.

Out of the corner of my eye, I caught a number of silent gestures between the occupants of the gray velvet upholstered carriage. It was a well-loved but comfortable carriage, probably in need of some maintenance. The curtains were drawn over both windows, trapping the tension within the conveyance's confines.

There was a quiet thump in Mr. Wayland's direction. Beneath lowered lashes, I saw him rubbing his shin with discomfort. I did not blame him. I had been the recipient of Kate's frustration on more than one occasion, and she was stronger than she appeared.

Moved to speak under the threat of further violence, "So" —a pause to clear his throat— "Have you been well since the ball?"

"Yes," I said into my lap, voice thick, ignoring the repeated question.

There was a lengthy pause, a scuffle, and some sort of thunk—this time, she hit the carriage.

"Unseasonably warm weather we're having," Mr. Wayland murmured.

"Yes." More gesturing.

"As I recall, you knew more than one word when we last spoke."

"Michael..." the viscount warned. This was followed by head tilts and flailing hands, this time from the viscount's corner as well. I could only discern hints of meanings because I maintained the meticulous study of my glove. Though not torn, the forefinger was threadbare and in need of repair.

Mr. Wayland—Michael—the viscount called him, released

a barely concealed sigh of frustration. "I brought a novel I thought might interest you."

I couldn't keep my head down at that. "You did?" I could not conceal the eagerness in my voice.

At my side, Kate's shoulders relaxed, tension easing.

"Yes, I quite enjoyed it myself."

He passed me a small book across the carriage.

"Thank you," I was earnest in my appreciation. I returned my gaze to my lap, this time filled with *The Romance of the Forest*. Rubbing my thumbs reverently over the cover, I was eager to crack it open. Unfortunately, manners prevailed. Though, honestly, I was being quite rude as it was, refusing to so much as look at anyone.

"Jules," Kate said with a more plaintive tone than I was accustomed to from her. "You can read it. No one will mind."

I glanced at Mr. Wayland, seeking approval for some unknown reason. He merely nodded encouragingly and pulled out a book of his own. With his permission, I greedily turned to the first page.

MICHAEL

I COULD NOT RECALL a single plot in my novel, ironically titled *Self-Control*. Clearly, I had none. But I was mere meters from her. Jules. Kate had called her Jules. It fit her, elegant in its simplicity.

In the dim light of the carriage, she was even more striking than she had been in the drawing room. Or perhaps time had dulled the memory of her slightly. Her hair had escaped her coiffeur with the London dampness and was curling intriguingly about her temples and neck. The carriage air was thick with an enticing citrus scent, the one I identified as hers. It competed with Hugh's cloying cedar-scented soap.

I couldn't help but sneak glances at her. She was the most expressive reader I had ever seen, biting her lip to hold back a grin, covering her mouth to stifle a gasp. I recalled enjoying the novel but not to this extent; I had never enjoyed anything to this extent. Her reactions were fascinating. I wanted to catalog each and every one. I desired her thoughts on each of the novel's characters. I needed to discuss the events with her. Our chaperones were the only thing preventing me from crossing the carriage to her, from reading at her side.

The novel seemed to have served its intended purpose, distracting her from her previous ire. I should have ridden separately, given her time to adjust to the idea of me without my presence. I was anxious to see her, though, to prove that her allurements were all in my head—clearly wishful thinking.

It was fortunate that Hugh and Kate had both fallen asleep quickly once the tension in the carriage faded. Neither would have been able to keep silent about my obvious infatuation. She was just so passionate. I couldn't help but wish to be the sole focus of that passion. No one looked at me with even an ounce of the longing she had displayed for the book. I craved that attention from her.

Aching to hear her voice once more, I considered and rejected more than a dozen topics while pretending to read my own novel. There was little I wouldn't do to experience the same scrutiny of my person she was showing that book. Her eyes widened with anticipation at something in the novel. Never in my life had I felt this kind of desperation for a woman's attention. I was reduced to repeatedly reminding myself that she deserved the opportunity to read in peace. Needling her would not endear me in her eyes. Kate would not hesitate to send me away if I upset her, or worse. I choked back a sigh and forced my attention toward my own reading.

"Not enjoying your novel?" Her quiet voice drew my gaze across the rocking carriage.

"Honestly?"

She nodded.

"I haven't comprehended a word. I'm a bit distracted at present."

Her cheeks flushed, but she forged on with feigned ignorance. "Distracted? Do you have difficulty reading in a carriage?"

I felt a grin spreading and caught my lower lip between my teeth to snuff it. "Something like that. Are you enjoying your novel?"

"Yes, very much. Thank you for bringing it. You mentioned you had read it?"

"I have. I quite enjoyed it."

"May I ask an impertinent question?"

"My favorite kind."

"Have you been visiting the library at Grayson House?"

Warmth filled my chest. I swore to myself that I was merely offering suggestions to a fellow reader, convincing myself that it was better if she did not know the identity of her personal curator. Clearly, I was a liar.

"I visit a great many places. It's difficult to recall."

My evasion earned an eye roll. I was fooling no one. Least of all her.

"So, you have not been leaving several carefully selected novels on the table for someone, definitely not me, to find and borrow."

"I'm a busy man, Duchess. I don't have time to scour libraries in the hopes of choosing a novel that a hypothetical visitor to said library would enjoy."

"Too many fortunes to steal? And, again, I am not a duchess." The words and tone were incongruous. There was none of the clipped irritation I had become accustomed to with her. Still, the epithet was a good one. Better to remember where she belonged, far away from the likes of me.

"Fortunes to win. And, from my understanding, soon-to-be one. You certainly act the part well."

"*Humph*," she pouted, sinking just the slightest bit lower in her seat, perfect posture collapsing an infinitesimal amount. "Well, if, on your travels, you come across a lady or gentleman who selects novels for others' perusal, you should let them know they have excellent taste. And their efforts are appreciated."

"If I meet such a person, I'll be sure to let them know."

Her gaze met mine, steady, sincere. "Thank you."

Playful banter evaporated in the face of such earnestness and all I could do was nod. Hugh chose that moment to let out a shamefully loud snore, startling us both and waking Kate. Juliet's spine stiffened ramrod straight, and she froze at the sound. Her eyes wide and unblinking on Hugh's form.

Her response would have been appropriate if my lips had found their way under her chemise as they had in my dreams or if we were digging a grave for a victim of murder. It was a substantial overreaction to my brother, a man who could not actually remember her name, possibly waking. Particularly while we did nothing more incriminating than speak across a carriage—a discussion that consisted entirely of thinly veiled implications about novels.

Not for the first time, I wondered at her life under Dalton. Wondered and seethed. What had he done to this beautiful, witty, passionate woman to make her scared of her own shadow? Would she help me bury the body if I killed him for it? She had practice reacting if we were caught mid-shovel.

Kate watched her worriedly, only calming once she turned back to her novel. Her face was buried so far in the book I knew she would not come up for air again, not to speak with me anyway. Gone was the expressive reading, the wide-eyed gasps and eager page-turning. Instead, the dead-eyed, placid smile returned, spine straight, each page flipped with precise calm. Resigned, I turned back to my own reading. My attention, even more frayed, remained across the carriage with the shell of the woman left behind.

Twelve

MICHAEL

A STILTED SUPPER followed our arrival at Thornton Hall. After which, Kate all but kidnapped Juliet. They flitted off to do whatever it is ladies did, and Hugh and I were left to our own devices. I carried the resultant tension through to bed. Four courses of studiously even-tempered remarks from Lady Juliet had me straining to remember my place. It took all my fortitude to refrain from needling her, shaking her, kissing her —anything for a reaction.

Something about Juliet—Lady Juliet, always Lady Juliet— set my nerves aflame. Her proximity proved too great a temptation to allow for sleep. I abandoned the comfort of my bed, just down the hall from hers, in favor of the study some time ago.

Several hours spent in review of the ledgers showed the extent of Hugh's neglect. Even the many hours weren't enough to sort out the mess he had here. Whatever his organizational system, it was indecipherable to all but him. Desire to press him on the issue warred with the understanding that the finances were no longer my concern. No matter the responsibility I felt toward the servants and tenants. Still, I could not be faulted for visiting with them; we were friends, after all. I doubted Hugh would see it that way, but I was simultaneously too tired and edgy to care overly much. Particularly after his loud nasal passage ruined my progress in the carriage with Juliet—Lady Juliet. Not that there was anything to progress toward, because there wasn't.

WHEN I BROKE MY FAST, it was much too early for Hugh and Kate to be about. The morning sun streamed through the windows, the April chill receding with its light. Clearly, Kate hadn't had the opportunity to work her magic on this room. It still bore the ostentatious gold and navy markers of Agatha. The mahogany table remained obsessively long, plenty to seat at least ten. The entire situation was far too extravagant for a breakfast parlor.

The hearty scents of eggs, cold ham on the sideboard, and tea awaited. Along with fresh toast and butter, my plate was laden with delights. Even this simple fare was a treat in Mrs. Hudson's hands. I dug in with more enthusiasm than manner, thumbing through a ledger I'd borrowed from the study.

Without glancing up from my reading, I knew the quiet rustling from the doorway was sure to be Lady Juliet. She busied herself at the sideboard before taking a seat across from me with her plate. She was fresh-faced, pink-cheeked, and her eyes blurry with sleep. She had bound her hair in a simpler style than she usually favored. Her wayward curls were already plotting an escape from her coiffure. The placid mask of the night before was nowhere to be found. I was imminently glad for it.

"Good morning. Did you sleep well?" My voice was rough with disuse.

Her answering flush was unexpected.

"I must confess I did not." At my questioning brow, she continued. "I found myself far too distracted with the misadventures of Adeline to sleep."

Her tone was playful, and she bit her lip to cover a pleased grin. I found myself suppressing a similar smile at that.

My response was entirely inappropriate. "I had difficulty sleeping as well, but it wasn't thoughts of a desolate abbey that led me to distraction." I fought back a pleased smirk at her flush.

She waited until I had taken a sip of my tea before replying, "Theodore de Peyrou drove you to distraction then?"

I choked down my tea with an undignified cough. She covered a giggle with the back of her hand. Despite its appearance at my expense, it was the most beautiful sound I'd ever heard.

"Monsieur de Peyrou remains in a Parisian prison, while my distraction remains somewhat closer to home."

Her eyes fell to her plate, and her flush deepened. Her navy eyes return to mine, mischief still shining in them. I met her whimsy with a crooked grin of my own.

"Speaking of your distractions, I have something to show you if you have a few moments this morning."

Her reply was interrupted by Kate's appearance. "Good morning Jules, Michael. I trust you slept well?"

"Quite well, thank you," Juliet replied with a pointed look in my direction.

I struggled to keep my grin from deepening. I would keep any confidence she was willing to share with me. Even such a small secret felt... intimate.

Kate turned to me with a raised brow, loading her plate with breakfast treats. "Quite, as well."

"I have some preparations that need to be made for our stay here. Perhaps you would be so kind as to show Lady Juliet the estate and grounds?" Once again, I was reminded how far above himself my brother wed.

"Oh, I should not wish to impose," Juliet protested,

"While I should be consulting you for suggestions, after all, you've read every conduct guide ever written; thrice over. I think a tour would be best."

"Only because they were the only things in our library," she directed her attention toward Kate before turning to me. "I have more than enough embroidery to pass the time. You need not plan your day around me, Mr. Wayland."

"I have no other engagements. Also, as I mentioned before, I have something I think will interest you. It's in the library."

She perked up, eyes luminous with interest. "The library?"

"Yes, it's quite extensive."

"The library? Or the thing you wish to show me?" She bit back a smirk, amused at her entendre.

"Juliet!"

She turned to Kate with feigned innocence. If I hadn't seen the self-satisfied delight in her countenance mere seconds ago, I would have believed her ignorant facade. I liked this side of her. I wanted to learn all of her facets.

I rose and rounded the table to her side. She paused for a moment before taking the hand I provided. I could feel Kate's eyes burning my back as I escorted her to the library.

JULIET

IT WAS THE FIRST TIME WE HAD TOUCHED without a bloody handkerchief between us. My hand rested on his forearm, warm and solid beneath my touch. This was closer than he had ever been, at least when he was not rattling the foundations of my life. With a steadying breath, I was met with his scent for the first time. There was a hint of mint with vanilla and orange and the barest hint of ink underneath. The combination was sensual, masculine, intriguing.

My heart fluttered, and my stomach danced about. I had never felt like this at a man's touch before. Not when I danced with His Grace, not when he slid my betrothal ring onto my finger, nor any other time I could recall. We were not even touching, not really. He was in half-dress. There were at least two layers of cloth between my hand and his arm. Still, the feeling was similar to my panics, but my breathing was steady, and it was an altogether pleasant sensation.

He led me around a corner through an open set of dark mahogany doors. I was immensely grateful for his solid warmth underneath me, the only thing keeping me upright when I saw it. Every single wall of the room was covered in floor-to-ceiling bookshelves, painted a greenish blue. There were additional freestanding shelves, as well. A small cozy bench abutted one of them. Sunlight gleamed through each of the five windows, casting shadows. Charred ash, leather, and burnt candle scents perfumed the air. There were two small settees and a large, low mahogany table off in the corner near the expansive brick fireplace. And every single shelf was lined with books. I had thought the library at Grayson House was magnificent; it was nothing compared to this. This was the most beautiful room I had ever seen.

My strength returned. I broke away from his arm to peruse the nearest shelf. Seconds, minutes, and hours later, I had a pile on the nearby table. When I would find the time to embroider and mend my gowns was of little concern; not when faced with all this ink, paper, leather, and these stories. Mr. Wayland cleared his throat quietly, bringing me back to myself. Before I could offer apologies for my inattention, I caught sight of the fond, amused expression he wore.

In lieu of chastisement, he handed me another novel. I struggled to juggle the three in my hands to take his offering. With some effort, I managed to set those down on the table in favor of his, *Mansfield Park*.

"I believe you're fond of this author. This is her latest. It was published just a month ago."

I could feel the gaping expression on my face, unladylike in my floundering. There were no words, no way to express my gratitude. A book, so new, would have cost a fortune. I wished that I had worn my gloves. It felt wrong to touch something so precious with bare hands. I collapsed onto the nearest settee, reverently opening the cover—the tome cracked with disuse, no use. I had never held an untouched novel before. I brushed my fingers delicately over the title page with reverence.

I finally managed to stammer my gratitude and express a hope that he would allow me to read it when he finished.

"It's yours. I bought it for you."

I was speechless again. Never before had I received a gift of this magnitude. Reality slammed back into me with that thought. I could not possibly accept it.

The words that followed broke my heart. "I thank you, Mr. Wayland, but I could not possibly accept such a thing. It would be inappropriate."

He hid his disappointment well, but it was still discernible in his eyes. "If it would make you feel more comfortable, we could call it a loan. Given how quickly you devoured the others, I should think you'll need more reading material for your visit."

"A loan. That would be acceptable," I agreed, more eagerly than I should.

"A very long loan. It's possible you could borrow it for so long that I forget to ask after it."

I could not hide my smile at that thought.

"If you can bring yourself to leave the others behind, I thought we might take a tour of the grounds. There's a spot I find has excellent light for reading, and I thought you might find it agreeable."

"I should like that very much."

"I shall meet you at the front entry. Shall we say in twenty minutes?"

I nodded my assent, reluctant to leave my new haven but eager for the opportunity to open the novel. The promise of his company had nothing to do with my enthusiasm.

Thirteen

MICHAEL

I BRIBED Mrs. Hudson and Anna to put together a basket for the two of us to enjoy. I felt every bit the love-sick fool when I requested it. Of course, the two were quite willing to make miracles happen for a bottle of the good port, though not without a good-natured teasing.

My bribery was more efficient than I anticipated, and I was left to wait on Juliet's arrival. *Lady Juliet.* I must remember it was Lady Juliet. I paced the foyer, fiddling with my hat like a dolt. I was certain I looked every bit as graceless as I felt when I saw her at the top of the stairs. She had added a navy spencer and a matching floral bonnet to her day dress, and she danced down the stairs, book in hand, biting her lip— perhaps the barest hint of trepidation.

"I thought perhaps we might find a spot for a bit of luncheon on our tour." I lifted the basket in my hand before donning my hat and holding the door for her.

"That would be nice. Thank you."

The day was warmer than usual for the time of year, and

the sun burned bright. The air was fresh and floral compared to the thick, cloying scents of London. Confidently, she slid her hand to rest on my forearm, a significant change to her previous unease. Her hand felt at home there. The rest of her felt at home next to me as well. Her frame and small curves perfectly matched the dips in my own form. She was tall, the top of her bonnet reaching just under the brim of my hat.

She was responsible for maintaining the distance between us that propriety dictated; I would not be so fastidious. Propriety would also have demanded a chaperone, yet she did not comment on our lack. The numerous gardeners and stable hands wandering about were likely enough for her comfort.

"Where would you like to tour first?" Unable to resist the urge to tease her, I added, "There are several gardens and the stables I can show you."

She hesitated, and I fought back a grin. She clutched the novel closer to her, seemingly an unconscious gesture. She cared little about the flowers or the horses, wanting only my promised reading hideaway.

A testament to her unfailing decorum, she answered, "You would know best where to begin."

It was frustrating. In the rare instances she let her guard down, I had become addicted to her light teasing, her earnest sincerity, her adorable fury. I wanted that honesty from her, always. But I hadn't earned that from her yet, nor her trust. I had no right to demand it from her. I was quite unworthy of even the precious few instances gifted to me thus far.

"Or..." I drew the word out as I turned to her and rocked back on my heels. "I could take you to my favorite place. Nice breeze and shade to keep cool, excellent light."

She bit her lip, restraining a smile. The warmth in her eyes betrayed her. "Yes, please."

I missed the anxious tightness that settled into my muscles

with her first placid response. It eased with her honesty, and the relief in its absence was striking.

"You know, I think you'd be surprised at what I'm willing to do if you just ask."

"And what, pray tell, would you be willing to do for me?" She wore the self-satisfied archness well.

"I think the better question is, what wouldn't I be willing to do for you?"

"And what would you refuse me?"

"I'll let you know the first time you ask me for something, and I find myself unwilling."

A pleased flush overtook her, and it was breathtaking. Offering my arm once more, she slipped hers gracefully through. She was pressed closer this time, just on the correct side of improper. It was a short walk to my sanctuary. In no more than ten minutes, we found our destination, and I couldn't help but wish I'd found a longer route.

The path was slightly overgrown. I was forced to release her to lift a tree branch from her way. In doing so, I missed her first sight of the little clearing surrounding the slow-moving creek and the worn bridge that crossed it. Her quiet gasp made up for it.

Trailing after her, I was treated to the first sight of my favorite refuge in years. The trees had grown in my absence, buds displaying the first brush of spring. The raspberry bushes on the opposite bank had overtaken it. Wildflowers bloomed in the sunlight filtering through ash branches. The dogwood had begun to drop a few petals into the creek; they floated lazily past. The simple oak bridge fared better than I had hoped in my absence. Though it was weathered, it remained sturdy. I had worried it would be overwrought.

I built the bridge in my youth using scrap wood. It served as a method to sneak across to the Revello property for raspberries. And raspberries meant Anna's raspberry tarts. That family had complained heartily until they abandoned the house, ostensibly seeking a tenant. I was more than willing to risk their wrath for Anna's tarts. As far as I was aware, the home remained empty to this day more than a decade unoccupied.

I could not bring myself to turn for her reaction, instead hurrying to my weatherbeaten bridge. Carefully, I tested the sturdiness with a foot before putting my full weight on it. Satisfied with its strength, I knelt to brush some of the debris off. After pulling out the blanket Mrs. Hudson had packed, I covered the worn wood, thankful she had thought of it. I never indulged in such flights of whimsy. I turned to find Juliet already on my heels, head tipped back as she took in the scenery. I handed her down to join me on the blanket. A small part of me feared that my proper duchess would refuse such an undignified, humble seat. At the very least, I expected her to sit primly, perfectly posed.

Instead, she gathered the slightest bit of her skirts up, flashing a tantalizing hint of stocking, and allowed her feet to dangle at the edge, legs bent at the knees. She pulled off her gloves, loosening one finger at a time before leaning back with her weight on one hand, the other at the ties of her bonnet, tugging it off. She tipped her head farther back, eyes closed, basking in the sun's warmth on her face.

My heart stopped at the sight before resuming its work with fervor. Several of her dark curls pulled free with her bonnet, caressing her neck and cheek with the soft breeze. The barest hint of cinnamon shone in the locks where the sun hit. Long, dark lashes and elegant brows served as a vivid contrast to her pale skin. Her cheeks retained that peachy flush. Her lips were bitten to the same red as the raspberries along the bank.

I returned to myself when she sat up, turning her eyes to me. Caught with my mouth open in wonder at the sight of her, I struggled for purpose. I pulled the basket between us for something to do. Mrs. Hudson had packed fruits, cheeses, loaves of bread, spreads, and other assorted treasures, and I pulled them out one by one, an offering to my Juliet.

"What would you like?"

She studied me, searching my face for the answer to some unknown question. Whatever she found must have pleased her because she offered me a small smile. She tipped her head toward the book at her side. "I'll serve. Would you read to me?"

"I must confess, I never thought you'd ask that of me."

I could feel the wry grin as I took the proffered book. It was a pleasant, warm feeling, that she'd asked something of me, and I fulfilled that request.

I cleared my throat before beginning, "'*About thirty years ago, Miss Maria Ward, of Huntingdon, of only seven thousand pounds, had the good luck to captivate Sir Thomas Bertram, of Mansfield Park...*'"

JULIET

I HAD SHOCKED HIM with my impertinent display, but I could not muster a care for it. The day was too beautiful, the location too enchanting, to stand on ceremony. He should have considered himself fortunate that I only removed my bonnet and gloves. I yearned to free my toes from the confines of shoes and stockings and dip them into the lazy creek below.

All my life, I toured perfectly cultivated and tamed gardens at great houses. Not a single one could touch the wild, natural beauty surrounding me. The only artificial touch in the clearing was the bridge supporting me. It was simple but well made, with no elaborate coverings or railings, merely two boards across with smaller boards atop. A little weatherbeaten, but it was not the weaker for it. The late-morning sun warmed the timber, seeping through the blanket. The familiar ache in my lower back that signaled my menses made its presence, and the heat was soothing against the pain.

The breeze brushed my curls against my skin, but I could not summon the irritation I usually felt at their misbehavior. They had an infuriating habit of coiling themselves into the straw of my favorite bonnet and pulling free from my coiffure the moment I removed it. No matter how I lined the thing, they still found a way. I thought the trimmings and shape of it favored my face and coloring. I had not anticipated removing it in his presence, so vanity defeated practicality when I dressed for the occasion. I could not regret it in the face of such a lovely setting. I luxuriated in the sun's rays on my face before a thought that sounded remarkably like my father reminded me of my freckles.

With a sigh, I pressed myself back up to sit from my half-lounging position before turning my gaze on him. He gaped slightly. I had never seen anyone gape handsomely before, but he managed it. My first assumption was displeasure at my brash display. A moment's further study revealed something akin to awe in his gaze. No one had ever looked at me with such wonder. The warmth that thought caused had nothing to do with the sun. At first, the consideration was discomfiting, but in short order, I found myself reveling in his attentions.

Unfortunately for my newfound desires, he recovered slightly and presented me the entire contents of his basket for the taking. His voice was rough with disuse. The sound warmed me deep in my chest. I was struck with a wholly impertinent request. Before considering the consequences, I asked him to read to me. It was an ideal solution to the issue I had been pondering, how to discuss the work with him when he had not read it.

With a sardonic comment and half smile, he began to read. A skilled orator, his raspy baritone rose and fell with the prose. His entire face was animated. Thick, dark brows rose skeptically at some comment or other. The wry, crooked grin made a frequent appearance. I was becoming rather fond of that grin. He had displayed a few others during our short acquaintance, but this one was most frequently directed toward me.

This was my first opportunity to observe him without interruption, and I made full use of it. His hair, thick and dark like burnt umber, was mussed from his long since removed hat. The typically immaculate locks still fell in their usual soft waves across his forehead, but they were flattened slightly at the sides. His eyes were warmer than I thought them previously. In the sun, they shone a bright caramel, and I noticed a shadowed hickory ring around the outside of the irises. The bruising from our first meeting was long healed, and his warm olive-toned complexion was clear and bright. His nose was slightly crooked, suggesting prior injury and lending interest. His lower lip was slightly fuller than his upper, and the pair seemed perpetually raised at the right corner. Contrasted with his frequently lifted left brow, it served to balance his face. His jaw was clean shaven, and strong. His smokey, graveled voice fit the masculine, dark features, and I lost myself in the music of his words and the expressions dancing across his face.

He read for some time, pausing only occasionally for a sip of wine or a bite of food before I realized I was completely adrift from the story. I was lost in his honeyed voice and dazed by his handsome features. The combination awakened a pleasant heat inside me sweet and new.

I was attracted to him. The thought was striking—new. Just as alarming was the understanding that I had never been attracted to a man before. His Grace was considered by all to be one of the most agreeable gentlemen of the ton. To me, he was an amalgamation of fine features. I saw and appreciated each distinctly from the other. Before this moment, I thought that was handsome. I knew better now. Michael was something different, something more.

Fourteen

THORNTON HALL, KENT - APRIL 2, 1814

JULIET

"How did you find the grounds?" Kate asked after my return.

"They're quite lovely, Kate. If I were you, I would never leave for town. They are so well settled, and there is true natural beauty to be found."

The drawing room was well situated with a dedicated view of a beautiful lake that Michael—Mr. Wayland—neglected on our tour. It was a clear blue green surrounded by reeds with an occasional break in the tall stalks.

Kate had made fewer changes to this house than to the London home. This room clearly reflected the dowager's tastes; bright oranges and purples everywhere. The bones of the room were lovely, though. An oversized brick fireplace was positioned to the side of the massive windows. A mahogany writing desk overlooked the view in one corner. Quality furnishings with gaudy upholstery abounded. Though overwhelming, I was sure Kate would adapt this room to her preferences as well.

"How was Michael?" Kate asked, an unusual tone in that question I couldn't quite read.

My response was cautious. "He was very attentive." I sipped my tea, buying time to assess her response.

"He and Hugh have such a strained relationship. I thought simple weekly suppers would rebuild the broken bonds, but seems as though I've made little progress."

"I'm certain that's not the case."

"As my dearest friend, you're a rather biased source, and I adore you for it. I think perhaps they've reached a cease-fire. I've had less success with Agatha. Forced proximity doesn't seem to have endeared me to her."

Kate's predecessor's welcome was anything but warm. I knew it was a source of hurt and frustration from the early letters of her marriage, but I hoped time had eased the strain somewhat. It seemed that was not the case. I was unsure why she had not been moved to the dowager house. It must have been cloying to watch each day as Kate ran the household in a manner she disapproved of.

"Still, she is worse to Michael. It's a wonder I can get him to attend our weekly engagements."

"Why should she be rude to Mr. Wayland?"

Kate glanced around to ensure the drawing-room door was closed before responding in a loud whisper. "Well, you know he's the late viscount's natural-born son. He was raised as a ward but look at the three of them. She could hardly be ignorant of it."

An unease settled in my stomach. I had no right to this intelligence offered from lips other than his. Still, I could not bring myself to interrupt or reprimand her. Not when I was desperate for any intelligence she offered.

"She has no right to be so rude to him, though. He was just a boy."

"She is truly so awful?"

"Oh yes, I've never seen its like."

Before I could respond, the door opened, and Mr. Wayland entered.

~

MICHAEL

THE LADIES SPRANG APART LIKE RABBITS, snapping up from the settee. There was absolutely no doubt in my mind that they were gossiping. About me, if the guilty blush rising up Lady Juliet's cheeks was any indication. I would have found it fetching if it were not at my expense. Faced with the choice of allowing them their confidence or watching the flush spread down to Lady Juliet's chest, I chose the latter.

"Good lord, Katherine, what on earth are you telling her about me?" I asked, willing her to join me in my teasing.

"Only your deepest sins," she said. She was a delight, as always.

"So, the envy and pride then?"

"Naturally"

"I hope you left out the lust. She looks easily shocked."

"Oh no, I gave her a full report of your lustful appetites."

"Oh dear, shall I have the carriage readied, Lady Juliet? I cannot imagine you should like to stay in the same house with such a reprobate."

"Actually, I believe I require more details of these appetites before I go so far as to vacate the county."

With that comment, the flush reached the edge of her bodice and below. There was a genuine smile on her face as she stepped toward me, not the forced one I had often seen. Embarrassed but amused then, still willing to play, to tease.

"I'd be thrilled to provide a demonstration at your earliest convenience."

"I believe my plans are quite fixed this evening. Shall we say tomorrow?"

"I serve at your pleasure."

It may have been my imagination, but her eyes darkened slightly at my comment. I wouldn't go so far as to label the look desire, but it was in the vicinity. My feelings were more firmly fixed in the realm of craving. I had spent the hours since we returned from the bridge in the kitchens, thrashing Hugh's valet, Stevens, at hazard. I needed an outlet for the tension the sight of her in the sunlight had induced. It was far too early in the day to take myself in hand. The sight of her flushed chest rising with her now heavier breathing, made me regret that choice.

A pointed cough came from off to the side. Juliet sprang back from me, burned, and I realized just how close we had gotten. Her retreat was hampered by the presence of the settee at the back of her knees. We were far nearer than propriety dictated. Kate's wordless reproach was well warranted.

"Apologies for my behavior Lady Juliet. I thought we might have the cribbage lesson we discussed earlier, but perhaps now is not the best time for such things."

She glanced at Kate for approval.

"Actually, I should speak to Mrs. Hudson about some of the meals for our visit. You two enjoy yourselves."

I was shocked she allowed this without a chaperone, but she pointedly left the door open, and moments later, a footman appeared in the hall, hovering just outside. Not the most adequate chaperonage, but effective nonetheless.

I rummaged through the mahogany shelves abutting the fireplace while Juliet wordlessly cleared the table. Once I'd located the deck and board, I joined her by the window. The afternoon sunlight streaming through set her curls aflame, brightening her upturned face.

I was unable to resist the urge to impress her, just a little. I shuffled the deck with more flourish than I would in my club. Once she appeared suitably awe-struck with my efforts, I began instruction.

"Typically, we would cut the deck to see who deals, but I thought it might be easier if I deal this first round?"

She agreed while leaning forward in her chair with interest. I enjoyed her attentions too much. They were entirely innocent, but her lips were parted with intrigue, and her sky-bright eyes were warm with enthusiasm. No one had ever placed such import on my words and actions, except when trying to outmaneuver me at the card table. Her intentions were entirely guileless; she had no plan to leave me gulled.

I dealt us each six cards before I explained that two cards went in the crib. "Cards are worth their face value; face cards are ten, aces are one."

She nodded at me to continue, and I elaborated further. If I were studying her with less enthusiasm, I would have missed the brief flash of worry before her eyes dropped to the table, and her chest rose with a deep inhale.

"Does that make sense?"

"Yes, please continue." Her voice was a little tighter than before as well. She returned her gaze to mine, and that infuriatingly blank smile was back. My stomach twisted at the sight of it. It hadn't made an appearance since the night before. I nearly forgot how much I loathed it until it returned.

"I wish you would tell me what's troubling you. If you don't wish to play, we can choose another game. Or I can leave you to your own devices."

The smile dropped at that. Even though it was replaced by a distressed countenance, I was relieved to see it gone.

She bit her lower lip before starting with a deep breath, "It is just that—you see—I am not particularly skilled with arithmetic." She rushed to explain. "I know my addition. It is just, I am rather slow at it. It can be rather frustrating to deal with me while I work it out."

Her eyes didn't leave the table for the entire speech. I couldn't determine whether I was more honored that she was willing to share with me or more enraged at whoever made her feel inadequate. After a moment's consideration, and with no enemy before me, I was left to discard the latter and focus on the former.

"You're in luck then; we're in absolutely no hurry."

She offered me a skeptical smile in return. I continued with the rules explaining play while she listened intently. I refrained from further efforts to show off. When we finally began, I prepared myself for a lengthy struggle with each additional card.

For the first few rounds, that was precisely what I found. She contemplated each additional card, occasionally taping each finger against her thumb in sequence. She announced her total with a slight look of trepidation. Even with the delay, she took no longer than most gentlemen after they'd enjoyed a drink—or several. As the rounds passed, and she quickly became more confident in the rules, her responses sped up. Her fingers ceased to tap. The apprehension disappeared. She played with the same speed as the gentlemen who regularly frequented my establishment before they had imbibed. She was still slower than I was, but I made my entire fortune with these cards.

When she apologized for the third time, I'd had enough. "You know, you're faster than my patrons who've been playing for years. It's a good thing you'll never set foot in my establishment. With a bit of practice, I would lose everything to you."

"You are too kind. A terrible liar, but kind." Even with her denial, her smile was pleased, and the flush returned to her cheeks.

"Take it back!"

She looked up with alarm.

"You've just destroyed my carefully cultivated reputation as a liar, a cheat, a rake, and a brute. Take it back."

That earned me a delighted laugh, and it took effort to retain the stern facade I'd adopted.

Our play was only interrupted by the bell to dress for dinner. She helped clear our game before I escorted her up the stairs. Her small hand rested in the crook of my arm where it belonged. Before we parted at the top, I gathered my courage.

"Lady Juliet, I quite enjoyed our time together today. I was wondering if perhaps we might repeat it tomorrow? If you're not otherwise engaged."

Her acceptance and genuine grin brightened her countenance and eased the anxiety in my chest. With that promise, we parted ways.

Fifteen

JULIET

TWO HOURS AND FOURTEEN MINUTES. It felt like an eternity. I had been trying and failing to find sleep. Every single tick of the clock was beginning to agitate. One twenty-five, I was sure to have dark circles tomorrow. I rolled to my other side, flipping and punching my pillow for the seven hundred and fifty-sixth time. When the ache in my shoulder returned, even more quickly than the last time, I finally gave up with a performative sigh for an imagined audience.

Lighting a candle, I grabbed my dressing gown and made for the library in desperate search of something dull enough to quiet my mind. Padding barefoot down the cold hall, I regretted my lack of stockings. In my haste to escape the frigid ice of the hall, I missed the hint of candlelight seeping underneath the door to the library.

I pressed open the door, and I was met with the sight of Michael asleep on the settee, book propped open against his stomach and a flickering candle low on the table behind his head. His body flopped across the furnishing, while his feet dangled over the edge. His neck was bent at an awkward angle that could not possibly be comfortable. Far from being formally attired, he was clad in only his shirt sleeves and breeches, suspenders hung over the side of the seat. Even his feet were only in stockings. A lone lock of hair made itself at home on his forehead.

He was more peaceful than I had ever seen him. My feet dragged me to his side without permission. From a closer vantage, I could see the shirt open low on his chest, a dusting of dark hair and freckles called it home. A collection of sonnets from Sir Philip Sidney rose and fell gently on his stomach with each soft breath. For a moment, I was paralyzed with indecision. His situation could not possibly be comfortable. But our position was scandalous enough with his unconscious state. For him to awaken—to see me as such—it was too much to contemplate. But to leave...

My uncertainty forced my decision. With an inelegant snort, he startled awake, flailing in his unbalanced position on the settee. He rose to sit before I could react, bringing us impossibly closer.

"Juliet?" His voice was bleary with sleep but softer, raspier than I was used to when he was reading to me.

The word startled me into action, and I straightened to pull away.

"Oh, I should not be here. I'm sorry. Please, forget you saw me."

Before I stepped fully back, he grasped my wrist, tying me to him. With his free hand, he wiped the sleep from his eyes.

"Unlikely. What are you doing here?"

His eyes, hot and real as any physical touch, dragged their way down my body. With alarm, I recalled my present state of undress. I pulled back once more. His hand tightened on my wrist, pinning me in place.

"I couldn't sleep. I came for something to read." My voice was barely more than a whisper in the darkness.

He handed me the book that had fallen to his lap when he sat up. "This seems to be an effective sedative."

I moved to take it, to retreat to my room.

He stopped me with a single word. "Stay?"

I should not. I knew I should not, but *oh, how I wanted to.* He shifted to one side of the settee, his back remaining against the arm while he curled a leg under the other, leaving half for me. My body made my decision for me. I folded myself into the opposite half, mimicking his position. His arm lined the back of the settee and, in my effort to replicate his unstudied air, our fingers brushed briefly. That single touch was everything. My heart stopped—my stomach dropped. My breath caught in the best possible way. All symptoms of one of my hysteric episodes, but the result was nothing like the same. I never wanted these feelings to stop. Instead of pulling away as I should, I let my fingers follow his retreat, repeating the graze. His eyes met mine and reflected a fever that was entirely disproportional to the innocent touch. I had never experienced such intense scrutiny. His stare warmed me deep inside; a feminine awareness unfurled in my belly.

He broke our eye contact while clearing his throat but made no move to part our fingertips. "You couldn't sleep?" His words were little more than a murmur. "Any reason?"

"Too many thoughts. I cannot seem to shut them off since we arrived."

His thumb and forefinger found the callous on the inside of my left ring finger, hardened from the prick of my embroidery needle. It was worsened by my stubborn refusal to wear a guard. He rubbed it gently with his thumb, quirking an eyebrow in question.

"Embroidery needle," I explained quietly.

His crooked grin made an appearance then, but the stroking of my fingertips continued.

"What kind of thoughts?"

"The kind I should keep to myself."

"I'm intrigued now," he said as he leaned forward, catching my gaze again.

In the quiet of the night, blanketed only in the glow of two candles, we were the only two beings in the world. I could trust him with my secrets.

"Dreams I didn't realize I had until it was far too late. Feelings I didn't want but now cannot imagine living without. Fear in the face of the future I thought I wanted when I didn't know better."

He abandoned the stroking of my fingers in favor of lacing them together, rubbing his thumb against the hummingbird pulse in my wrist.

"Nothing serious then?" His joke fell flat in the stillness between us. "What kind of dreams?"

My sigh breached the quiet as I considered how to explain. "Kate was the romantic. She was the one determined to marry for love. I just dreamed of anywhere else. I thought the best I could hope for was a husband who would treat me a little better than Father did. Perhaps one who was frequently away. Indifference in a spouse would be ideal. Now though, I am faced with the reality of marriage to a husband. His Grace is, by all indications, my former definition of perfection. And I am just... *miserable*."

"You don't wish to be married?"

"No, that's not it. I still want to be out of my father's house. I just—We're not well suited, Rosehill and I. He's so... glamorous. Somehow, I am the only one who can see that we have nothing in common. It should be perfect. My only qualification in a husband was far from my father, and it seems his

ALLY HUDSON

only qualification in a wife is breathing. But now that it's real, I can't help but want—I don't know—more?"

I had not understood exactly what was distressing me until I gave it voice. Now that I had, I could only hold my breath, waiting for his response.

His voice was low and thoughtful. "It's so bad then? At home?"

"He does not hit me if that is what you are asking. He just has these..." My free hand cast about, searching for the word. "Triggers. They change all the time. But if anything goes wrong, it sets off something inside him, and he rages. Some days he's wonderful, kind, and generous. The next, he stalks around, almost searching for something to erupt over. It can vary minute by minute. So, I spend every second of every day just waiting. It's only words, but he never fails to find the most hurtful combination. It's not always in a rage that he says them, either. Often they're a sort of joke—but not really. He means them, but if they hurt me, I'm too sensitive. And I can never be hurt or angry at him because he's always more angry at something I've done. And by the next morning, it's as though nothing happened. And I am just so tired from being wary all the time."

It was, perhaps, more than I had ever said in his presence. His eyes were thoughtful, caring in the flickering light.

"Is it... Did I make it worse? The debts?"

I contemplated that question, filling the silence with a worn sigh. "Yes. And no. I knew something was different. He didn't do anything worse than usual, just more tension, I suppose. But he was also avoiding the house and avoiding you, I suspect, so that was a relief."

"I'm going to forgive the debt."

"Don't. I have to marry His Grace either way. Father may as well have fewer pounds to lose when I'm gone."

He didn't respond to that. Somehow, I knew he would forgive it anyway.

The silence of the night, the certainty that the books would keep my confidences, and the way his thumb was soothing the outside of mine, it was too much. The words I had been holding back for weeks, months, and years burst forth.

"Sometimes I hate the person he made me."

Now that I had started talking, it seemed I could not stop, did not want to stop. I felt lighter for unburdening. I wanted to feel lighter still, to float away.

"What do you mean?" His brow furrowed, concerned, I suppose.

"So unforgiving that I want him to suffer."

"I have to disagree with that. You've been very forgiving with me."

"You hardly count. You did nothing wrong."

"I threatened your father in the middle of a ball."

"In retrospect, I quite applaud your efforts." That gained me a laugh.

"He's made me hateful too." The confessions would not stop.

"How so?"

I looked down at my lap. I wanted to confide in him. But, I could not bear to watch his admiration wash away. "My baby brother. My stepmother, Sophie, gave birth to a boy before she died. He only lived a few moments, but seeing my father so proud of the boy in his arms—I hated him. He did nothing more than exist, and in doing so, he earned the only thing I ever wanted. My list of failings began the moment I was born a girl. Nothing I will ever do can atone for that first sin. I still feel sick thinking about the hate in my heart for those moments. I don't want to be like this."

I stared at my lap, unable to look away. That was when his

hand tightened around mine. He slid two fingers under my chin with his other hand, directing my eyes back to his.

"That's your great sin? That you were envious for a single moment after a lifetime of vitriol directed at you? If that's all that's necessary for a trip to hell, I think you shall find yourself with a great deal of company. If the babe had lived, you wouldn't even remember the momentary lapse."

There was passion behind his speech, willing me to believe him, and, lord help me, a part of me did. His eyes were so sincere, no lie in them.

"You don't think me terrible?"

He scoffed in response. "I'm envious and hateful all the time. I can hardly judge you for a momentary lapse. I hate Agatha every time I'm in her presence and my father every time I see his judgmental face above the desk in the study. I'm envious of Hugh frequently."

"You are?"

"Has anyone explained to you our relation?"

"No, not really."

"I don't know my mother. I believe her to be an opera singer, but I can't know for certain. I was the late viscount's ward for years before he married Agatha. I was treated as a son in every way. If he never had a legitimate son— Well, who can know? When Hugh was born, I was cast aside entirely. Some days I hate him."

"You don't act as though you want to be viscount. I had no idea."

"What would be the point? Wanting something, someone doesn't change the situation."

"Someone?"

He cupped my cheek with his free hand. My heart pounded. I was certain he would kiss me, and I wanted it desperately.

"I'm envious of Rosehill, also. Not the clothes—those are ridiculous—but of his choice of fiancée."

"You are?"

He shifted closer still.

"Some days, I wonder what would have happened if I had found your father before he made his agreement with Rosehill. Would he have offered you as payment for his debts? Would I have been strong enough to resist?"

"What have you decided?"

"I'm not a good man, Duchess. I'm not in the practice of self-denial. But, I prefer my women willing and eager."

A delicious thrill ran through me at the turn of this conversation.

"So, you would have had me for your own?"

"I'm not certain. I worry your interest at the moment is primarily because I am not your fiancé. If we were betrothed, perhaps you would feel about me the way you do Rosehill now."

"Never." It was a vow I made to him, and he swallowed in response to my certainty.

His fingers tucked around my jaw and pulled me closer. My breath caught at the certainty that he was going to kiss me. And he did. Just not where I was desperate for him. Instead, he dropped a soft press to my forehead before releasing me and pulling back entirely—the sudden distance between us a chasm. I didn't know how to cross it or how to reclaim the ground.

"I suppose we'll never know. You should return to bed now, little Duchess, while I still have the strength to let you go."

"But..." Ignoring my protestations, he stood and grabbed my candle and pressed it into my hand. He strode over to the door, holding it and brokering no arguments. Unsteady, I reached him, turning to meet his gaze one last time.

"Good night, Juliet." There was a force behind his whisper, urging me away from him, pushing me a step back.

He shut the door gently behind me, and I was left gaping at it in the still-chilled hall, until I could bring myself to leave him. I did not find sleep any easier when I returned to my bed. This time, thoughts of his haunted gaze kept me awake.

Sixteen

THORNTON HALL, KENT - APRIL 24, 1814

MICHAEL

I SPENT the afternoon visiting tenants. It was not in a thinly veiled attempt to avoid Agatha's arrival. When I finally returned from my contemplative ride, the entire party was already entering the dining room. I trudged behind them, dragging my feet all the while. Juliet's bright smile at the sight of me was almost enough to counteract the irritation at Agatha's disgruntled squawk.

The dowager's distress at my existence served as a distraction. It was long enough for Kate to reach her place at the foot of the table without the usual tactless display from Agatha. Kate offered me a grateful smile. I ignored Agatha in favor of Tom's warm greeting before sitting. Kate had been kind to me, seating me across from Juliet and next to Tom.

"Where have you been all day?" Hugh queried distractedly, examining his soup with interest.

"I went for a ride, visited with a few tenants." My response was terser than I intended.

The day's events had left me more drained than I had real-

123

ized. I took a hearty sip of wine in an attempt to rally for the coming spat with Agatha. I was hopeful Hugh would leave off tonight. I didn't have the stamina for battle on two fronts.

"Why are you visiting tenants? This isn't your estate."

It was to be enemies on every side, then.

I replied into my soup, hoping to blend into the wallpaper, "I lived here for the better part of seventeen years, Hugh. They're friends." I was too weary for whatever fight Hugh was itching to start.

"What are you doing befriending tenants? You were a ward of the lord."

I refused to be baited, to let him know precisely when I became friends with his tenants—when I was running his estate for him. When I pulled the Tanner girl from their burning home. When I held down Matthew Lucas when the surgeon set his leg. Every year when I helped the Smiths till their field. Instead, I hedged, "You know me, friends everywhere."

Agatha's caw at that was even more peeved than the last. She was becoming more bird-like in her advancing years. "In the gutter," she added, not quite under her breath.

"Unseasonably warm weather we're having this year. Is it not?" Tom threw the observation out. He was too loud, hoping to cover his mother's comment. It was ineffective but appreciated nonetheless. Tom was the best of all brothers.

Juliet and Kate agreed with far more alacrity than the statement deserved. The former even went so far as to discuss the late freeze the year before. That distraction wouldn't last long, but I was grateful for the effort.

Kate chimed in with a litany of probable effects the freeze had on the harvest in Lincolnshire. I finally braved a glance from my plate. Juliet's sympathetic wide-eyed gaze only served to make it worse. I was usually better able to defend myself from the barbs, and I did not wish for her pity. Another swig of wine sent me back into the fray.

It was just in time for Agatha to be... well, Agatha. "Why would anyone give a fig about what last year's harvest produced in whatever backwoods town you hail from? They clearly failed to teach you to comport yourself properly. Do they not know what to do with a partridge in that county? Or do you refuse to serve it out of stubbornness?"

She turned on Kate in my distraction. I knew precisely why Kate didn't serve it any longer. Everyone hated the way Agatha insisted on having it prepared.

I was about to sacrifice myself to save her when she surprised me by saying, "Hugh isn't fond of partridge."

I internally applauded her effort but recognized the fraught territory she had just entered.

"Of course Hugh loves partridge."

"Then why does he merely pick at it when it's served?"

As impressed as I was with Kate's efforts, she would do better to ask when Hugh would step in. She should question when he intended to defend his wife from his mother's vitriol.

"You must have prepared it incorrectly!"

I was quite certain raw and still flapping would be a better cooking method than the way Agatha preferred it. Mrs. Hudson's partridge was exceptional for the kitchen staff, but Agatha expected it boiled without seasoning of any sort—some remnant from her youth. No support from Hugh appeared to be forthcoming, even with Kate's pleading gaze.

Into the fray again.

"We serve partridge in my club. It's my favorite."

That was a lie, but now she would never ask Kate to make it again, merely to spite me.

Agatha choked on her squawk, and I had to bite back a laugh. Then I felt it. Salvation. A tiny slippered foot brushed against my own under the table. I met Juliet's eyes with my

125

own and pressed back against hers. Her answering flush was so pretty, even in the dim light of Agatha's ugly chandelier.

"I do not believe it is partridge season, Mother." Tom, once again took up the shield in my defense.

"Of course, it is."

Juliet stepped in, buying Kate time to nurse her wounds. "No, ma'am, I believe it does not begin until the fall."

"What would you know of it? Miss..."

"Lady Juliet, ma'am. We've met several times." Hugh came by his inattention naturally. "My father is Richard Dalton, Earl of Westfield. He is quite fond of shooting and is always gone in the fall for the season." A lie from her corner also; Dalton was never far from the gaming table.

Agatha perked up at the title. "Earl, you say?"

"Yes."

"Daughter of an earl. Are you unwed?"

"Engaged, ma'am, to the Duke of Rosehill."

And, so, my Juliet caught her interest. Agatha leaned forward, practically salivating. She loved titles almost as much as she loathed me. I suspected that was one of her disappointments with Kate. She came without a title.

Suddenly, Juliet found her footing. She noted Agatha's interest and immediately shifted battle strategies. She was magnificent, resplendent, in this hideous dining room, surrounded by people who tolerated each other at best and loathed each other at worst.

She cast a spell. Through three more courses, she manipulated Agatha, luring her into traps so deft the woman did not even notice them.

"This custard is exemplary, Lady Grayson. Is it a favorite recipe of yours?" It was definitely Anna's recipe.

"Kate was just telling me the other day that you are responsible for the magnificent rose gardens by the east wall. I've never seen their like." Half-dead.

Juliet even managed to find the only item in the room that was not truly unfortunate to pay a compliment. "Kate, I must insist you keep that painting there if you make any changes to this room. It is perfectly situated." Her foot remained pressed to mine the entire time.

My expression was undoubtedly one of slack-jawed awe. Tom was utterly befuddled, never having attended a family dinner where he was not solely responsible for the prevention of bloodshed. Kate merely looked proud—she knew all along.

That was when the sinking feeling began. It connected, then, why Juliet was so skilled at parrying Agatha. The flattery, the appeasement, the distractions—she had done it her entire life. She managed her father's emotions with the same skill and poise with which she thwarted Agatha.

She hadn't faltered in the slightest. White lies and half-truths fell from her lips without so much as a blink. It would be alarming if I didn't recognize the skill's necessity. Even Hugh took note, eyes wide and unblinking, fork dangling limply from his hand.

She maintained the peace with ease, right up until it was time to separate after dinner. Unfortunately, my plate clanged when I stood, reminding Agatha of my existence.

"Shouldn't you be in the kitchens now, Michael?"

I had worried over that. Unlike during our weekly dinners, I had no escape route in the country.

"What do you mean?" Juliet's question lost the easy, bell-like tone she had adopted earlier. Instead, it was harsh, brokering no argument.

"Michael likes to hide in the kitchens with the servants after supper and thinks we do not notice," Hugh answered in a bitter tone.

I suppose my efforts hadn't been as surreptitious as I'd thought. Honestly, I would quite like to escape to the kitchens now. Tom offered me nothing more than an apologetic shrug.

"Well, I do love to reminisce," I added.

"What do you mean?" Juliet repeated more forcefully.

Agatha didn't deign to answer her, instead directing her vitriol to me. "You should still be taking your meals down there."

Juliet searched between us. It would have been comical. If only the reason for it was not an understanding that I would rather she not have.

"He ate with the servants? But he was a ward."

"It's better than the street where he belongs."

I didn't have a retort for that, not today. Instead, I rose without ceremony and strode toward the kitchens with feigned ease. What I never expected was the chair scraping across the floor, the quick, delicate footsteps that rushed after me, the tiny hand that brushed mine. Just like that, an entire afternoon's practice in resistance melted away at her touch. I grabbed her hand and pulled her with me toward the kitchens.

The room was over-hot with the oven fires. The long table at the far end was occupied by Anna, Mrs. Hudson, Mary, and Stevens. They maintained their relaxed stance, waving me over. When they saw Juliet beyond my shoulder, they jumped to attention. Sheepish at the response, she urged them back down.

Mrs. Hudson began her usual fussing, pulling out a plate of lemon tarts from heaven knew where and setting them in front of an empty place for me. Sitting down, I loosened my cravat before tucking in.

"How did I know we'd be seeing you tonight?" Anna threw in my direction.

"No idea. After all, I'm the most unpredictable of men."

"Your guest is a bit of a surprise. Do you like lemon tarts, Lady Juliet?"

"I do. I hope I'm not interrupting."

"Not at all." I could hear the lie in Anna's voice, but it was a kindly meant fib. "Am I to assume dinner was a disaster?"

"Oh, it was delightful as always."

Stevens pulled a deck of cards from a pocket, dealing to me for a game of cribbage. When Juliet leaned forward with interest, he dealt her in as well. The others were content to watch, and Mary hopped up to fetch something.

With a forced casual cheer, Anna asked, "How is Augie?"

It took a good bit of effort to restrain a chuckle. "Underpaid and overworked."

"You should do something about that," Anna retorted.

Mary returned with glasses and beer and poured one for all present.

"I would, but then I would actually have to run my club instead of allowing him to do it for me. Then where would we be?"

"You would be substantially less wealthy," Anna answered.

"Almost certainly," I retorted with a sip of the bitter brew. "He's primarily occupied with asking after you, if I'm honest. Do you intend to put him out of his misery at some point?"

I won the first hand easily. I made it a practice not to wager among the staff, so the stakes were nonexistent.

"To put him out of his misery, he would actually have to ask for my hand. A step he's neglected thus far."

Augie... "He hasn't asked you? I've been listening to sonnets about your hair, eyes, and pastries for years, and he hasn't asked you? I hope you weren't intending to marry him because I'll have to kill him before he can get around to asking."

"The poor lad just stares at her every week until he has a few drinks in him," Stevens added.

I scraped an exhausted hand across my face. Juliet won this round and beamed at me in excitement, and my exasperation was forgotten.

129

"Augie?" Juliet questioned.

"My superintendent. He supervises play in my club and acts in my stead. He was a footman here in his younger days before I stole him away. Anna and I grew up with him. He's been in love with her forever."

"He has not!" Anna objected, tossing the last bite of tart crust at my head. I caught it in my mouth before it had a chance to hit me, and Juliet's laugh was suitably impressed.

Striving for a less personal subject, Anna continued, "How upset is Kate going to be when I help her ready for bed? Was it truly terrible?"

"I deflected the worst of it during dinner, and Lady Juliet was magnificent. I'm sure Agatha was in fine form after we left, though. Does Hugh never check her?"

Stevens' negative response was full of disapproval.

At once, the bells started ringing for the servants, and our game was finished. I shoved the last tart in my mouth whole—Mrs. Hudson tutted in dismay at the display. Everyone scattered to their respective duties, and I helped her clear the table before leading Juliet away, back down the hall.

"They're your family." Her whisper echoed in the empty hallway.

"I suppose. Though when Agatha is elsewhere, Hugh and I manage well enough. And Tom and I are genuinely close. I quite like Kate as well. She's far better than my brother deserves."

"Oh, she is the very best of friends. I feel terrible. She told me she struggled with Lady Grayson, but I had no idea. I fear my advice was woefully inadequate for the situation."

"All advice for managing Agatha is woefully inadequate unless it includes large quantities of brandy."

I was rewarded with a tinkling laugh, and my chest swelled with no small amount of pride. We reached the top of the stairs though, and I was forced to release her to her evening rituals.

"Good night, Duchess."

"Good night, Michael," she whispered back. My name. With that single word, all my earlier efforts at excising her from my thoughts were ruined. I couldn't bring myself to lament it.

Seventeen

JULIET

KATE WAS desperate to escape Agatha's company. In an attempt to flee, she asked that I join her to visit tenants. *Asked* was a weak word. *Begged* or *pleaded* might have been more apt.

She had a basket at the ready as soon as Michael and I returned from the bridge, grabbing my arm and half-dragging me back out the door.

"Where are you two off to in such a hurry?" Michael called after us.

Kate turned to answer him, calling out, "Mariah Doll had her twins the other day. We're bringing blankets and such for the babes, and Mrs. Hudson made up a basket."

"She married the butcher's son? John Doll?" he asked.

Kate's surprise was plain in her raised brows. "Yes."

"Didn't they only wed about six months ago?"

"It's impolite to do arithmetic when babies are involved, Michael Wayland."

He merely laughed in answer, and stepped forward.

"You're joining us?"

"I have as much reason to avoid the shrew as you, more even. Besides, John deserves a scolding for the arithmetic I'm pointedly not doing."

Kate led the charge down the walk, seemingly convinced of Michael's determination to join us. She maintained a brisk pace until we turned out of view of the house. Where her walk slowed to a more sedate stroll.

The day was warm and pleasant. With a brief, surreptitious glance about, I untied the ribbons of my bonnet, letting it sway back and forth with my arm as we walked.

Kate considered Michael thoughtfully as we meandered. "You visit the tenants frequently, don't you?"

"It depends on what you consider frequent. Less often than I ought, I suppose. Also, the Dolls aren't tenants."

He scratched the back of his neck in a gesture that was rather... sweet. His discomfort with the praise implicit in Kate's statement made me smile, if only to myself.

"More often than Hugh. Or Agatha. And the way I've heard it mentioned, you've cared for everyone at one time or another, tenant or not."

"Well, Agatha's neglect is a blessing to the entire county," he said.

"And my husband's?"

"He's young."

"So were you. You are still spoken of very highly. By everyone," Kate said.

"I'm a charming fellow."

"Something like that..."

"You're not going to say anything? To Hugh, I mean. I don't fancy the quarrel that will result if he finds out," Michael worried.

"I won't say anything. But you should."

"And why would I do that?"

"Because he needs to hear it," she said.

"Kate... I adore you. But Hugh and I are never going to have the relationship you seem to want for us."

His assertion saddened me. I wanted that for him as much as Kate. The easy friendship between the two of them was nice to see, though. The way Agatha treated him—treated them both... I was glad they had each other for support.

It was what I imagined having a sibling to be like. It made sense, Kate was the closest thing I had to a sister, and she was very, very good at it. Of course, she would be so for Michael as well.

I trailed along, content to observe their jovial, false bickering. If it offered me the opportunity to appreciate Michael in motion, well, there was no one to scold me for it.

He moved with a graceful confidence I had never appreciated before. Spinning, he walked backward to continue to snipe teasingly at Kate. Turning back, he would walk forward for a few steps before rounding once more. He flipped his hair out of his eyes continuously, not bothering to tuck it but just flinging his head instead. It was a boyish gesture and quite charming.

Michael had taken the basket from Kate's hands without comment early on our journey, swinging it at his side.

"If you ruin anything in that basket, Michael Wayland, I will..."

"You'll what?"

"Barr you from the library."

"Katherine, my dearest sister, if you think you know every way to sneak in and out of that library, you're very, very mistaken. Some of us have been avoiding Agatha for decades. And, the servants may adore you, but they owe me money."

"You're a nuisance."

His eyes caught mine, warm as amber honey and full of mirth. He knew of my observations. His crooked grin

134

confirmed it. "What do you think, Duchess? Am I a nuisance? Or brilliant?"

"A brilliant nuisance? And I'm not a duchess."

Our path took us beside a field of wildflowers, similar to the ones by the bridge. There was a thick carpet of pinks, purples, blues, and yellows. He bent down at the waist. I had never appreciated a man's backside before Michael, but I rather thought he had a nice one.

Michael plucked one then two flowers from the field. He handed a yellow one to Kate with an overly formal bow.

"A truce, milady?"

"Temporary only."

"Agreed," he answered.

He stepped toward me. Rather than handing me the flower with another ridiculous bow, he tucked it behind my ear in a loose curl. The gesture made my stomach flip pleasantly, and I had never been so glad to have my bonnet fisted in my hand, rather than on my head.

"Lovely, Your Grace."

"I am still not a duchess, Michael."

"So you say."

Ahead on the left was a well cared for wooden cottage. Michael slipped my hand into the crook his arm, steering me toward the path. Kate stepped forward, and knocked on the door.

It popped open to reveal a kindly looking woman of perhaps fifty years with warm brown eyes, graying hair, and a delighted smile. She was familiar, but I could not place her in this context.

"Oh, Kate! It's so good of you to visit. Do come in, all of you... Michael Wayland? Is that you?"

She ushered us into the room, grabbing the basket from Michael and our bonnets.

"Mrs. Hughes, you look well," he answered.

"I would look better if you had come to see me. I've heard from everyone else that you're in the country. But I've had not a single sight of you."

"Sorry, ma'am." He did not sound sorry at all, when he pressed a kiss to her cheek.

"Oh Kate, this must be your friend, Lady Juliet. I'm Mrs. Hughes. I'm the vicar's wife. I've seen you at church, but I've never had a moment to ask Kate to introduce us."

"It's a pleasure to make your acquaintance."

And it was. Her complete lack of guile was so refreshing after interacting with Agatha for the past several days.

A young woman, perhaps younger than me, slipped out of another room, a babe in her arms. She was willowy, with soft brown hair and eyes. She smiled and mouthed "Hello," lifting the bundle in her arms to explain away any lack of manners.

She handed the bundle to Kate whose arms had reached out the second she spotted the swaddled babe. Tucking the baby tight against her chest, she made gentle cooing noises while the child snuffled before settling in against her. Running a delicate finger along his nose and cheek, she expressed silent delight at the woman, Mariah.

An entire conversation occurred in complete silence, delight over the adorable features and sweet demeanor was expressed in wordless gestures. Suddenly, a warbling cry came from across the room.

"That'll be Margaret," Mrs. Hughes whispered softly. She urged Mariah and Kate to sit down while she went to tend to the girl.

"This is Finnian, for my grandfather," Mariah whispered. "He's the quiet one. Meg makes her opinions known."

Mrs. Hughes returned, second bundle in hand. She stepped straight up to Michael and pressed the baby into his arms. I expected a protest or some display of awkwardness. Instead, he slipped one arm beneath her to support while wrapping the other around her, bracing her to his chest. He smiled easily, bouncing Meg gently until she quieted.

"I expected a bit of protesting and dancing about. You usually see it with men and babes," Mrs. Hughes whispered conspiratorially. "Michael, there, is something of a disappointment."

I disagreed. I did not know if there was anything I had ever disagreed with more. He was a natural, confident and sure with the girl in his arms.

Her tiny fist reached from her blankets to grab at his dangling cravat. She gave a mighty tug and he pulled it from her hand with a delighted laugh. My heart gave an uncomfortable lurch. Michael turned to me, seeking out a laugh at his predicament most likely. When he found none, he must have misread my expression. He bounced over with Meg, holding her out to me.

"Oh, no. I couldn't."

"Of course you can. You just make sure to support her head, like this."

He leaned back slightly, using gravity to keep her against his chest. With his free hand, he laid one of mine out along my chest. Gently, he laid her along my arm, her tiny head in my hand. He wrapped my other arm around the outside, ensuring Meg stayed put.

It was too much. It was everything, and it would never be enough. *I wanted this.* Desperately. Until right this moment, my fears had been an abstract problem for a future married Juliet.

But now, this second, I wanted this man's arm around my shoulder, just as it was now. With a baby in my arms. Our baby. With sleek dark waves and bright blue eyes. His more olive complexion would look very fine with my eyes.

My throat was closing, knotted tight. Years and years of my father's promises and complaints swirled around me.

"Your mother was barren. All she managed, after years and years, was you. A sniveling girl. You'll be just the same, just as fruitless to a husband. If anyone puts it together, I'll never be rid of you." Or worse still, *"It's a blessing that you won't breed. Then you can't inflict your hysterics on my grandchildren."*

Tears were welling up, and I blinked them back before he noticed. There was no explaining this. Not to Michael or Kate. Not to anyone.

Small, adorable whines began to escape the sweet girl in my arms. Her mother rose, reaching for her. It took everything in me to fix the placid smile on my face. To hand over the tiny bundle in my arms that cost me everything. In mere moments, I gave over a dream I never knew I had.

Because even if I was able to have a child, it would never be with the man whose arm just left my shoulder bereft. And try as I might, as easily as the image of the child Michael and I would create appeared, I couldn't see Rosehill's son in my arms.

Eventually, Kate was convinced to return Finn to his mother as well, and we set back off toward the house.

The jovial attitude from earlier had escaped us all. I could barely manage the effort of holding back the tears. Michael and Kate were equally quiet.

When we approached the house, Michael slowed. "I think I'm going to ride this afternoon, ladies."

"Will you join us for dinner?"

"Tomorrow, perhaps. Duchess, I'll see you in the morning?" There was a tinny quality to his voice. When I nodded, genuine and eager, he smiled. "Good."

He turned off, heading toward the stables. Kate and I continued our trudge up to the house in silence.

I had not had one of my fits since I had arrived in the country. Desperate to stave it off, I breathed in and back out for five. Twice more and the knot began to recede.

I decided to think no more of it, to lock those thoughts back in the box they came from. It was either the truth, or it was not. And regardless, the truth was that the child with the blue eyes and dark waves was never to be. No matter the state of my womb.

Eighteen

JULIET

THE SUN'S RAYS, warbling in the reflection on the lake, warmed my back as I embroidered in the drawing room. With some skill, I managed to avoid thinking of the events of that afternoon, of the little boy or girl who would never be. Today was no different.

Kate's talented fingers plucked out a new tune on the pianoforte off to the side. I did not recognize it, but I could recognize the beginnings of something lovely. Mr. Tom Grayson seemed to be playing a game of chess against himself. Not being a player myself, I could only assume he was winning. Agatha had kindly feigned a megrim once again. Those seemed to be a regular occurrence and a gift to all involved. And, once again, the viscount was nowhere to be found.

I was in the midst of my second attempt at the periwinkle gown's bodice. Kate had gifted me more of the shimmery golden silk thread, and I had chosen to create an appliqué rather than stitching directly into the gown, the source of my

140

failing previously. Inspired by mornings at the bridge, I used forget-me-nots and dogwood blooms in place of the indistinct flowers and vines of the previous design.

I filled in a petal with vertical satin stitch to catch the light, intending it to contrast the more textured French knots. I was pulled from my work by the sight before me. Michael. More specifically, Michael's forearms. He had shucked his coat and rolled his sleeves before pulling a writing desk over to the window, ostensibly for more light.

He occupied himself writing to Augie. I had never met the man, but I was unreasonably invested in his relationship with Anna. The unconscious, giddy smile that crossed her face whenever he was mentioned in her presence was more than enough for me to wish them well.

Thoughts of their budding romance floated away when Michael flexed his hand, stretching cramped fingers. Long, straight cramped fingers with square, well manicured nails, attached to wide strong hands—lord, what was wrong with me? Lusting after a man's hands. Hands with defined muscles and veins running along the back into muscular forearms.

I turned back to my work, determined to focus. Then he rolled his shoulders and crooked his neck to one side, glancing out the window. Oh! He must be doing this on purpose, he simply must be.

The quill dropped from his hand with a clatter, ink splashing across the pages and pooling beneath it. The wooden chair clattered to the ground as Michael startled with a wordless cry, racing to the door.

The tinkling of the piano ceased. For an overlong moment, the three of us remaining merely stared at the door. Then, nearly simultaneously, we turned toward each other, wearing matching looks of confusion. There was another wordless cry in the corridor, this one female, along with the clang of teacups on a tray. It was followed by the bang of someone throwing themselves against a door. Anna's "Michael!" followed behind. The door slammed closed.

It was Mr. Grayson, with the best view of the window, who made the connection. His own wordless cry drew our attention to the sight of Michael, sprinting from the house toward the lake some two hundred feet away, Anna not far behind. He turned to sprint after Michael. Kate and I raced out as well, close on his heels.

In the time it took for the three of us to follow, Michael was already stumbling into the muck and mire at the bank. The distance was such that I could just barely make out another person in the water. Anna skittered to a stop just before the edge, calling his name all the while, but it was too late. Michael was already waist deep in the water and struggling to free his still boot-clad feet from the mud to swim toward the person.

I slipped in the wet of the bank, nearly toppling in myself before Kate caught me, righting me. Mr. Grayson was not so lucky; his feet slid from under him and he landed, bottom first, in the wet, soggy, filth. Finally, close enough to discern the shape. It was the viscount. His arms pulled him through the water easily, feet propelling him along. He was oblivious to the chaos behind him, unaware of Michael, flailing after him.

Over the rush in my ears, I heard Anna. "Michael! Stop! He's not drowning, Michael! Come back!" Over and over.

Michael could not hear it. Not when he finally reached the viscount with his inelegant thrashing. Michael grabbed him by the shoulder and pulled him close. In response, the viscount reared back, startled. He shoved back against his presumed attacker, inhaling the water and coughing. Michael was undeterred, yanking his brother's struggling form back toward the shore, kicking with all his might.

Mr. Grayson waded farther into the sludge, reaching the two struggling men. He pulled the viscount free from

Michael's desperate grasp. The man heaved, coughing and cursing and coughing once more. Kate rushed from my side to help her husband upright. Anna and I reached Michael at the same time, grabbing a shoulder and hefting him to the bank with all our might. He took great gasping breaths before heaving himself farther onto the bank, ignoring our further attempts at assistance. Anna's tear-filled reassurances, "He's fine, Michael. He's unhurt," went unnoticed. Unheard over his attempts to crawl toward the viscount.

The viscount had abandoned the coughing entirely in favor of raspy cursing, "What the devil are you doing?"

Michael, seemingly unable to hear him in his terror, choked out, "Is he breathing? Is he breathing?" in between desperate gulps of air.

The viscount managed to shake off Kate and Mr. Grayson, dragging himself to standing.

"Michael! What the hell?"

Michael heaved himself upright, swaying slightly. Anna and I both rose to steady him, but he lurched forward toward his brother before either of us could reach him. He grasped the viscount in both hands, inspecting him frantically for injury.

"You're alright? You're unharmed?"

"Of course, I am unharmed. I was swimming. What are you doing? You nearly killed me!"

Michael, apparently unsatisfied with that, kept checking him over. The viscount's complaints grew louder with every word.

Mr. Grayson interrupted from his seat in the filth, "Hugh, let it go."

I glanced his way. The stricken expression was heartbreaking, perhaps, even more so than Michael's frantic, unhearing inspection. Realization crashed over me, and I knew. The truth burned through me, filling in the missing pieces of the picture I had created of this man. Michael pulled his father from this very lake.

Kate tried to drag her husband from Michael's grasp, before the viscount resorted to violence.

"Hugh, please." Michael shook her off, ignoring her efforts.

Mr. Grayson finally managed to scramble to his feet, pulling his brother away.

Resolutely, I approached Michael from behind. It was probably a poor choice, approaching a man lost to the world with worry and long held grief, but I gripped his shoulder firmly. Every muscle in his body was coiled tight, ready to spring into action.

I whispered, "Michael."

That was all it took. The tension evaporated, as if it had never been there. He turned to me, clarity returning to his eyes slowly. His damp hands grasped my cheeks, my shoulders, my waist, my hips, performing his own inspection, confirming my safety.

He swallowed thickly, choking out nothing more than my name.

MICHAEL

MRS. HUDSON JOINED US WITH BLANKETS a few minutes after realization and humiliation crashed over me in equal measure, tutting as she ushered the lot of us inside to clean up. After tossing my wet clothing in a corner for some poor footman to sort out at a later date, and likely discard entirely, I dunked myself into the warm bath that had been filled for me. The heat from the water burned my still-cold extremities, and I didn't linger. Tossing on whatever was nearby, I headed out toward my bridge, checking corridors to be sure I was alone.

Rounding the clearing, I was surprised, but somehow not, to find Juliet seated on the bridge, waiting for me. I paused, enjoying the view of her lazing in the sun's rays, bare feet swinging over the edge, I knew it would be the last time. She would not wish to spend time with such an unstable individual after all. I had nearly killed Hugh in my attempt to "rescue" him. Time and reflection had made that clear.

Without turning her gaze to me, she said, "Michael, come join me."

And I was powerless to do anything but obey. I hadn't been lying when I told her there was little I wouldn't do for her. Including coming closer, so she could break my heart more easily.

"Sit with me," she said, indicating a place at her side with her hand.

With a great, heaving sigh, I did.

We sat in silence for several moments. Her basking in the sun, me basking in her. Eventually, far too soon, she pushed herself to be seated, turning to meet my gaze. Whatever she found there, she had no comment for it. Instead, she gripped my shoulder, pulling me to turn and lay my head on her lap.

I blinked up at her, in stunned silence, for some time before the feeling of her fingers running through my hair registered. Her expression was unreadable as she peered down at me. The combination of the sun's warmth and her fingers was too much for me, and I allowed my eyes to fall closed. It could have been minutes, hours, days before she spoke.

"You pulled him from the lake?"

I swallowed hard, nodding. Her delicate fingers never ceased carding through my hair.

"I still send a servant into my stepmother's chambers if I need anything. I cannot go in."

"I'm sorry."

"That is not what I meant. I just... I understand."

"I know. I feel quite foolish. Hugh may never forgive me."

"Does he know?"

"I don't know what Agatha told him. I wasn't forthcoming with the details, and we never discussed it."

Her gentle hand never ceased its efforts.

"He... it was on purpose."

That stilled her. Just for a second.

"It was February. He couldn't swim. His suit coat was filled with rocks. Big, not small."

I heard a quiet intake of breath. Now that I had begun, I could no more stop my confession than I could stop the sun from setting.

"There were debts, massive debts. We were months, perhaps days, away from losing everything."

Her trailing fingers ceased now, and she cupped my cheek in her hand. I opened my eyes, waiting for her response. All I received was a thick, warm, "Michael." In her gaze I could read everything she left unsaid—her hurt, her desire to comfort, something akin to love perhaps. I was surely mistaken on the last, but I clung to it nonetheless.

I continued, unbidden. "That was how the gambling started. I was always good, of course, but Augie took me to Temple Bar, to the gaming hells one night. I returned with enough to pay off Agatha's modiste bill. It spiraled from there. It took years, but I made enough to clear the debts. I moved up to the silver hells in Piccadilly, playing against the gentry. Over a few more years, I acquired a nice savings, enough for the estate to comfortably live on for years. I made improvements to the tenant cottages, upgraded the irrigation systems, set up everything for Hugh. Then the idea of Wayland's took hold. By the time Hugh reached his majority, I had enough to open the place. He didn't approve, of course, but it was the first thing, the only thing, that has always been mine."

All I could see was sky and Juliet. Her eyes were brighter, more brilliant than the blue of the sky. They were slightly glassy, with unshed tears. Her skin was a delicate peach color, flushed with some kind of emotion. Her tongue darted between her lips, wetting them.

"And your bridge, mustn't forget that. Thank you for sharing it with me. And thank you for telling me."

I just nodded, closing my eyes once more. At some point, I fell asleep, lulled there by the gentle combing of her fingers and whispers of her breath.

Nineteen

THORNTON HALL, KENT - JUNE 3, 1814

JULIET

THAT AFTERNOON SHATTERED any barrier to intimacy. Touch between us was more common, more free than ever. Michael—Mr. Wayland—and I continued to delve into *Mansfield Park*. As a voracious reader, I typically finished novels at a rapid pace. His dark voice and eloquent reading style more than compensated for the slower pace.

Some days, we spent the entire morning reading on the bridge. On other days, when the sun became too warm, we moved to the shade of the nearby dogwood, now dropping its petals at a brisk pace. I took to plucking raspberries from the bushes for us to enjoy. They were still just short of ripe, but the sour bite was addicting. Forget-me-nots and cornflowers surrounded the base of the tree perfuming the air. This little hideaway was quickly becoming my favorite place in the world.

Day by day, I felt my tension easing. It had been a part of me for so long that I noticed more the absence of it than its presence. I brought embroidery and small stitching projects with me. I studiously refused to consider the implications. That I was spending several unchaperoned hours each day working diligently on my trousseau in the presence of a man other than my fiancé.

Michael and I established a rapport. I had been given leave to make frequent interjections and he did the same. "'*Her curiosity was all awake, and she ran through it with an eagerness which was suspended only by intervals of astonishment, that it could be chosen in the present instance, that it could be proposed and accepted in a private theater!*'"

"I have not read *Lovers' Vows*. Have you made a study of it? Is it truly so scandalous? Or is Fanny being insipid again?"

It was an ongoing discussion between us. I found Fanny to be meek and banal. He saw more good in her than I did.

"I believe there is a copy of it either here or in the London house. I can find it for you if you wish."

I should not. I knew my father would not approve. I agreed anyway.

"As for whether the material is scandalous or not, I don't know where your sensibilities lie. It deals extensively with illegitimate birth. Given my own situation, I hardly find that particularly distressing."

It was the second time Michael had openly acknowledged the situation of his birth to me. His matter-of-fact tone, paired with his nonchalant shrug, was too studied. It pained me. He was bracing himself. As though he was certain I would find his circumstances shameful. Worried that the reminder of them would send me running. Worse still, not so very long ago, they might have. I felt a pang of shame at that acknowledgment.

I waited a beat, until he raised his eyes to mine.

"I should not find that upsetting."

I infused my words with the sincerity I felt, willing him to understand my meaning. His posture softened, almost imperceptibly. I enjoyed the warmth of my success.

"There is also a rather frank discussion of certain... immoral behaviors."

It took me a moment to parse his meaning, and I felt the flush rising in my cheeks. I cursed them for exposing my naiveté.

"Personally, I find them to be rather tame, but I am a known reprobate. I'm rather difficult to shock."

He had grown to enjoy teasing me with implications of his degenerate behavior. He also had yet to provide me with any concrete examples, which led me to believe he was more talk than substance in this respect.

"What do reprobates find shocking then?"

"I'll alert you the first time I find myself shocked," he teased.

My lips were pressed tight in an effort to fight a smile. It was blooming, and I offered a reproachful shake of my head in its stead. I should not encourage such brash speeches. I enjoyed his flirtations more than I ought. Indeed, were he anyone else, I would discourage such behavior. It was necessary to avoid the appearance of encouraging affections where I could not reciprocate.

Still, he was a self-acknowledged rake, and I, little more than a disinteresting debutant. Nothing so extraordinary as the women he must surely entertain. My heart was the only one at risk of feeling more than I ought. And it was at risk. I had to pull more than a few stitches out of my work the last few days, when I found myself distracted by the warmth behind his eyes and thoughts of his crooked mouth.

It was an impossibly dangerous game I played with myself. It was one thing when what I felt for him was mere attraction. But I was forced to acknowledge it has gone much farther than that. Every night since we arrived, I had laid awake, distracted by thoughts of him. Each morning, I rose impossibly early, eager to see him again.

By all rights I should have been exhausted, but I was not. I was energized in his presence, strung tight and tetchy, but also soothed. It could have been the reprieve from the pressures of town, but I suspected it was him. I felt... extraordinary in his presence, intelligent and witty and beautiful and everything I ever wished to feel about myself. It was an addicting sensation. The flip my insides performed when he glanced up at me from underneath his dark lashes and paired it with a self-deprecating grin.

This flirtation between us was entirely inappropriate. Even if I were not betrothed, even if he did not have my father on the rocks, it would still be improper. My father would have a fit of apoplexy at the idea of such a connection. No, the entire idea was insupportable. Fortunately, Michael could have no serious designs on me. As he said, he could not be shocked. I, in my naiveté, would have no appeal to such a worldly gentleman, at least not beyond an amusing flirtation. With that distressing thought, I managed to pierce my ring finger with my needle.

~

MICHAEL

ONE WOULD THINK her effect would become less striking with repeated exposure. It had not. If anything, her power over me was growing. She accidentally stabbed herself with the needle, and then she popped her ring finger in her mouth. Steel will was all that held back the groan that sight induced.

I glanced down, looking away in a desperate attempt to keep myself in check. She was working on embroidery today. She brought this piece with her several days in a row. It was an intricate series of flowers, vines, and leaves in a shimmering burnt-gold thread. When she first started, I thought it was rather more plain than the rest of her works, with just one color. Now I could see the intent, the different tiny stitches and knots forming unique textures, the density manipulating the tone. Previously, I had only ever seen Agatha's work. Her stitching was plain and primitive in comparison. Juliet was stitching art.

"This is lovely. Do you have an intention for it?"

I was drawn back to her face where her finger was still at home between her lips.

She hesitated before responding, "It's an appliqué, for a gown. I originally stitched it directly onto the gown while I was tailoring it, but I made quite the mess of it."

"I'm certain that's not the case. I'm sure the gown will be lovely. What's the occasion for it?"

Apprehension crossed her face and realization washed over me. Her wedding gown. She spent days embroidering it for her wedding gown. She would wear it for another man. There was an instinctive pang at that thought before I reminded myself I had no right to feel such hurt, such jealousy. Even if her engagement to Rosehill were not in place before we met, she was the daughter of an earl. I was still a bastard whose only claim to fortune was bamboozling the Beau Monde out of their coin. Thinking I had a claim to envy was as ridiculous as thinking I had a claim to a star if I just stretched my arm a bit farther. I had no more right to pluck those stars from the sky than I did to entertain thoughts of her.

"Right, I'm sure he'll be appreciative of your efforts." My voice was more strained than I liked, and I cleared my throat and gestured toward the novel as an excuse.

"Michael—"

She cut herself off as soon as she realized her error. That didn't change the fact that she used my Christian name. Again. The intimacy in that single word was breathtaking.

152

Perhaps even more so in the harsh light of day, no candlelight and shadows to hide behind.

"This really is a work of art. I've never seen so many different stitches."

She studied me intently with her head cocked slightly to the side. Our days in the sun had given her a light dusting of freckles across the bridge of her nose and cheeks. I adored them. Each and every one of them was evidence of our time together. They would linger even after she returned to town, a reminder of us. I didn't know what answers she found from her observation, but she moved to put her work away. My stomach dropped, thinking our time was over. A second later it righted itself, as she pulled out something new.

"Would you... I owe you a new handkerchief. From that day in the drawing room with the teacup. I intended to surprise you with it, but perhaps you'd like to learn? I know it may not interest you, but you've been so kind teaching me hazard and cribbage. If you've any inclination."

She was grasping a square of fine white linen. She had penciled an intricate pattern of swirls directing the eye to the corner where the initials *M. W.* were drawn with a feminine flourish. I traced a finger over the design. Until I watched her work, I would have asserted to my grave that embroidery was useless women's finery. I never had the slightest inclination to learn, but she wanted to teach me. She wanted to share something with me, and that was a precious thought.

"I think I'd like this to be your work. I would hate to mar it. I would like to learn though, perhaps on something less fine?"

Her grin at my response was infectious, and she started to root through her basket. That was when the first raindrop marked her cheek.

Twenty

THORNTON HALL, KENT - JUNE 3, 1814

MICHAEL

THAT SINGLE RAINDROP became thousands instantly as the skies opened up. I shoved the novel and her embroidery into the picnic basket and slammed the lid. As soon as her efforts were safe, I scrambled up, helping her along the way. Clutching the basket and our blanket, I ushered her toward the relative safety of the dogwood. The tree offered little in the way of safety from a downpour this severe. Her back was pressed against the trunk of the tree, seeking as much cover as possible. I dropped the basket and lifted the blanket over our heads, sheltering her a little from the torrent with the fabric and my body. It was only after I pressed my hands to the trunk, her head between them, as I held the blanket taut, that I realized what I'd done.

I'd slotted myself against her sodden frame, no more than six inches between us. It was dark under our little makeshift tent. But I was so close that the dim light was no impediment to studying her. Her once vivacious, now damp, curls were stuck to her forehead and neck. Raindrops clung to her eyelashes, drawing my attention to her eyes, now midnight in the shadows. Her mirthful grin fell, and her lips parted as she registered our proximity. In the mere moments we were without cover, her gown was soaked. It dipped lower with the weight of the water and clung tighter than it did when dry. Her chest rose and fell with her heaving breaths.

My body reacted to the sight. Our frames were too close for her to mistake my interest. I attempted to shuffle my lower half to the side without her notice, but the distance didn't allow for it. I miscalculated the allotted space, and thigh brushed between hers. Her corresponding gasp was everything. My heart stopped, and I froze, searching her face for reproach. Instead, I found her eyes even wider than before and filled with heat, her lips parted with something akin to want. It was a heady, exhilarating feeling.

"Juliet—" Her name was a harsh, strained thing in my throat.

She swallowed roughly. "Yes."

"Yes?" I clarified.

She nodded her agreement but it was a tentative little movement. My heart pounded, and I was certain she could hear it. My breathing grew even more erratic than hers. But I needed to be clear with her.

"Yes, more?"

Another nod, and this one more definitive. Desire spread rapidly through my entire being.

"I need the words, Duchess. Do you understand?"

"Yes, I understand. Kate explained— Yes, I want more— not everything—but more. Please?"

Not even the mention of my brother's errant wife could dampen the need burning through me with that request. I couldn't be certain in the dim light of our damp retreat, but I suspected the peach of her flush had made its way under her chemise.

"Have you ever been kissed?" I had no reason to find as much joy in her negative response as I did. "May I?"

"Yes," her voice was barely a whisper, but it was clear as a bell in the damp air between us.

Permission granted, I dropped one hand from the tree. The sodden blanket collapsed onto our heads. My hand trembled, and it was a nearly imperceptible thing as I *finally* cupped her jaw. Her eyes drifted closed as she leaned into my touch. Awe at her trust in me overwhelmed the lust surging through me. The enormity of what she offered me crashed over me.

Before my flawed morals could slake my lust, I pressed my lips against hers. Nothing in my life had ever felt right in this way. I slid her lower lip between mine, and *this* was where I belonged. I would give anything to stay here for eternity. Pressed against her, her lips against mine, shrouded in our damp haven. It took everything I had not to lose myself in the kiss, to devour her, to press her for more than she was ready to give. I forced myself to pull back after the simple caress. She defied my good intentions, following my lips with hers. She crashed her mouth against mine with more enthusiasm than skill. Her actions were paired with a soft whimper, and all at once, the fervor returned.

I took control of the kiss. My touch on her jaw became a grasp. I directed her to tip her head brushing my tongue across her lip. She tasted of raspberries and an intoxicating paradox of rain and sunshine. I had no power to stop the groan that escaped when her tongue tentatively brushed mine. I granted her entry, determined to let her explore at her own pace. Her delightful little hands found their way to me. One clutched in the folds of my shirt. The other tangled in the overgrown hair at the nape of my neck. She tugged me impossibly closer. She broke from me with a startled gasp when my thigh slid more firmly against her center with her frantic movements.

Her breathing was heavy, and I could taste it in our close-ness. Her eyes met mine as we shared air, both of us panting. For a moment this simple kiss was the most erotic moment of my life. Then she rocked against me, against the thigh trapped between hers and several dampened layers of skirts. And it was instantly replaced with that new moment.

I couldn't contain the hoarse curse that escaped me. "Jules."

Her eyes widened in response, and I was prepared to apol-ogize, but she yanked my mouth back to hers. It was a slight challenge to kiss her the way she deserved with her smile in the way. I wasn't certain whether it was the curse, the use of her nickname, or my loss of control that caused it but I appreci-ated it regardless.

Once I gathered myself, I tipped her head farther back and kissed her more thoroughly. She was clearly enjoying her power over me. Now it was my turn. I tangled my lips and tongue with hers, any attempt at slow long gone. This time when my thigh rubbed between hers it was deliberate. She pulled away with a whimper of my name, and I used the opportunity to explore her jaw with my lips and tongue and teeth. She tasted of apples and some sort of citrus there. By the time I reached the hinge where her jaw met her neck, she was panting my name between desperate whimpers.

"Jules, is this alright—do you like this?"

She tried to pull my mouth back to hers in response, but I resisted.

"I need the words. Do you want this?"

I pressed my leg harder against her core to illustrate my meaning. And perhaps add to her conviction.

She buried her head in my chest before mumbling agree-ment. Seconds ago, she was wantonly pressing herself against me, but the words had made her shy. The juxtaposition was charming, but I needed her to trust me with her desires, her pleasure.

With the hand on her jaw, I tipped her back slightly. "Tell me. I want to give you what you want. Everything you want."

She whimpered before swallowing harshly. "I want... I need..." She trailed off, her voice breaking with desire. She darted her tongue out to wet her lips before closing her eyes and trying again. "Your leg. My... I... I don't know the words." With that she tried to pull me closer and bore down against my thigh.

I pressed a quick kiss to her forehead before taking pity on her, satisfied that she was nearly in the desperate state I wanted for her. I dropped my other hand from the tree behind her, unable to sacrifice touch for the sake of the tentatively balanced blanket. It fell by the wayside. Fortunately, the rain had slowed, and we were only assaulted with sporadic drips from the branches above us. The fresh air did nothing to slake the heat running through me, and I doubt the full downpour would have either.

My now free hand brushed down her side. I made the difficult decision not to linger, destination in mind, before falling to her hip. With a gentle hand, I directed her frantic, disjointed movements, into orderly circles. The groan that escaped her as I guided her movements was entirely unladylike, and I wanted more of them.

The words fell from me unbidden. "That's it. Just like that. That's what I'm here for. Take what you need. Everything you need. I've got you."

Mewls were falling from her between pants of my name. She sounded as broken as I felt, and I was greedy for more still. "Michael, I—more. Please."

"Alright. Here, is this better?"

I began to move my leg, thrusting in time against her frantic circles. Her nod was distracted as she chased her pleasure. I couldn't tear my eyes away from the vision before me, her ecstasy building. Because of me.

"Don't fight it. Let it build. It's good. I promise. I'll make it so good for you. Give you everything."

Her hand fisted in my hair, just the right side of painful. Her other twisted in my shirt. With a wordless cry she fell apart in my arms, and it was the single most beautiful thing I had ever seen. She went slightly boneless. Her grip slackened on my hair, and I regretted the loss before she collapsed into my arms, face buried in my chest. My heart swelled at the sight of damp wayward curls pressed against me. A new feeling of belonging peace washed over me.

JULIET

MICHAEL'S ARMS WERE THE ONLY THING keeping me up. I was pressed against the curve of his neck and chest. It was delightful here. I only caught hints of his scent before, when the breeze blew just right, or he brushed past me in the hall. It surrounded me now, vanilla and mint as usual with just a hint of petrichor from the damp earth beneath us. His body was warm and solid even in the damp. His embrace was more substantial than I expected from his moderate size.

He pressed a kiss to my damp head before tightening his arms even further. My heart fluttered at the movement, the innocent gesture somehow all the more meaningful after everything we had just shared.

"Jules..." he uttered in a throaty whisper that was probably not intended for me to hear. The single syllable had warmth pooling in my belly again. His voice was still as ravaged as when we were entwined. We were still tangled in each other, but the urgency had died down. That was nothing at all like

Kate described. She mentioned a man's hardness and pleasure. I did not have the words for what I had just experienced, but "pleasure" was insufficient. Even now, giddy euphoria, boneless peace, and warm tenderness filled me. We were all wrapped in a bubble of joy. The bubble was almost full to bursting, but I was too sated to care about the impending explosion.

"Are you planning to surface anytime soon?" His tone was less strained. I could hear the smile in it.

As much as I wanted to see the crooked grin, I was too comfortable here. Easy, loose in a way I had never known before. I sensed rather than heard the deep chuckle that greeted me when I pressed myself closer. He brushed his hand through my wet curls and added another kiss to them, almost cherishing me.

"I'm perfect right here. Thank you." I infused my tone with as much prim assurance as I could muster.

His response, pressed into the top of my head, was so quiet that I nearly missed it. "Yes, you are." Though it took my head a moment to parse his meaning, my heart responded instinctively with an erratic skip. Suddenly, I needed to see him. I couldn't help but press a kiss to my new spot, just above his cravat on his neck, before I pulled back.

I was met with a real smile, not the crooked grin I had grown to love. He had always been handsome, but this was something more. Masculine pride and tender affection mixed in his countenance, the force of the combination directed toward me was overwhelming. With a whispered "Come here" and an accompanying hand gesture, he pulled my smiling lips to his own. There was less heat behind the kiss than its predecessors, more a pressing of smiles together. Then his hand cupped my jaw again, and he directed it into something deeper. Now that I was less frantic, I could appreciate the actual act, the pleasant heat, the teasing flip of my stomach at his efforts. Before I had my fill, he pulled back and tipped my head to press another kiss, this time to my forehead. He made to separate us, but I tightened my grip to keep him with me, not ready to be out of his arms yet.

"That was... different from what I expected. Not how Kate described it."

He dropped his forehead to mine, untangling one of my fists from the fine linen of his shirt to lace with his own.

"Dare I ask what she told you?"

"Well, she said there was pain the first time, and a lot of thrusting. And that it was quite messy. Then sometimes there was pleasure."

While I spoke, he pulled my grasped hand up to his lips. Untangling our fingers, he took each one in turn and pressed his lips gently to the tip. His eyes were intent on mine throughout. The simple action had an ache forming in my center anew.

"Michael?"

"There should always be pleasure. Always." His gaze was heated, and his tone harsh, and I found myself clenching on nothing. "She's not terribly wrong about the rest though."

"I don't... but that's not..."

"We didn't complete the... marital act. Just a precursor."

"Oh." In this I was ignorant, and I despised the feeling.

Before I questioned him further, he continued, drawing the words out. "You can't be... with child from what we did."

"Oh," I repeated again stupidly. "Can you... Will you explain?"

"I shouldn't." I was about to protest. "But I will. You should know. All women should know. I don't understand the secrecy. Not today though. It looks like the rain will begin again shortly. We should return to the house."

Appeased for now, I allowed him to assist with setting my clothing to rights. As much as possible anyway. As my dress had begun to dry, the wrinkles became set in the fabric. There was no fighting my curls in this state, and my bonnet, left behind on the bridge, was unsalvageable. Once we made ourselves as presentable as the situation allowed, he offered me his arm. I rejected it in favor of wrapping both arms around his chest. He slipped his offered hand around my waist and guided me through to the clearing.

Once we reached the edge he paused. "Time to let go now."

I shook my head, and he dropped a firm kiss to my head before disentangling us. My heart gave a disgruntled pang as he enforced the space propriety dictated.

Twenty-One

THORNTON HALL, KENT - JUNE 3, 1814

MICHAEL

My smalls were chafing. The discomfort was well deserved, and it was the least of my problems. I couldn't leave one rule unbroken. I had lied, cheated, stolen, and gambled. But I had never seduced a lady before, an innocent one at that. Against a tree no less. Now I needed to find a way to sneak her back into the house without notice. Could she even dress and right her hair without a lady's maid?

I risked a peek at her, and the state of her was even worse than I had expected. Her thick curls formed a nest on her head, her lips were bruised red, there was a distinct burn where my whiskers had rubbed her neck raw, and her skirts were wrinkled to hell and caked in mud. She had never looked more beautiful. And she had never looked more thoroughly tupped. As if sensing my gaze, she tilted her head to mine and greeted me with a bright grin. I struggled to offer her an answering smile through the thick knot in my throat.

It was a dangerous game I played, spending so much time with her. I knew it was wrong, and I continued anyway. I couldn't stay away from her. No, I didn't want to. Any moment now she would realize what I had done and castigate me as I deserved. A sick part of me prayed she never came down from the euphoria that seemed to have overtaken her. I shoved down the swelling of distinctly male pride that filled me at that thought.

The rain kept the household staff inside, and we were fortunate not to encounter anyone on the grounds. I set her by a tree just out of view of the house before checking the back entrance. There was a staircase that was rarely used by family or servants, and with luck I would be able to get her in unnoticed. For once, luck did have it, and no one was milling about. I gestured for her to join me. I ushered her up the stairs, abandoning her at the top to check for servants. When none were forthcoming, I pulled her toward the best guest room, certain that was where Kate had placed her. I took a step back from her, her closeness too enticing.

"Do you need me to find a maid?"

"No, I can manage." Her small hand pulled my chin down to meet her eyes. "Michael? Is something wrong?"

"Nothing."

"You're not upset with me, are you?" The open vulnerability in her tone and expression split my heart open.

"Never! You're perfect, as always."

I couldn't help but press one last kiss to her forehead, certain she would never let me touch her again once she realized what I had taken from her. Instead of allowing me to pull back, she grabbed me closer, hand fisted in my shirt, directing my lips to hers. It was a gentle press; she tried to deepen it, but I kept it shallow. Finally, I released her with a nod towards the door.

"I'll see you at dinner?"

The best I could offer her was a vague, noncommittal nod. It satisfied her though, and she finally closed the door between us. The click of the lock sliding into place was loud in the empty hallway. Determined. Final.

JULIET

ONCE IN MY ROOM, I collapsed onto the bed with a dramatic sigh, the kind Kate used to produce when discussing her newest love. I had no idea. None. I knew I should be overcome with an abundance of guilt and shame, but I could not put forth the effort to summon the emotions. At this moment, it seemed as though everything was possible, that there were no obstacles between Michael and myself.

I should set about removing my damp garments, but instead I lay there, tracing the path his lips took on my skin with my fingers. Reliving the wondrous sensations seemed a far more pressing concern than making myself presentable in the moment. If I was found in this state I would be ruined. A part of me welcomed it. I was certain I had never been such a mess. My hair would never recover, my gown and shoes were destroyed, and my skin was certainly flushed from Michael's attentions. I was a wanton mess. I had strived for perfection my entire life, and in spite of my disheveled state, I finally felt it—perfection. It was nothing like I had expected, and everything I never dared to hope for. I resisted pressing my face into the pillows to unleash a girlish squeal.

After an extended period of rapture, I finally rose to address the condition of my hair and clothing. My chemise was the only layer that had escaped the deluge. I splayed the rest of it out in front of the fire. Seated before the mirror for my toilette, I was forced to acknowledge the enormity of the task before me. My hair had never seen such a state. My lips, neck, and jaw all bore the marks of Michael's admiration. I hardly recognized the woman before me. There was a lightness to her countenance I had not ever seen in my reflection.

With a sigh, less put upon than the one I typically reserved for sorting out my curls, I began the onerous task of righting them. Brush in hand, I attacked each in turn. I had foregone the assistance of a lady's maid for nearly two years so the task was familiar. I was grateful for the experience now. One by one they gave way until I had them in order.

I had yet to develop an attack strategy for the reddened marks across my décolleté and neck. I settled for pressing a towel dipped in the cool water of the nearby basin to the irritation. I couldn't bring myself to regret their existence, not when I was still reliving their creation with giddy, lustful ardor. Eventually, my efforts proved effective and the redness gave way.

A knock sounded at the door followed by a timid "My lady?" Anna, Kate's lady's maid poked her head in when I granted her entry. "Stevens suggested I might be of assistance to you?"

If the servants knew enough to suspect I needed assistance, my misdeeds were certainly all over the house by now. I felt the flush of embarrassment but not the accompanying panic I expected from the acknowledgment.

"Thank you, Anna. Your assistance would be much appreciated."

"Of course! Have you considered what you might like to put on this afternoon?"

"I'll leave it to your judgment."

"Of course. May I assist with your coiffure as well?"

I couldn't stop the huff of laughter at that. "You may certainly try, but I think it may be beyond even your considerable talents at this point."

She cracked a small smile but politely denied the trouble

for which my unruly curls were famous and started to pin them into place.

"That was quite the storm, my lady. I'm glad you and Michael—Mr. Wayland—were safe," she said, confirming what I already knew.

A few of my curls escaped her pins, and she removed the pins calmly. I usually found myself frustrated at this point but her touch remained gentle.

"May I ask, is there a great deal of talk downstairs? About my whereabouts this morning? And Mr. Wayland's?"

I was not certain we had developed enough of a repertoire for her to speak candidly with me, but I had no other way of discerning the extent of the damage to my reputation.

"Oh! None at all my lady." Her answer was too quick and too bright to be the full truth. "I don't think anyone knew you were out in the storm until Stevens went to search for Michael. He pulled me aside and said you might require assistance because of the rain. I won't say a word, I swear it. And Stevens is a vault. But no one downstairs would say anything anyway. We quite like you, you see. It's clear that Michael adores you and— Oh, my mouth has run off with me."

I had no reason at all to believe in her sworn discretion, but something about her suggested that she wouldn't betray my confidence.

"Oh, please go on. Is my reputation quite in tatters?"

"No, my lady, of course not. Mama and I were beginning to despair of him ever taking a wife. But then we saw the way he is with you, and... we're just hoping for the best for the both of you."

"I hope you will tell me if there's any... untoward gossip downstairs."

"Of course, my lady, but no one would speak so about Michael, and you, as well, of course."

"Thank you."

She was going in for a third attempt with the pins, still as patient as the first.

"I think you should wear the light blue gown for supper. It flatters your eyes."

"I will then. Thank you."

There was a pleased flutter at the thought of displaying myself for Michael's perusal. At showing any of my features to advantage for his gaze. She finally managed to tame my curls on the fourth attempt, and I had to admit they looked beautiful. She abandoned the fashionable, tight, face-framing curls. Instead, my larger, disorderly curls were left to escape my coiffure naturally. The effect was quite enchanting. Certainly Michael would agree.

Twenty-Two

MICHAEL

I MANAGED my flight to the family wing without incident. As soon as I shut the door behind me, harder than intended, I tore at my cravat. The still-damp fabric clung, making breathing difficult. Although my efforts resulted in mild strangulation, I managed to escape my fabric prison. The effort didn't lessen my shortness of breath though. I fought out of my jacket and ripped several buttons of my shirt in my attempt to escape. I stripped down to my unmentionables, while my lungs regained function once more. In spite of all of this, I was still half hard. I had never been more grateful to forego a valet. No one else needed to appreciate my deranged state. I collapsed into the nearby chair, still breathing much too heavy.

I'd ruined her. If anyone found out, if anyone saw us... She was meant to be a duchess. Literally. She trusted me. And at the first opportunity, I took advantage of that trust. I was so naive, thinking I could control myself around her. Instead of leaving well enough alone, I kept pressing closer and closer, spending more and more time with her.

The worst part of all was that if I had it to do over again, I would not be able to make different choices. She was the sun, and I was Icarus. My head knew to stay away, but every other part of me longed for her warmth. I wanted to take everything she had to give and more.

And lord, everything she had to give was glorious. She was passion and inexperienced enthusiasm and shy tenderness, wrapped in an achingly beautiful package. Even in the midst of my self-castigation I could not escape thoughts of her exquisite form, pressed tight against me. I needed to put a stop to such maddening thoughts before my self-control slipped and I sought her out once more.

I launched myself from the chair over to the wash basin, splashing the cool water over myself. A desperate, ineffective, effort to slake my lust. I repeated it once more when it failed to produce the desired effect, driving her from my thoughts. Finally, I was forced to submerge my entire head in the basin. This effort, too, proved ineffective. I was about to pour the water over my head as a last resort the servants would certainly not appreciate, when there was a knock on my door.

"Sir?"

"Come in, Stevens."

Hugh's valet had developed an efficiency that sometimes startled. I'd barely finished toweling my hair before he had new clothes laid out for me. He knew better than to assist me in dressing at this point and set about collecting my dampened garments from where I had dropped them on the floor.

"Apologies, I hadn't intended to leave them there."

"It's no matter, sir." His tone suggested otherwise, dry and judgmental.

"We've discussed this," I said.

"It's not appropriate outside of the kitchens, sir." I shot him a look he knew well. "Very well, Michael."

"Thank you."

"His Lordship has requested your presence in the study at your earliest convenience."

I managed to mostly dress myself. He took over my cravat, batting my hands away in irritation, tying a ridiculously complicated knot. I would be lucky not to strangle myself trying to undo it tonight. No loss.

"Very well."

"What shall I tell His Lordship?"

"Tell him that he can summon me like a misbehaving child when his own bollocks drop."

That earned me an exasperated look. I couldn't restrain the eye roll that followed.

"There's no need to report anything. I'll go there directly."

He nodded approvingly and held out my coat for me to slip into. He let out a disgruntled huff when I opened my own door, then hurried to keep up with me down the stairs, through the hall and to the study. I was about to wrench open the double doors when he reached around me to pressed them closed from behind. There was a brief struggle between us before he knocked with a customary, "Sir?"

"Just let him through, Stevens." Hugh sounded irritated even through the door.

Without warning Stevens released his weight from the doors, and they went flying open from my own yanking. I sent him a disapproving glare as I struggled to restrain my laugh. He had managed to improve my blackened mood, and I was grateful. He offered a brief smile in return before setting off back down the hall.

I turned my attention back to Hugh.

"Close the door."

Viscount voice then. He rarely used it in my direction after he took over the role. In fact, I thought the only time was to express his disapproval of Wayland's as a venture. That scene did not end in his favor.

"Have a seat."

I tried not to let it grate on me, my younger brother offering me a seat in the study that once as served mine. I refused the directed seat and instead leaned against the nearby bookshelf. Just as in the London study, there was a massive portrait of my father behind him, regal and imposing. So I had two Viscounts Grayson staring at me disapprovingly. I snagged a book by my side at random and flipped through it. Desperate for something to distract me from the chafing irritation of whatever scolding Hugh was working toward. Out of the corner of my eye, I noticed the way he started and stopped several times before finally beginning.

"She's engaged, Michael."

Those three words, and my stomach sank. I never considered Juliet would be the subject of this lecture. I deserved any flagellation he offered, but my pride could not abide its source. Instead, choosing to needle him, I asked, "Who is engaged, Hugh?"

"You know damn well who! She is engaged and here as my guest, under my protection."

Hugh had a tight leash on his temper, but it was there now, boiling under the surface, evident in his strained tone.

"Oh, Lady Juliet? I hadn't heard she was affianced. What of it?"

"You spend hours each day with her. Alone. I assumed you were in the rose garden, but I learned today that none of the servants know where you take her. Tell me!"

His face was getting tighter, but I welcomed his anger. I deserved it. I encouraged it.

"Here and there," I offered with a studied indifference.

"Damn it all, Michael. This is not a joke. If anyone were to catch even a hint of this... You would ruin that girl!"

"Catch what? What exactly am I going to do to her?" The lie tasted like ash in my mouth. Exactly what I had already done. But the self-loathing part of me needed to hear it from someone else.

"You know damn well what you're going to do to her! Even being seen with you is enough in some circles."

Hugh was losing control now, growing louder with his anger, unable to keep his seat in his rage. In this, we were opposites.

"Let's not be coy here, Hugh. Say it." The words were little more than a hiss. I abandoned my casual stance, stalking to the desk.

"You're a bastard! Everyone knows it. All of London! You're a dishonorable bastard whose own living comes at the expense of the gullibility and dishonor of others."

He called me a bastard once before father died. I hit him once, just once and never again. The switching the viscountess insisted on had left an impression on me. I was going to hit him now though, consequences be damned.

Then he finished. "She is not for you!"

Just like that the fight went out of me.

That summed the situation up nicely. Everything I had been striving not to think of since the moment we left the clearing. Juliet wasn't mine. She would never be mine. I could not give her the things she needed, let alone the things she deserved. My place was never at her side. I crumpled into the chair he had originally indicated. He remained standing, fists clenched, braced for the punch that wouldn't come.

His expression shifted to something dumbfounded. It would have made me laugh if I weren't so disgusted with myself.

"Sit." My throat was tight, but I shoved the word out with a nod toward the chair.

He was still tense as he took the seat, waiting for the ploy.

"I'm not going to hit you." Even to my own ears I sounded defeated.

"What just happened?"

"You won."

"What?"

"You won. You can wipe the befuddled look off your face now." I cradled my head in my hand. There was a throbbing behind my eyes, and I was exhausted.

"I do not know what I have won." His tone was cautious as he finally sat.

"You're right. I'm spending too much time with her. Unchaperoned. I just.... I can't stay away from her, Hugh." It was the first time I had ever said such a thing outside of my own head. The relief the confession brought was accompanied by nausea.

"Oh, lord."

"You have the right of it."

"Michael, I had no idea. I thought you were toying with her. Perhaps to get at her father."

"That's flattering." My comment was brittle, harsh.

"I did not mean..."

"No, you did mean it. And why would you think otherwise? After all, I am a dishonorable bastard." I couldn't hide the bitter undertone.

"I did not mean that." I shot him a withering look. "Alright, I did mean it. But you do not need to run the club, Michael. You can do something respectable. You know I would fund you..."

I couldn't restrain my bitter laugh. "The club is everything I have, Hugh. I built it from nothing, and it's mine. There's nothing else, nothing in the entire world that's just mine."

"But if you just tried your hand at a respectable occupation—"

"Seven years. I was viscount in all but title for seven years. In seven years the ton never once forgot. And neither did you, so don't try to deny it."

"I did not know you wished to be thought of as such."

I couldn't hold back the acidic laugh that escaped.

"Yes, who would want a title and wealth and power handed to them at birth? Who would want the chance to marry the woman he cares for? I had four years before he married your mother. Four years where no one treated me as lesser than. Four years where I thought I could do anything I dreamed. Then he married Agatha. Then I was banished from her sight. Worse still, she had a son, and everything that could've been mine was handed to you. I never, not once, complained. But don't for one second mistake my silence for lack of feeling."

I was breathless. And worse still, I had said too much. As soon as the words left my mouth, I regretted each one more than the last. I never wanted him to know these things.

"Michael, I... I don't know what to say."

I couldn't bring myself to look at him.

"It doesn't matter. The things I wanted were never mine to dream of in the first place. She's not mine to wish for either."

"Do you... Has she been compromised?"

"Not irrevocably."

"What do you consider to be irrevocably?"

"She's not with child, Hugh."

"Is that a possibility?"

"Not unless her offspring is the son of God."

"I have to ask these questions, Michael. She is a guest of my wife. She is under my protection whether you like it or not."

An exhausted sigh escaped. "I'm not a seducer, Hugh. I've never touched an innocent."

"As far as I know, you never cared for a woman until now either. Are you going to offer for her?"

"What do you mean, offer for her?"

"Are you going to ask her to marry you?" he asked it slowly, as though the words were foreign rather than their meaning.

"She's already promised to Rosehill. And more besides, as you so kindly pointed out, she's not for me." There was a resentfulness in my voice I couldn't restrict.

"Damn it all, Michael, I did not know you actually felt for her."

"My feelings hardly change the situation."

"You could ask her. She might say yes."

"She. Is. Already. Promised. To. Rosehill. And even if she were not, do you really think a father, even one so poor as Dalton, would allow his daughter to marry a man of my reputation and situation? Even if I hadn't threatened him bodily little more than two months ago?"

"I had forgotten that part."

"Yes, well, he will not have. I made sure of it." The sharp irony of that wasn't lost on me.

"She is two and twenty. She can wed without his permission."

"She'd never wed without it. She's terrified of him."

"Has it occurred to you that she may be expecting your address? You say you compromised her, even if not irrevocably —whatever that means."

"She's not."

"How do you know?"

"Because she's smart, Hugh. She knows this isn't anything real, just stolen moments before she weds the man of her dreams."

"Rosehill is the man of her dreams? Are you certain?"

"He's the man of every woman's dreams. Your own wife stated so at dinner the other night. Remember?"

"That was Kate being Kate. I did not hear Juliet rhapsodizing on her fiancé's merits."

"She didn't deny them either."

"No, how could she? As you stated, she's engaged to the man. She can hardly disparage him publicly at the dinner table. That does not mean she would not make a different choice if it were presented to her."

"Even if she wanted to, I could never ask it of her. She would not understand what a life with me would mean. She would be ruined. Never to be accepted in polite society again. I couldn't do that to her."

That was the inescapable truth. Even if she wanted to be with me, the price was too high for her to pay.

"You are determined then? Nothing I can say will convince you?"

"I won't drag her to hell with me."

"Very well then. I must ask you to refrain from engaging with her unchaperoned. No more strolls to places unknown. No more cards in the drawing room without Kate or myself present. The strictest proprieties must be followed."

I couldn't manage it. I knew I wouldn't be able to be so close to her and not have her. Not after this afternoon.

"I'll leave."

"What?"

"I'll go back to London."

"That is not what I said, Michael."

"I can't stay here. I can't be this close to her and not be with her."

"Are you certain?" His words were more sigh than speech.

"Yes."

"When?"

"Tomorrow, first light."

After a too-long pause, he agreed. "I will have the carriage readied for you. I just have to say one last thing, then I will never mention it again. I think you are underestimating her. I think you should tell her how you feel and let her choose. She deserves the truth."

"Are you finished?"

"Yes."

"I have packing to do."

"I will send Stevens in to assist you."

"That's unnecessary."

"Try telling that to him."

"Fine."

It took a few moments to force my legs to respond to my commands in order to stand. Eventually I managed the effort and with heavy steps I left the study, and the still disapproving eyes of two viscounts.

Twenty-Three

THORNTON HALL, KENT - JUNE 4, 1814

JULIET

I WOKE EARLY the next morning more rested than I could ever recall. I missed Michael at supper last night, and a small part of me was disappointed to hear no knock on my door later that evening. Still, it was probably best to avoid talk. Eager as I was for another visit to our bridge, I rose well before the appropriate hour. I dressed with care and fussed with my curls longer than usual.

When it was finally *nearly* an acceptable hour to break my fast, I left in search of a cup of tea. I rounded the stairs only to nearly run smack into Stevens carrying a hefty trunk. A trunk with the initials *M. W.* printed on the front. My blissful mood soured instantly, stomach dropping to the floor.

"Stevens? Is someone leaving?"

His face was grave, confirming what I knew from the sight of the trunk. "Mr. Wayland left early this morning, ma'am."

"I see... He will not be returning?"

"I do not believe so."

"Did he say why he left?"

My answer came from behind. "He had business to attend to in London. He had been away from his club too long." The viscount's voice was stern, brokering no room for further questions. When I turned, his expression was more sympathetic than I would have expected from the tone.

My throat was tight with emotion, and I knew I could not get words out. I respond with a solemn nod instead.

"Lady Juliet, I know you and my brother have grown... closer over the last few weeks. I do hope you will be able to find some other diversion while you're here. I'm certain Kate would be happy to assist you with your trousseau."

I forced the words through a thick voice, "Thank you. I'm sure she will." My breath was catching once more, tight in my chest. I needed out of this house. "I believe I will take a walk this morning. Would you be so kind as to let Kate know?"

"Certainly."

With his acceptance, I took the bonnet Stevens fetched at my mention of a walk, escaping from the open doors. I could not bring myself to don one more piece of clothing, so I kept it in hand.

I maintained a measured pace until I passed out of sight of the house, breaking out into a run. The effort was difficult with my breath still hitching, but my need to escape outweighed my need for air. Without decision, I found myself rounding the corner at our bridge. Tossing my bonnet with all my might, it caught in the air and floated gently down in a most unsatisfying manner. In retaliation for my bonnet's defiance I kicked my slippers off, flinging them at the tree where they made a satisfying thump against the bark. I stomped over to the bridge before flopping down in the middle in an unladylike display, legs hanging over the side. My lungs obeyed me, my run having overruled the hitch, but they were heaving with the effort.

There were a great number of emotions jockeying for

priority with every inhale. Anger, sadness, resignation, hurt all manifested. As one, my lungs began to relax, and my heart made itself known. There was, instead, an aching want spreading from deep in my chest all the way through my arm to my fingertips. Numbly, I stared as the dogwood petals floated gently past me, dancing in the current of the creek. There were tiny drips plopping between the rosy petals. My first thought was that once more it had started to rain. Instead, I realized they were tears dripping off my nose, only discovered when I rubbed the back of my wrist against it rudely.

I had no idea how long I had been sitting here, staring at water bubbling past when I heard a throat clear from over by the tree. For one brief, beautiful moment my heart soared and I thought Michael had returned, that it was a misunderstanding. When I looked up to see Mr. Tom Grayson my heart fell once more.

"Sorry to interrupt. I just wanted to see if you were alright."

Frantically, I wiped tears and other, more disgusting discharges from my face with the back of my hand.

"You're not interrupting anything, Mr. Grayson. I'm perfectly well." My voice was hoarse, and my face was certainly red. Even if he missed the other tell-tale signs of crying, these would not escape his notice. Still, I hoped my assurance was enough for him to recognize my desire for privacy and assuage his guilt at leaving a lady in such a state.

"Tom, please. May I sit?"

No luck then. He gestured toward the bridge beside me, and my ingrained manners answered with an automatic nod before I could refuse him. He sat silently, matching my position, legs resting over the side. He was tall, his legs long enough that his boots skimmed the top of the water. He set his hat beside him before beginning.

"I've always loved this place. I was so impressed when

Michael built it."

"Michael made it?"

"Yes, one summer before Father passed. When my mother was being particularly rough on him."

"He never told me."

He just shook his head in response. "Of course not. I take it he's gone?"

I tried to form the "yes" but my voice cracked. Suddenly, the flood of tears that had been only a trickle before broke free, and before I knew it I was sobbing. Tom pulled me into his chest where I blubbered into his fine linen shirt. Without realization or understanding I was voicing all my questions.

"What did I do wrong? Why did he leave? Why am I not enough for him? Why am I not enough for anyone?"

Tom's response was little more than a gentle shushing.

"Do you know the worst of it? I wasn't surprised. Some part of me knew he wouldn't be there this morning. I tried to ignore it, but it was there."

"I love my brother. He's been a father to me. But he's not a perfect man. He's quick to run away. He ran from here when mother was difficult. He ran to his club when Hugh was too much. Now he's running again."

"I'm too much? Is that it?"

"No, but you are affianced, Lady Juliet. To a duke. The title would be a concern for him. I'm confident he's convinced himself that Rosehill can make you happier than he can and he is leaving before you get too invested."

"Too late, and just Juliet, please." At some point, my tears dried and I pulled free from his shirt.

"I'm sorry to hear that. In some ways he's right. Rosehill can give you a life of respectability my brother would never be able to offer. You would never again be accepted in polite society if you broke an engagement. Let alone for a man such as my brother."

"I don't care a fig for society."

"You say that now, but you've never been rejected by the ton. You don't know the consequences. To be snubbed by people who now curry your favor. It's not a burden every woman could endure. I suspect that is why he's never seriously courted anyone. You're everything society could want in a lady, and you've worked hard to become so. Are you truly willing to give that up?"

"Yes..." I intended a certain tone, but the result was more unsure than I liked. Tom's brow rose again, clearly finding my enthusiasm wanting.

"Consider it. There's no wrong answer." He rose abruptly, brushing off non-existent dust and retrieving his hat. He offered me a hand. "May I escort you back inside?"

I shook my head. "No, thank you. I think I'll stay a while longer."

He nodded thoughtfully. "If you've not returned by midday, I will be back for you."

I gave him my thanks before I returned to staring at the water. As much as I loathed to admit it, Tom wasn't wrong. I hadn't truly considered the implications of my feelings for Michael. I had stubbornly refused to think of His Grace, to recognize what a marriage to the most notorious club owner in London would mean. My father would never speak to me again. As much as the thought appealed to me frequently, would the reality cut deeper? I would never be invited to another ball, never accepted into another drawing room. The rest of my life would very much follow the trajectory of the last several years, nursing Sophie, and mourning. A life perpetually watching from the outside. Of course, all of these thoughts were in vain. Michael had made me no offer, no promise.

~

MICHAEL

I'D SWITCHED TO THE CHEAP Scotch several glasses ago but hadn't found the taste particularly objectionable. I was down £150 to a Baron Something-Or-Other but there was little cause for concern. Someone must have alerted Augie to my return, because he came out of the office looking rather flushed. He took one look at me and sent Baron What's-His-Name away with a promise of payment and dragged me off to my study. I didn't recall the walls of my club being so prone to switching with the floor and ceiling but I had been away some time.

"I was just about to take Baron Pompous-Face for all he had. Why did you pull me away?" My enunciation was spectacular, if I did say so myself. I expected a bit more slurring with the six... seven drinks I'd enjoyed.

Augie set me down in my office chair and the walls and floor did their spin once again before righting into a consistent swirl.

"The Earl of Southerton and I saw your hand. You had nothing. Why are you back? You weren't supposed to return for another fortnight."

One of the two Augies seemed disappointed in me so I directed my response to the other.

"Hugh kindly reminded me that the woman I'm in love with is betrothed to a duke, and I'm nothing more than a viscount's by-blow. That I can offer her nothing except ruin and humiliation."

There was a hint of surprise when I parsed my words after. I hadn't realized that "love" would be so easy to say, that it would feel so right. Heart-achingly right. And wrong—so, so wrong.

"You're in love with Lady Juliet? I hadn't thought it went that far." Now both Augies were concerned.

"It didn't until it did."

He poured me a glass of water from a nearby pitcher, and I drank it reluctantly. I didn't particularly wish to be sober. Even in my drunken state, I was barely holding myself together and burdened by thoughts of Juliet. She awoke to find me gone. My stomach soured at the thought with no relation to the drink. Then the organ gave a full revolt, and I retched pathetically, desperately, into the nearby dustbin.

Several minutes of unproductive heaving followed before a now-singular Augie offered me a handkerchief. I wiped my mouth with disgust and lay my head on the cool desk. With the expulsion of the scotch my head was tragically clearer. It was so long before Augie spoke that I'd forgotten his presence.

"Any better?"

"No."

"Tell me what happened."

"I'd rather not."

"I wasn't asking."

I debated refusing him. He was unlikely to leave me to my self-loathing without a response though.

With an exaggerated sigh I answered. "She was just—there. All day, every day, being intelligent, and kind, and talented, and lovely. And I couldn't stay away. Every time I told myself I would leave her be, I found my feet heading in her direction without permission. Hugh dragged me into the study like a disobedient child and told me off for compromising her with my attentions. So, finally, I left."

He nodded thoughtfully for a moment. "How does she feel about all of this?"

"I'm certain she's relieved to find me gone."

Augie blinked owlishly at me for a full minute. "You didn't say goodbye? You didn't tell her you were leaving? You didn't discuss your feelings?"

I had never heard Augie take that tone with me in all our

years of friendship. I lifted my head from the cool respite of the desk to see that he was angry with me in a way I had never seen. I had experienced irritated Augie, exasperated Augie, patronizing Augie but never furious Augie.

"Of course not, she's engaged to Rosehill. What would I even say? 'Juliet, I know you're already promised to a man who can give you fortune and societal stature and children who won't be shunned by all of good society, but could you find it in your heart to give all that up for a degenerate gambling bastard who threatened your father with ruin and whose relation will bring you nothing but shame?'"

"I hadn't thought to put it that bluntly, but yes. That's what you say. And perhaps include your vast fortune, if you haven't lost all of it at the gaming table tonight."

"I haven't," I replied offhandedly. "And you, you're one to talk. How long have you been in love with Anna? Have you told her?"

He deflated a bit at that.

"Alright, it's easier to say it than to do it. But she must be upset. You truly left without a word?"

"That was badly done, I'll admit. But it's for the best. She'll see that."

"You cannot be convinced otherwise?"

"No, it's the right thing."

He raised a skeptical eyebrow.

"Then go home, before you do lose your entire fortune. I have no desire to clean any more sick than you've already provided."

He swept out the door, presumably to find a maid to assist in the cleaning. It was moments like this that I wished my office had a window. It did smell terrible in here. I knew I ought to take Augie's advice and return home, but after I cleaned myself up enough to face the world, I found my feet headed to Temple Bar, to the hells of days long past.

Twenty-Four

DALTON PLACE, LONDON · JUNE 19, 1814

JULIET

Tom's words echoed in my thoughts far longer than I would have liked. The entire fortnight I remained in Kent was spent in a perpetual state of angst. Even the night before I left for town I wavered. Then dawn broke, and I understood with the kind of certainty I had never experienced before. I knew the effects of a marriage without love. Every day I watched unhappiness eat away at Sophie, until she became a kind of wraith haunting the house rather than living. I did not believe His Grace to be anything like my father, but now that I had experienced it, I could not imagine a marriage without love. Even if that marriage was not with Michael.

Of course, now I would have to tell my father that I refused to marry His Grace. I had never courted his ire before nor purposefully disappointed him. I could not think that anything would fully prepare me for his reaction. Kate offered to let me stay at Grayson House in the, entirely likely, event that my father tossed me out. The length of the carriage ride back to London I rehearsed my words.

When we arrived, I entered the house with a strange, unexpected calm. Unfortunately for my nerves, my father had not seen fit to cooperate with his presence.

That was two days ago. He had not returned home at a reasonable hour once in that time. With the delay, my calm wavered. An irrational part of me, certain that he knew my plan, felt he was avoiding me to ensure the entire process was even more unbearable. I spent the intervening hours in a perpetual state of nausea. The only benefit of the delay was that the servants seemed to have picked up on my unspoken tension. They began preparing me, and the house, for the oncoming storm. Without a word, my trunks were already packed for the inevitable.

When Hannah's knock on the drawing room door finally came, I knew it was time. That didn't stop my stomach from offering a disgruntled flip or my heart from pounding in my ears. Even though I spent the last two days preparing for this moment, I struggled to find the gumption with which I had entered the house.

For the first time in weeks, I stared at the double doors, counting my inhale and then exhale. Hannah kindly accompanied me on my trip to the gallows.

"Hannah, please have the carriage readied with my trunks."

"It's already being done, my lady."

"Thank you." Another deep breath before I turned to face her. "No matter what you hear, I don't want you interrupting, do you understand?"

"But—"

"No. If you feel an intervention is necessary, you must send in at least two footmen. You are dismissed for the rest of the day."

I was shocked when Hannah, always one for propriety, wrapped me tightly in her arms. I couldn't help but return her embrace. As quickly as it had started, she pulled away and swept off without a word, presumably to alert the footmen.

Bolstered by Hannah's unexpected affection, I knocked on the door before I could talk myself out of it. I took one last fortifying breath as I waited for my father to bid me entry. When it came, I closed the door behind me, avoiding eye contact as long as possible.

When I turned, it was clear that my father was worse for wear. He was disheveled, still in last night's clothing and nursing a headache remedy with bleary eyes. Not the best moment for this conversation, but I refused to allow that to deter me. I had waited days for my opportunity, and there was no perfect moment in which my father would hear what I had to say with ready acceptance.

"Why are you here, Juliet?" he grunted.

In a tone that belied the tumultuous feelings inside, I said, "I have something I wish to discuss with you."

"Does it have to be now?"

Something about those loathsome words strengthened my resolve. "Yes, I need to discuss it now."

My words or resonance must have caught his attention because he actually looked up at me. He gestured for me to sit across from him with a grunt. I made my way farther into the room but refused his directive, instead remaining standing. Even with his interest peaked, he was my father and was therefore constitutionally incapable of fully committing to his daughter. He offered a dismissive "go-on" hand gesture. With a calm I had never before possessed, I spoke.

"I will not be marrying His Grace. I am aware of the arrangement between the two of you. I have no interest in being sold like chattel. Your gaming debts are your own, and they are for you to pay."

For a moment there was nothing but stunned silence from my father. The only sound was the painfully loud ticking of the clock and the unbearable drumming of my heart. For all the times he had accused me of defiance and disrespect, I had never actually defied or disrespected him. I had now. It took all my strength to bite my tongue, to refrain from desperate, fawning, attempts to soothe. Not this time.

When he finally spoke, it was not the shouting I had anticipated. Instead, it was a venomous whisper. "Excuse me?"

"I will not be marrying His Grace."

"You will not be marrying Rosehill? You think you can just walk in here and announce that? Just like the weather? You think to accuse me of accruing debts? You, the ungrateful, spiteful shrew that has been ruining my life since the day you were born? I don't care what you think you know. You will marry Rosehill, and you will do it with a smile. Do you understand? If you leave here right now without another word, I will graciously forget this entire conversation."

His words were hissed, droplets of spittle landing over his desk. The vein in his neck was ready to burst. His face turned a dark purplish color with ire. Suddenly, instead of terrifying, it was comical. The man whose approval I had strived for my entire life was utterly ridiculous. I wasted years of my life trying to do the impossible, and for what? The support of this spitting, throbbing, aubergine stuffed into a too small waistcoat? The good opinion of this depraved, abusive, lout who would be missed by no one but his debtors upon his demise?

In little more than a seething whisper, the words came tumbling out of me. "This ungrateful, spiteful shrew will not be marrying Rosehill. She will not be rectifying your debts with Mr. Wayland. She will not be your excuse to lure some other poor unsuspecting girl into a loveless marriage bed where you can once again fail to have a son. She will not be managing your estate with nonexistent funds because you've squandered them all at the gaming table. And she will not stand here and accept this abuse, not for one more second."

With that I whirled away toward the door in a flurry of skirts, opening and slamming the door in the face of my father's bluster. Both footmen stood outside at the ready, and I appreciated their efforts. One pressed his weight to the door in a preemptive measure while the other grabbed my upper arm and directed me quickly toward the carriage. I was already halfway down the hall when I heard the crash of a drinking glass against the study door. Before I escaped the house, I heard what I can only assume to be the entire contents of his study tossed about with a wordless snarl of rage.

The footman closed the door behind me, dampening the effect. The carriage pulled away before I was fully seated. I fell onto the bench and watched the only home I'd ever known shrinking smaller and smaller, knowing with resigned certainty that I would never set foot inside again.

Twenty-Five

JULIET

I SLEPT last night in a way I had not since the day Michael left Thornton Hall. It was a dreamless sleep driven by bone-deep exhaustion. Kate had been unbearably kind when I arrived at Grayson House yesterday. The viscount and his mother remained in Kent so it was just the two of us at supper and neither one of us spoke much.

Now though, I was once again feeling my stomach tumbling as I stared at the imposing visage of Hasket House. Much as I wanted to avoid this conversation and hide from His Grace until after the wedding date, it would be better that he hear this from me than my father. Though we were ill-suited, he had been kind to me during our betrothal and I loathed the idea of hurting him.

Eventually, I summoned the courage to knock and was once again greeted by the smartly dressed butler. The man looked at me with curiosity and peered behind me, searching for a chaperone. I had not felt it necessary to trouble Kate with the effort. My reputation would be in tatters regardless once I broke the engagement in a few minutes.

"May I speak with His Grace? Privately?"

He did not answer but instead gestured to wait in the drawing room before heading off down an equally imposing hall. I fidgeted uncomfortably in the harsh black and white of the room. Fortunately, His Grace arrived in only a few minutes. The butler pointedly left the door open, but His Grace closed it.

"Lady Juliet?" he asked with a bow before gesturing to a nearby chair.

"Your Grace."

"Is there something I can assist you with? I had not expected you." His tone was kind but concerned.

My heart gave a nervous lurch, and I waited for my uneven breathing that would surely follow, but, though rapid, it remained steady. Somehow, this was more difficult than speaking with my father.

"It is a matter of some delicacy... I should like to end our engagement." Though I managed the words, I could not bear to look upon him as I spoke, staring at my, once again, scuffed slippers.

His reply was a measured, "I see..." He paused for a fortifying breath before continuing. "Juliet, I'm sorry but I cannot release you."

My eyes snapped to his. I honestly hadn't considered that he might refuse. Who would want to marry someone who did not wish to marry them?

"I don't understand..."

"There are factors of which you're unaware."

"I know about the money and my father's debts."

He raised a surprised brow at that. "I had not thought he would tell you."

"He didn't. I overheard it."

"Regardless, I still cannot release you."

"But, Your Grace—"

"Xander, please. I think this conversation would benefit from a little familiarity. I prefer Xander to Alexander."

"Xander, I cannot marry you. I have feelings for someone else."

There's a muttered curse under his breath followed by a resigned sigh. "I'm sorry to hear that, but, Juliet, I cannot release you. I must marry and produce an heir. After that, you can be with whomever you choose. As long as you are discreet, I have no objection."

It took a moment to parse his meaning, and the result was horror. He would have no objections to an affair? He did not care if I loved another? "But surely you would wish for a wife who cares for you? Or, at least, one who does not long for another?"

"I would prefer a wife who did not have other attachments, it is true. But a wife who cares for me would be a... complication. I already had one failed courtship, Juliet. If you break the engagement, I will not find another bride. The ton will suspect there is something off about me."

"But it has nothing to do with you. You've been kind and gentlemanly. If I didn't have feelings for Michael, I could have been a good wife to you."

With yet another exasperated sigh he continued, "Juliet, may I speak frankly and rely on your discretion?"

"Of course."

"There is something about me the ton will not forgive. I will never have feelings for any wife I take."

He paused here with a significant look, clearly hoping I would draw some sort of conclusion, but none was forthcoming.

"I will never have romantic feelings for any woman."

Again, there was a pause, and again, I felt the weight of my own ignorance. He began once more after a surreptitious glance around the room. "Because I have those feelings for men."

"Oh." The word felt inadequate, but it was the only one that came. I did not fully understand the implications of what he told me, but I knew it was significant. Perhaps illegal as well. As the words began to arrange themselves in my mind, a great many things slipped into place. All this time, I had known why my father wished to marry me to Xander, but I had never understood why he cared to wed me. He was all eagerness to arrange a match but disinterested in becoming acquainted. How ignorant I was.

"Do you understand my meaning?"

"Yes, I believe so. Forgive me, but is that not... illegal?"

"The feelings are not. The expression of those feelings, however, would end in a hanging, yes. I'm relying on your discretion."

"Of course," I assured him readily.

As I took in the blatant relief on his face, my heart suddenly broke for him. I had fallen in love with Michael without trying, without my permission, against my judgment. While a future with him was uncertain at present, the possibility existed. Though an imprudent match, there was no law against it. But Xander... to know with absolute certainty that he could never have such a thing without risking his life, it was too much to contemplate.

"So, you see. I cannot afford the stain of two failed courtships. It would draw too much scrutiny. I must marry and produce an heir. There is no other option. You are a kind woman, Juliet, and you will be a good mother to any children. Everything that is within my power to give, it will be yours. Anything to make your situation tenable. After we produce an heir, you can take a lover. Any children would be recognized as mine, given all the appropriate distinctions. You can keep an entirely separate house. Anything you want. But I cannot release you. It would ruin me."

The desperation in his tone and countenance was unbearable, full of heart-aching agony. I could not abide hurting this man who had been nothing but kind to me. Months ago, when I first agreed to wed him, the arrangement he proposed now would have been perfectly acceptable to me. Now though, the thought of a marriage based on mutual respect but not love was agony, too.

"You will not release me then?"

"I'm sorry. I cannot. But please, consider everything I have said. Would it truly be so terrible being married to a man who respects and admires you?"

I nodded absentmindedly. We were at an impasse, and I needed time to consider my next course.

"I should be going then. I had thought to leave here a compromised woman by way of a broken engagement. Had I known you would refuse to release me I would have made the pretense of a chaperone."

He winced at that before taking my hand in his for the first time. There was none of the pleasant warmth and flutters, none of the giddy rush I felt the moment my fingers brushed Michael's. That realization solidified my decision in a way that nothing else could.

"May I call on you?"

"I have left my father's home. I'm staying with my friend Kate, Viscountess Grayson, at Grayson House. But I believe I require some time to make sense of all this."

"Very well. You will send a note when you've considered it further?"

"Yes," my response was curt, and I desperately needed to escape this house. With its maddening black-and-white floors and walls and ceilings and furnishings, I felt as though I had lost the ability to see colors.

He escorted me out of the drawing room to the door in a perfunctory fashion. Once outside, I was momentarily blinded by all the blue of the sky and the green of the elm tree in front of their home. Kate's carriage still awaited me, and a footman handed me in before setting off. I left the house every bit as engaged as when I had entered.

Twenty-Six

WAYLAND'S, LONDON - JUNE 22, 1814

JULIET

IN THE THREE days after my visit to Hasket House, I had come no closer to a solution than when I first left. As a lady, I could jilt Xander without the legal repercussions a man would face under similar circumstances. Two failed courtships, though, would draw unwanted attention to any young man. Especially a duke, as handsome and charming as he was wealthy. The gossipmongers would circle like sharks scenting blood, searching for the ruinous wound.

Could I do that to any person? At best, his line would end with him. At worst—I could hardly think the worst. For the hundredth time, I cursed the laws and rules that created this situation. My heart ached for Xander. He asked too much of me, though. He asked for the rest of my life. Now that I had experienced the first flutterings of love in all its rapturous, heart-breaking beauty, a marriage without it would be unbearable. I knew I must end the engagement, that was certain, but the "how" eluded me.

The one constant in my tumultuous thoughts was a

desperate desire for Michael's mere presence. And now, in an increasingly blatant attempt to ruin myself, I was outside Michael's club. I had chosen mid-morning for my visit. My father frequently returned home at that time, so I hoped the club would be slightly less crowded. Unfortunately, I had not considered that a gaming-hell might keep different hours than a tea shop, and the entrance was locked. I stood, staring stupidly at the door for much longer than I cared to admit before deciding a knock was the only option.

It was less than a minute before the door opened to reveal a strangely familiar man. He was tall and stout, with a bald head. I was absolutely certain I had never been introduced to him but equally certain I had seen him somewhere before. My suspicion was confirmed when he bowed politely and addressed me by name, urging me inside and closing the door behind us. I was not certain what I expected, but it was not this. Rich mahogany furnishings, luxurious sage fabrics, elegant gaming tables filled the enormous room with a glass domed ceiling. The place was bright and airy in the sun of the skylight, not the dark, musty tobacco scent of my father's study.

I was distracted from my perusal by the addition of another gentleman who was also suspiciously familiar to me. This one was portly, with a curly mop of red hair and freckles. When he, too, addressed me by name, recollection dawned suddenly. Months before, I saw them both outside of Dalton Place. Frequently. Michael must have had the house watched.

I was equal parts irritation and amusement at that realization when I replied, "Do you gentlemen often lurk outside a lady's home prior to an introduction?"

Simultaneously they realized their critical error, the first coughing uncomfortably and the latter turning an alarming shade of red. They were spared further scolding by another calling my name from behind.

"Lady Juliet? May I assist you with something?"

Though I had never met this man either, I knew instantly that he was the infamous Augie. He confirmed it a moment later, insisting I call him such. He was already half ushering, half dragging me up a flight of stairs and into what I could only assume was an office before I could answer.

"Michael isn't here right now, Lady Juliet. Can I help you with something?"

The floor dropped out from under me with that intelligence. I hadn't realized just how desperate I was to see him, to be with him again, until the promise of him was taken away. I sank into a nearby leather chair, unable to hide my despondent response. Augie fussed over me, first reaching toward me then aborting his efforts, before ringing for tea and perching uncomfortably on the edge of the adjacent chair, clearly at a loss.

"When do you expect him to return?"

He hesitated, and my heart lurched with understanding. "He hasn't been here in some time... But I would be happy to assist you with anything, absolutely anything."

"I had hoped to get his advice, it's a matter of some delicacy. Do you know how to deliver a note to him?"

"I don't. I'm dreadfully sorry."

"It's certainly no fault of yours, Augie."

"Are you certain there's nothing I can assist you with? I'm responsible for all of Michael's best ideas."

That drew a chuckle out of me. I appreciated his efforts. He was the kind of person who put one instantly at ease, and I understood both Michael's and Anna's affection for the man.

With a resigned sigh I rose while replying, "Unless you can get me out of an engagement where the bridegroom refuses to be jilted, I'm afraid not."

He stood with a start, blurting, "You're trying to end your engagement? With Rosehill?"

"Yes..." I dragged the word out, trying to parse his sudden urgency.

"Sit back down. We'll figure this out."

"We will?"

"Yes. You say he won't release you. Did he tell you why?"

"Yes, but I won't share it. His reasons are fair, and I cannot see him ruined as a result of my actions. He has done nothing to warrant it. My desires to end the engagement have nothing to do with his actions or situation."

He considered me thoughtfully. For a moment I worried I had said too much.

When he spoke again, it was with a measured thoughtfulness. "You are prepared for the consequences of ending an engagement? If you end it with Rosehill, you will be ruined. No respectable gentleman will have you."

"I am quite aware of the consequences. To be honest, I hoped an entirely disreputable gentleman of our acquaintance might consider me. I do know he may not. He has made me no promises or declarations, quite the opposite. Regardless, I am prepared."

He blinked slowly in response, contemplating my meaning before continuing. "You're prepared for ruin, but you're not yet ruined... What if you sped up the process? What if your reputation was in such tatters that no one could blame Rosehill for throwing you over?"

I flushed with the idea of what that ruin would entail, with the understanding that if anyone knew of the events at our bridge, Xander would have little choice.

"Oh lord, not like that!" he rushed to add.

"What did you mean then?"

"Please don't tell Michael I implied that. I meant financial ruin—have your father's debts called in."

"What would that entail?"

"Well, he owes the club more than enough to put him in

the fleet. I'm sure there are others outstanding, as well. We could purchase them and have him arrested for them."

I blanched. Though I knew the vast sum he owed, the idea of debtor's prison had never occurred to me. Somehow, I had not grasped the magnitude of my father's vices, not even when he offered me in exchange for payment of his debts. It brought clarity to his erratic moods and desperation over the last months.

"You want to have my father thrown into debtor's prison?"

"I don't want to. It's bad for the club's image. We try to settle these matters in other manners. But we could, if it was something you were willing to do. We wouldn't have to leave him long. We're trying to ruin his reputation—and your's by extension—not leave the man to rot."

My first instinct was a vehement objection. Then, the idea took hold in a vindictive part of me, a part of which I was ashamed. He was perfectly willing to sell me to pay his own debts. Was this not merely him facing his own consequences?

"I am wretched for even considering this. How long do you suppose he would have to remain there?"

"Long enough for the gossip to spread. Perhaps a fortnight?"

A fortnight? My father would never survive it. Surely the ton moved faster than that. I had seen rumors spread across a ballroom in minutes. Oh— "What if we made a spectacle of it? What if the entire ton was there to witness his arrest? Could he not be released quickly after that?"

"What did you have in mind?"

I parsed my mental social calendar. I had been dreading Lady James's ball for weeks; it was next week. My father would be there. Since I had bungled his plans for Xander to pay his debts, he would be in search of a wealthy bride.

"Lady Charlotte James has a ball Friday next. Would that be enough time?"

"Certainly. Are you sure? I will need to begin the arrangements immediately."

"Yes. Can he be arrested at a ball, though? I've never heard of such a thing."

"I have friends. I can make it happen. Especially since he's been so efficient at dodging us for months."

Without pausing to give myself time to change my mind I answered, "Do it." With two words I had ensured my father's ruin. And my own.

Twenty-Seven

PICCADILLY, LONDON - JULY 1, 1814

MICHAEL

IT WAS TRULY astounding just how much money one could lose in such a brief time. I was down more than £500 this evening with no end in sight. Even that sum was paltry to me, but I really ought to work up some concern. Some of these men remembered me from my misspent youth. Some of their losses helped build my fortune. There were still some who were wary of me. They hadn't forgotten my skill in the four years I had been away. The majority were taking advantage of my string of bad luck. It was not so much bad luck as apathy, but I saw no reason to correct their misconception.

Augie and Tom had both been trying to reach me, if the stack of calling cards I found at my house on the rare occasions I returned were any measure.

I made no effort to remain presentable. I could not recall ever having so much growth on my face. I had long lost my cravat and had no interest in its location. If I employed a valet, he would be in a fit about the smell of liquor and cigars seeping from my very skin.

It was no wonder that the man who made himself comfortable across from me didn't recognize me in my current state. I recognized him, though. I would recognize him anywhere. He was nearly as bedraggled as I was, rumbled and sloppy with drink too. Stouter with age and sin, even more than he had been a few months ago. He was paler too—a sickly yellow. Richard Dalton.

"Dalton."

He startled, squinting at me through hazed, beady eyes. When recognition sank in, he stumbled to his feet, swaying slightly, lurching toward an escape. The crush surrounding us was too much for him, and he slopped back into his chair, the furnishing groaning under the mistreatment.

He finally responded with a resigned tone. "Wayland, I don't have your money."

The reminder of how he planned to get my money, the still impending nuptials, made the ale and scotch roll in my stomach. Unbidden thoughts of untamed, sun-lit curls and bluer-than-sky eyes came forth, and I swallowed the bile with another sip of scotch.

"I'm not here for your money. At least no more than you're prepared to lose at present."

He blinked slowly, stupidly, not taking my meaning in the slightest. The caster to my right began the roll.

"I won't have your money. Least not right away," he said.

"I know—not until after the happy day." I struggled to keep the bitterness out of my tone and was not remotely successful.

I should not start a fight with the man here. Neither of us were in a state for it, and while I was relatively confident the crowd would side with me, I had taken a great deal of money from them over the years.

He swallowed back the rest of his drink and signaled for another while I cast, losing once more.

"Not going to be a happy day."

My thoughts, cloudy with drink, were slow to understand. When comprehension dawned, the haze cleared in a rush, too quick with urgency and blinding with import. Juliet—had her reputation been tarnished by my association? Had Rosehill thrown her over? Fuck!

My hands were around his collar, no thought necessary, interrupting the game and dragging him to face me. "What do you mean?" The words were little more than a growl through clenched teeth, but my rough handling seemed to have had a sobering effect on him as well, and he took my meaning.

"There is not going to be a wedding," he spoke slowly, enunciating each word. It only served to further enrage me.

"Not that," I spit out before continuing. "Why won't there be a wedding?"

He struggled to free himself. "Not sure why you care; you're not getting your funds regardless. My ungrateful, disobedient, urchin of a daughter is refusing to marry the man. Somehow learned of my arrangement with Rosehill. Claims she won't be sold. She's my daughter, and I can do what I want with her. But she's run off and she's of age. Solicitor says there is nothing I can do."

I released him as abruptly as I had grabbed him. His words echoed in my ears, my heart pounding with the beginnings of something like hope. She was free. She had ended it. For the first time in our acquaintance, there was no other man with a claim on her. She could be mine. A match between us would still be imprudent, of course. But perhaps, just this once, if I loved her with everything I had, it would be enough. *I* would be enough.

Without warning I stood, clinking my glass against his where it rested on the table before knocking mine back. I tossed an obscenely large pile of bank notes on the table without consideration before pressing my way through the crowd that had thickened at the promise of fisticuffs. Finally, I stepped into the day, hope blooming with every step.

THE CLUB WAS STILL STANDING, at least. Everything appeared to be in order on the main gaming floor. Augie was more than capable of managing Wayland's without my input, and the evidence was plain in the clean, organized tables. It was all set for tonight. I asked a passing maid to bring coffee to the office at her convenience, and she scurried off with a nod. I knocked on the frame of the open door, and could see that Augie had made himself comfortable in my absence. Numerous files were piled high on the desk in front of him while he perused some document.

Glancing up, he startled. "Where the hell have you been?"

"Piccadilly."

The response was met with only a tired palm wiping over his equally tired eyes.

"Should have known. How bad is it?"

"I managed to avoid losing the club, at least."

"I suppose that's better than I expected. Tom and I have been trying to reach you."

"I saw. Does it have anything to do with Juliet leaving her father's home?"

"So, you've heard?"

"Ran into Dalton at the gaming table."

"What did you say?" his tone had abruptly shifted to concern.

Fear and confusion rushed through me in equal measure. "Just that I knew he wouldn't have my funds until the wedding, and he informed me that no wedding will take place.

The details are a bit fuzzy, we'd both had more than enough to drink."

He sank back in my chair, more relaxed. "Your Lady Juliet and I have been working together. Her father cannot know."

"What do you mean you've been working with Juliet?"

"Rosehill won't release her from the engagement. Left it up to her to jilt him at the altar or go through with the marriage."

"Why on earth not?"

"She won't say." His look was significant, further confirming my previous suspicions.

I felt for the man, but I wouldn't allow him to solve his own problems at the expense of my Juliet.

"She came here looking for you last week. Since the obvious solution wasn't available in your absence, we had to choose another option."

Joy, worry, and self-loathing warred for supremacy inside me. She came to find me, risking injury to travel here, alone. And all the while I was trying and failing to drink and game away thoughts of her.

I forced myself back to the present. "Obvious solution?"

"If you had been here, you could have married her. Gotten a special license or skipped off to Gretna Green. Can't jilt a groom when you've already found one, and Rosehill would be all but forgotten in the scandal of your marriage."

Oh, the pang of want that sent through me. Juliet walking down an aisle toward me, all dark curls and bright eyes and tempting grin. Once again, I cursed my absence.

"Why is it too late for that?" The thought was too infinitely appealing to leave me easily.

"Our other plan is already underway. She's a game one. I'll give you that."

Before he could continue, we were interrupted by a knock. Instead of the maid with coffee, I was faced with Tom.

He began questioning Augie before he even recognized my presence. "Is everything all set for tonight?"

I coughed pointedly before he noticed me.

"Michael! Where the hell have you been?" It was the closest he had ever come to raising his voice at me.

"Not important, what is happening tonight?"

Augie sighed. "Hadn't had a chance to fill him in yet, Tom. We've called in Dalton's debts. He's going to be arrested tonight."

I was all confusion and anger. "No, absolutely not. Juliet will be ruined!"

He continued, "That's the plan. She's agreed to it. If she's ruined, Rosehill will be forced to release her, and no one will question it."

"But—"

"But nothing." Tom interjected. "The plan is all set. It cannot be changed now. If you wanted a different outcome, you should have been here."

He was angry with me. I wouldn't have thought him capable of that emotion. Augie made an unsubtle exit with a mumble about confirming with the constable. I took his vacated seat behind my desk before offering Tom the one opposite. For the first time in four years, the chair felt foreign to me, like I didn't belong in it.

Before I could follow that thought, Tom continued, "You just left her without a word. She was devastated. Did you know that? Did you even think?"

"Of course, I did. I thought too much. Couldn't turn the thoughts off. She was engaged, what was I to do?"

"Ask her what she wanted!" He was fully yelling at me now. He seemed to have startled himself with his tone. It would be comical if it wasn't so deserved. He sighed deeply before continuing, more sedately. "What are you going to do?"

I paused, giving the question the consideration it was due.

"Whatever she wants. If she'll have me, I'll wed her tomorrow. If she wishes me gone, then so be it."

"Promise me."

My gaze shot to his. I agreed with solemnity. Adding, "I didn't think you knew her well."

His response was curt. "We had a moment."

I could feel the irritation rolling off him at my slow blink. "What kind of moment?"

He merely glared. "You cannot run again. She needs you to fight for her. She deserves it."

My throat was thick with the sudden understanding of the hurt I'd left in my wake. All I could manage was a nod.

Tom accepted it. "You've been a father to me, Michael. I'm grateful. I don't know if I've ever told you that. I'm sorry if I haven't."

I was still without words, this time with affection for the man my brother was becoming.

He cleared his throat before abruptly changing course. "I know about the money, Michael."

It took me a moment to comprehend his meaning. "How?"

"You forgot a ledger. I was looking for an example for my studies."

"How long have you known?"

"A while."

"Does anyone else?"

"I think Kate suspects. She's smarter than Hugh realizes. Hugh is getting close. If he hasn't gotten there yet."

I merely nodded. Even with that surprise, I was still unprepared for his next question.

"It wasn't an accident was it?"

I knew exactly what he was referring to, but I questioned to buy time. "What wasn't an accident?"

"Father. It wasn't an accident."

Tom and I had many uncomfortable conversations throughout his youth. None of them came close to preparing me for this.

"No. I never wanted you to know. I'm sorry, Tom."

His only response was a resigned swallow. He was thoughtful for a moment before he shocked me yet again. "You saved us all from ruin, and you asked for nothing in return. You saved a viscounty that was never going to be yours, and you never said a word. You let two young boys grow in blissful ignorance of their father's flaws. You let a widow who hated you remember her husband with pride. You're a much better man than you give yourself credit for, Michael. Don't let anyone tell you that you don't deserve the woman you love, not even yourself."

My heart ached with affection for my brother, and no small amount of pride. This entire conversation was becoming far too sincere for my comfort. I was forced to break the tension. "What happened to the lad who used to throw his peas at me?"

"He's still here, disrespecting the furnishings," he replied before throwing his feet on my desk with a laugh. I shoved them off in mock irritation just as Augie returned with a tentative knock.

"Well?" Tom questioned.

"Everything is ready."

"What's ready? You forgot to fill me in on the plan."

Augie's answering grin was too mischievous for my comfort. "How do you feel about attending Lady Charity James's ball tonight?"

"Charlotte," Tom corrected.

"What?"

"Lady Charlotte James. Not Charity."

"I thought it was Charmaine," I interjected.

"It's definitely Charlotte," Tom insisted.

"It doesn't matter," Augie interrupted, frustrated. "You're going to the chit's ball tonight."

"What on earth for?"

"The show."

Twenty-Eight

JULIET

THE JULY NIGHT air was unexpectedly chilled. My gooseflesh, however, was from an entirely different cause. I had expected I would spend this entire week in a state of indecision and dismay. Instead, once I made my choice, I never wavered even the slightest.

Tonight, I stood outside the Grayson carriage, flanked by Tom and Augie. Anna had dressed me in the periwinkle gown I had worked on for months, and flecks of gold from the embroidery shone in the lamplight, flickering. My wedding gown. She had pulled my curls into a romantic loose style with matching gold pins and forget-me-nots. Though neither was strictly in-fashion, the effect was enchanting, and I felt lovely.

Grayson House had emptied in recent days with Hugh remaining in the country with his mother and Kate taking to Lincolnshire to assist her sister with her confinement. Though she worried about leaving me alone in town, I was even more sure of my decision in this moment than I had been a week ago. A part of me had been desperately holding out hope for

Michael's presence, as though he would be summoned merely by my need for him. He would appear and press a comforting hand to the base of my spine, supporting me. I had not seen or heard from him since that rainy day in Kent, and his absence was a palpable loss tonight.

Tom checked his pocket watch for the third time in as many minutes. He seemed more anxious than I, pacing to and fro. We had arrived with some time to spare before the constables made their appearance. The men had entered the home a few moments ago. I wasn't certain how long their efforts would take, but I couldn't imagine what would take them more than a handful of minutes. Perhaps that was optimistic; hoping, for my father's sake, that his humiliation would be short-lived.

As if summoned by my thoughts, the double doors opened with the assistance of two footmen. My father, circumscribed by three constables, was shoved unceremoniously out. Through the window, I could see a number of faces of the ton pressed against the glass. It seemed our efforts had been successful. He stumbled a bit down the stairs, clearly intoxicated, before righting himself at the base.

Finally, he caught sight of me, and all color drained from his cheeks. It had been less than a fortnight since I left home. In that time my father had gained weight, centered low on his form, and it seemed to be due to scotch more than food. His skin had taken on a sallow tone, waxy in the lamplight. A small part of me worried after his health before I forcibly silenced the thoughts.

"Hello, Father." My voice was steady once more. With the constables at his side and my champions at mine, I felt none of the rising panic I should.

"You..." he slurred.

"Me."

"You did this to me? You and Wayland?" I was fortunate

that he was far enough away that his spittle missed me completely. The vein was making its presence apparent again, and I found it just as amusing as the last time.

Augie moved forward and started as though to cut in, but when I raised a hand in front of him, he paused.

"You did this to yourself. I merely chose not to help you."

"I've given you everything. Found you a duke to marry. And you couldn't do this one thing in return? There's a place in hell for daughters like you." The constable tightened his grip on my father in response to his hissed predictions.

"You didn't give me anything. Sophie gave me everything I needed. In spite of your best efforts, I might add. If I'm bound for hell, I imagine I'll see you there."

Apparently, the constables had enough of our shared vitriol and dragged my father by the elbow farther down toward their wagon. They heaved him into the back with no apparent gentleness before slamming the door against his groan. They were nothing if not efficient. One of the men tipped his cap toward Augie in the moonlit night before joining his brethren in the front. The horses started off at a sedate pace, my father's groans of displeasure audible for some time over the hoof beats.

As the wagon turned the corner out of sight, Augie and Tom turned to face me. Tom began, "Well, that was pleasant. Are we certain he bears no relation to my mother?"

"Lord, I hope not," Augie replied. "Are you certain you wish to go in? The scandal appears to be quite effective regardless of whether you make an appearance." He gestured toward the faces still pressed against the window, slightly smaller in number than when my father was present.

"This dress was not made for hiding outside, gentlemen. We discussed this. The scandal will be all the greater for my brazen appearance."

"Still, I should go with you," Tom offered.

"I cannot be seen to have the public support of a viscount's brother. It will lessen the impact." He made a noise of protest before I continued. "I must face society eventually. At least here, I can ruin Charlotte's ball even more thoroughly, and Anna's efforts toward taming my hair will not have been in vain."

"I knew it was Charlotte!" Tom added haughtily toward Augie who handed over a five-pound note with a grumble. I chose not to question them, merely chuckling in response. "At least let us escort you to the door," he tacked on, sheepish at his forgotten manners.

With one man on each arm, I took the steps to the entry of James Place. The footmen held the doors for me, and my protectors stepped aside as I made my way in alone, the doors closing quietly behind me.

I was going to walk into this ballroom now as though I had every right to be here. Because I did.

RUINATION DIDN'T FEEL at all the way I had expected. All that was left was relief. Relief and a few nerves. Just beyond those double doors was Lady Charlotte's ball. The one I just ensured was infinitely more interesting than whatever spectacle she had planned. I doubted she appreciated my efforts. Her canapés would certainly be forgotten in drawing room gossip tomorrow in favor of the Earl of Westfield's arrest and subsequent bodily removal from the dance floor. Every single one of those gossipmongers was about to express awe at my defiant audacity. Just as soon as I gathered the courage to open the doors.

"I suppose I should release you now. That was what you wanted, wasn't it?" the lilting voice of Xander came from behind. I turned to face him and the consequences of my choice. He was halfway into a glass of something amber colored, leaning heavily against a doorframe. He didn't look angry though, just resigned.

"I'm sorry it had to be this way." And I was. He would have been a good husband to me. I would have been a good wife for him. Though there never would have been any romantic love between us, we could have been happy. I had destroyed that possibility tonight. And with its destruction I lost any chance of friendship with this kind gentleman.

"I know you are." He accompanied the statement with a resigned sigh. "You know it's quite difficult to be angry with you. How can I rage at you for refusing to resign yourself to a life without love, now that you know what it's like? All that besides, you've punished yourself far more than you've hurt me. I hope he's worth it."

"I don't know if he is yet. I hope so. I know that I am, though."

"Aye, you are. Next time I'm going to insist on an elopement. Can't keep giving you ladies time to beg off."

"You know you're worth it, too, Xander."

"I know. Society disagrees, though."

"Society is wrong," I retorted.

He tilted his drink toward me in a silent toast before finishing the glass in one swallow.

"What will you do now?" I asked.

He answered with a nonchalant shrug. "I suspect I have some time before the situation becomes untenable. I'll try to enjoy myself while I can. Then... Well, I've got some independent property in Scotland. Perhaps I will go there."

"If there's ever anything I can do for you..."

"Besides marriage?"

That broke a soft chuckle from me.

"Besides marriage."

"I do not think you're in a position to offer anyone

anything right now. I don't know if you've noticed, but you're destitute. Also, ruined."

"I thought I heard something of that nature this evening. I will let you know what it's like. Being cast from society." I turned back to the doors and squared my shoulders.

"Do you want some company? Entering the wolves' den?"

"Thank you, but this is something I need to do for myself."

He offered me a silent nod before wandering lazily back where he had come from, I suspected in search of another drink.

Alone in the empty hall once more, I stared up at the intimidating arched doors. I was surprised when I realized I felt no need to count. I expected more panic. With a single deep inhale, no lung hitch to be felt, I grasped both handles and pulled them open. Though I was more confident than I had expected, I couldn't help but close my eyes, bracing as I stepped into society's wrath.

The ballroom was deathly quiet, a feat I had previously thought unimaginable. I had stunned the entire ton into silence with my shamelessness. The instinct to count still remained quiet. Just as I was about to open my eyes, I heard a soft whisper in my ear. "Just breathe, Duchess." Instantly my eyes flew open, meeting his on a gasp.

"Michael! What are you doing here?"

He hesitated only a moment before replying, "I'm here for you. I was hoping you might favor me with a dance." His expression was more earnest than I could ever recall seeing. I liked it on him.

"You don't dance."

He slipped two ungloved fingers under my chin, tipping my head back to meet his smoky gaze. "I think you'd be surprised by what I'm willing to do for you."

My heart skipped, and my stomach flipped at the

reminder. My lips parted on a gasp, and I was entirely without words. I ached for him to pull me closer, to press his lips to mine. I was about to do it myself, pull him close, take matters into my own hands, when the whispers of the ton penetrated my romance-addled mind. Lady Charlotte's infuriated complaints rose above the rest. He must have noted them, too, because he dropped his hand as though burned. Before he pulled too far away, I caught his fingers in mine.

"I would love a dance. But I do not know if you heard, I am not to be a duchess any longer." I tried to infuse the statement with humor, but there was a small, insecure, irrational, voice inside me. It whispered that he would not want me now that I was ruined.

He banished it in the next moment, sliding my hand into the crook of his elbow as he escorted me gracefully down the stairs to the dance floor. The room was elegant with a slightly overpowering, rose scent perfuming the air. That was no surprise since every available surface was covered with the blooms in every color of the rainbow.

"I heard something to that effect," he muttered with a thoughtfully furrowed brow. "I can't say I'm overly saddened by the news." He leaned closer, offering a rough whisper for my ears only. "If you were someone else's duchess, the things I'm dying to do with you would be most improper."

A delightful shiver ran through me at the thoughts of what things he might want us to do together. He lined us up on the dance floor for the upcoming waltz. He thoughtfully placed my left hand on his shoulder before lacing the fingers of my right hand through his. Poor form but the intimacy of the gesture left me giddy.

"Why do I suspect the things you're referring to are most improper, regardless of my situation?"

His answering smirk was wicked. My body responded in kind, heat coursing through me to gather in my center. He slipped his free hand to my waist, pulling me too close for propriety but not close enough for my senses. That devilish hand slid lower, eventually finding a scandalous home low on my hip.

Lady Charlotte and her guests seemed to have taken our lead and lined up on the floor. Their attention remained on Michael and me. We were pressed shamefully close. I suspected the couples were hoping for a better view of our shocking behavior to report on the morrow. With three succinct taps on the stand, the conductor directed the orchestra to begin. Michael's lead was steady and graceful. I doubted I would have sensed the trepidation in his direction had I not been already familiar with the confidence underlying his ministrations. That thought warmed in more ways than one. That he would undertake efforts he was so unsure of for my pleasure, in front of the entire ton no less, sent a burst of affection through me. The reminder of that afternoon, on the other hand, shot a searing heat through my veins.

He huffed out a throaty chuckle. "Why do I suspect your thoughts are just as improper as mine, Duchess?"

I could feel the flush building in my cheeks, but I summoned my courage. "Perhaps more so..." His answering smile was brighter, adoring, and less seductive than the one I had expected. I felt my own tugging at the corners of my lips in response. "But I'm not a duchess, remember?"

"Oh, I'm not likely to forget that any time soon." His voice was low and sensual, but his expression was still ardent, almost... loving. Oh, a luscious glow filled my chest to bursting at that thought. "You're my duchess, though." His voice was a low, erotic purr as the dance came to a close. "So, tell me, my duchess, how long must we remain here, under the watchful eyes of the ton, to prevent scandal, ruination, and gossip?"

With the end of the set, he reluctantly released my hip, but I could not bring myself to step back, to increase the distance between us. Neither one of us made an effort to separate our joined hands.

My reply was dripping with feigned sincerity. "I'm afraid to tell you it's much too late to avoid such a terrible fate. In fact, I think it best to offer them some truly delectable gossip fodder."

"Is that so? How do you suggest we court scandal?"

He was contemplating my hand now, slipping our interlaced fingers apart. He shocked even me when he gently, deliberately, loosened my glove's grip on each of my fingers before sliding it off my hand entirely and set about stripping me of the other. The movement was far too sensual for a ballroom, and I honestly could not say whether my resultant flush was from embarrassment or arousal.

"You're—" my hoarse voice cut out on me and I was forced to start again. "You're doing a fine job of it right now."

"Oh, good. I would hate for my efforts to be in vain."

"Michael..." I intended it to be a stern repudiation, instead it was a needy whisper. "Michael, take me away from here."

He straightened, suddenly serious before slipping my ungloved hand into his elbow to guide me gently out into the London night.

Twenty-Nine

MICHAEL

I TUGGED her along faster than I ought, down the hall and out onto the temperate streets of Grosvenor's Square. In the London night, she pressed closer to me, seeking my warmth. After shrugging out of my tailcoat, I wrapped it around her. It was a worthy sacrifice for her company. She tucked gratefully into the coat. I quite liked the sight—the entirely improper attire, marking her as mine for all to see. Underneath my coat, I caught sight of delicate gold thread vines and flowers, the one she had been embroidering that day in the rain. I was immensely grateful to see it. Now it was for me and not her wedding gown to Rosehill.

She was even more beautiful than I remembered. Angst had dulled the memory of her slightly. But here in the lamp lit night of the street, she was exquisite. She had left her curls primarily to their own devices, wild and free. A few escaped the delicate gold pins, catching the light, a halo around her. Her eyes darkened in the night. That darkness lent a sensual quality to her gaze. Her expression had pooled something inside, encouraging ungentlemanly thoughts I couldn't shake.

"I suppose I should see you home?"

"I'm not certain I have a home at present."

"You mean..."

"He wagered the deed to the house, yes."

My stomach clenched at that thought. Of her without a roof, without comfort. My doing.

"Not at my club. Surely no one accepted that?" I dreaded the answer but needed it all the same.

"No. He chose other, less reputable venues for his riskier wagers."

The relief was mild compared to the frustration at her circumstances, the ones I could have prevented.

"Juliet, I... How can I begin to make amends for what I have cost you?"

"You cost me nothing, Michael. My father made his choices. He made his priorities quite clear. You are no more responsible for his actions than I am." She paused here, directing my gaze back to hers with a delicate hand on my jaw. "Kate has kindly offered to let me stay with them until I find a more permanent situation. Perhaps you can walk me to Grayson House?"

I nodded distractedly, grateful for the destination, the purpose. "A more permanent situation?"

"Yes. I had thought to apply for governess positions. Not in town obviously, but there may be some less particular families in the country."

The ton would condemn her for her father's dishonor and the display at the ball, assign blame to her when nothing could be further from the truth.

"Governess? Why would you be a governess?"

"Well, I must find some way to provide for myself. I can

hardly spend the rest of my life relying on your family's charity."

"But you will marry."

She pulled me to a stop now under one of the street lamps, insisting on my full attention.

"I'm quite ruined, Michael. And there is the other problem of course."

"Problem?"

"Quite a serious one. When I agreed to marry Rosehill, I had never known love. Now that I know the feeling, of course, I could only abide a marriage based on the very deepest of loves. In fact, I believe there is but one gentleman in all the world I could consider for my husband." Her earnest expression left no question in her meaning. "But you see, I have no way of knowing if this gentleman returns my regard."

"Jules, Duchess..." I pressed my forehead against hers, the distance between us too much. "I don't think I will ever deserve you. But if you let me try—if you do me the great honor of becoming my wife, I swear to you, I will spend every second of every minute loving you."

"I decide who deserves me. I deserve to be with the man I love, who loves me in return. Can you be that man?"

"The only requirement is to love you?"

"With your whole heart."

"I think I may safely promise that."

"Then yes, I would very much like to marry you."

My answering kiss was more of a pressing of smiles than an actual kiss. When we parted, she threw her arms around me. My heart was full to bursting. She was whispering words of love in my ears, and it was the happiest I had ever been.

"I should get you back to Grayson House, Duchess."

"You're not going to stay?" Her eyes were round, pleading, offering.

"I hadn't planned on it. Hugh and Kate aren't likely to approve of my presence if you're to be married from their house."

"They're not there. The viscount is at Thornton Hall, and Kate left for her sister's confinement in Lincolnshire."

We would be there—alone. The thought drew a groan from me.

"Duchess, if you'd like to make it to the altar without anticipating our vows you shouldn't tell me things like that."

"Michael, I was very much hoping to anticipate our vows."

My only response to that was a low curse. All blood required for thought left my brain for more essential areas. I finally found the wherewithal to continue toward the house. If I stopped every few steps for a kiss, there was no one afoot to see.

Finally, after far more kisses than were appropriate, we reached the house. I aimed for the front door but, instead, she pulled me down the alley to the servants' entrance.

"I gave them the night off," she whispered before knocking.

I was all astonishment when Augie opened the door. He was alone in the kitchens but for Anna.

"Looks like the ball went well then?" I didn't mind his smug tone in this instance.

"You could say that. Why are you here? Shouldn't you be watching my club?"

"I've been watching your club for nearly three months. It's my night off."

"Since when do you have a night off?"

"Since I'm at least partially responsible for the foolish smile on your face. Now that you've returned, Anna and I will be leaving for the evening."

"Unless you need assistance, my lady," Anna piped in, and Augie grimaced at the thought. On closer examination, they were both slightly disheveled. I supposed Augie had a magnificent evening as well then.

"No, no, I will be fine Anna."

At Juliet's dismissal, Anna appeared ready to press the issue, but Augie reached around and covered her mouth with his hand. I expected violence from Anna at the gesture, but she put up only the mildest of token struggles.

"We'll be going then. Enjoy your evening. I'll see you at the club tomorrow, Michael."

The last comment was pointed but fair. I had been away too long. I offered a nod in acknowledgment before he pulled Anna out the door and into the night.

Juliet and I were alone. A thick quiet settled between us. The anticipation was tangible, neither of us fully confident in the next steps. Always braver than I, she slid her delicate hand into mine, pulling me out of the kitchens. The press of her palm was enough to encourage bravery. I slipped a hand to her lower back to guide her through the house. We were almost to the stairs when she paused, turning to me with affectionate mischief in her eyes. Wearing a soft smile, she pulled me to the right, opening the double doors there, and guiding me into the library. The room where everything had changed.

She set about lighting several candles. I stared at her in all her loveliness, unhelpful in my awe. She was on the last one when I managed to force my legs to obey commands, to carry me to her. Her breath caught when I crowded behind her, pinning her against the table, her former hiding place. I grasped the shoulders of my coat, large on her form, and pulled it down her arms to land on the carpet between us. The back of her gown hit low on her shoulder blades, and I was presented with all sorts of delicious skin to sample. I settled for brushing aside the silky curls that escaped her coiffure, pushing them to one shoulder.

The freckle just behind her ear on her hairline was my first mark. I pressed a damp kiss to it. She rewarded my efforts with a shiver, and I made my way down her neck, only pausing to breathe her name against damp skin when I reached the place where her neck and shoulder met. The one that made her groan my name once before. The effect was instantaneous. She softened against me whimpering my name. The sound sent heat pooling to the hardness I had been striving to ignore.

"Juliet, darling, I'd very much like to pleasure you. Would that be alright?"

As much as I appreciated her enthusiastic nod, I was selfish. I wanted to hear her beg for me before the night was over. I trailed my fingertips along her collarbone, dipping them lower with each pass, finally tracing the neckline of her gown, mapping the curve of her breasts.

"Jules, I need the words. Tell me what you want, Duchess."

I heard the whisper of her tongue against her lips before she answered. "My gown. Take it off." Her voice was steadier than I'd anticipated. She was not nearly as desperate as I wanted her.

I allowed one finger to map the column of her spine that was visible before it hit the top of her gown. I took the opportunity to explore her form with my other hand before joining them at the dress hooks along her back. One by one, they gave way to my efforts. Finally, I slid the garment off her shoulders to pool on the floor alongside my coat. As erotic as the sight of our clothes crumpled together was, her gown was too lovely, her efforts too exquisite, to treat so callously.

"Step for me, Duchess."

Her answer was nothing but a distraught murmur, before following my instructions. Reluctantly I stepped away to lay her gown on the nearby settee before kicking my own coat out of my path back to her side. Her voice was thick, heavy with want, when she whispered my name.

"Yes?"

She started, shaking her head before continuing. "My petticoat."

"What about it, love?"

"Take it off, please."

She received a gentle nip at the joining of her neck and shoulder. I had become so fond of that spot. I freed her from the fastenings of her petticoat. Her long stays were revealed beneath. She tensed once more, nearly imperceptibly. Concerned that nerves were rising, I paused in my undressing to free her hair from its jeweled pins and flowers. I brushed the wayward curls that were revealed over her shoulder before aligning her back to my front. I offered a gentle kiss to the top of her crown, rubbing her arms and shoulders in silent comfort.

"Jules, Duchess, should I stop?" Her negative shake was decisive, but I wouldn't proceed until she told me to continue. "Juliet?"

"I want this, Michael. I do. I'm just nervous. I've never... No one has ever... Well, of course, you know that. And, of course, you've... Well, you've done this before. Which is good; one of us should know what we're doing. It's just that... You're so good at this, and I'm... I don't know what to do. And before, by the bridge, I didn't... I didn't do anything, and I wanted to, but I didn't know what to do and I just—"

I turned her to face me, tipping her delicate cleft chin up with a finger and silenced her panic with a kiss. She met my lips enthusiastically. I made to pull away, and she continued, "I just want to..."

"Clearly, I'm not doing this properly if you can still think all that, Duchess."

"But—"

"Juliet, I need you to listen carefully. If you want to stop right now, send me on my way, and head to bed, this will still be the best night of my entire life."

I couldn't help but press a kiss to her shy smile.

"If you want me to take you upstairs and hold you all night, this will still be the best night of my entire life. If you want me to love you right here on this table until neither one of us can walk, it will still be the best night of my entire life. There is nothing you can do to make this evening anything but perfect."

I had to pause when she buried her face in my chest and wrapped her arms tight around me in a warm embrace.

"Stop trying to distract me. I don't need you to do anything. Believe me when I say being in your presence is more than arousing. In fact, if you tried to do anything, this would all be over embarrassingly quickly." A soft pile of curls brushed my chin with her huffed laugh.

"But I want to please you."

"You do please me, Duchess. If, while we're together, there's something you want to try, talk to me, and we will discuss how to go about it."

She peeked her head out from my chest with that. "So... If, say, I wanted to undress you, all I would have to do is say so?"

"Yes." I could feel my grin shift to one side. I was pleased she seemed to have overcome some of her shyness.

"I want to take off your cravat."

"Do you want assistance, or would you like to try on your own?"

"I can do it."

"Very well," I offered with a gesture toward my neck.

Her delicate hands slid up my chest, burning a path toward my neck. She gently began to tug at the knot until it gave way. Unwrapping it once, twice, before she pulled it free from my starched collar, dropping it aside.

"I'm going to take off your waistcoat now."

I offered a nod of agreement before her hands traced their previous path. Starting from the bottom, she worked over the series of buttons. Once she reached the top, she pushed it off my shoulders.

"Your shirt?"

She tugged it loose from my breeches before I could respond. I helped her tug it up and over my head.

"Oh!" Her eyes were wide and beseeching, her mouth still rounded on the sound. She was staring at my chest with what I was fairly certain was a mixture of arousal and confusion.

"Good oh?" I questioned with a crooked grin.

She nodded absently, dragging her eyes back to mine. Her hands hovered no more than an inch off my chest. The not-quite-touch was more arousing than any actual touch I had ever received. Finally, when I could take no more of the exquisite torture, I caught one of her hands in mine. Lacing our fingers together, I pressed them over my heart. The fierce pounding beneath was all her doing. She needed to know the havoc she wrought.

With my unoccupied hand I tipped her chin back. "You can touch, Duchess. If you want."

"Anywhere?"

She was eager now, less tentative. That was how I wanted her, free to explore. The thought was unbearably arousing, and I could barely suppress a groan at the image of her hot hands on me.

"Everywhere," I promised solemnly. "Anywhere you want, I'm yours."

She surprised me by sliding her free hand to my wrist, pulling it free for inspection. Trailing delicate fingers up my forearm, I swallowed against the onslaught of unidentifiable emotion.

"Do you remember? That day at the bridge? It was so hot, and you rolled up your sleeves? It was most improper."

"I remember every minute at that bridge, but I only recall your actions. I assure you, that particular moment of impropriety was unconsciously done."

"I had... feelings about it. I didn't understand until that day in the rain, when they were so magnified. But that was the first moment I can recall experiencing them."

"You were... aroused?"

"Yes, I suppose that's the word for it."

"At the sight of forearms?"

"Your forearms. Not just forearms in general. Is that wrong?" Her brow furrowed with concern at the thought of her attractions being incorrect.

I rushed to correct her misconception. "No! No, certainly not. I quite like the thought of you being aroused by any part of my person. I'm excited by every inch of you. It's only fair."

She tightened her hands around said forearms. Even this innocent touch was unbearably affecting.

"You're excited by me?" Her expression was eager, charming. My heart warmed at the sight and I couldn't help but press a quick kiss to her smile.

"I wasn't aware that was in question. My most sincere apologies, Duchess. The very thought of you enflames me."

Her answering shimmy was pleased, a little cocky. She dragged her hand up my arm to caress my bicep and shoulder. Her tentative exploration stirred both affection and lust in equal measure, more than any skilled lover's touch ever could. She gave my upper arm a delicate, testing squeeze before continuing on to my chest.

"Are there places you like best?"

"I wasn't aware that a simple touch on my forearms could

be arousing until you discovered that a few moments ago. I suspect the places I like best are whichever ones your hands are on at present."

She took that as permission to slide her hands along my chest gently, glancing along the contours. I left her to her own exploration as long as I could withstand. I took the opportunity to run my hands through her curls. Now that they were free from their pins, the curls were even softer than I remembered. At length, I was forced to leave the lure of her silken hair for the temptation of flesh. First fingers, then lips, followed by tongue sought the sweet surface of her throat.

"Michael..." Her voice was a soft whine, and I needed to hear my name in that tone a thousand times again.

"Yes, Duchess?"

"I can't think when you do that." My answering chuckle was just shy of wicked.

"You're not supposed to." I nipped the delicate freckle dusting her collar bone. "May I remove your stays?"

Her breath caught before she offered a tentative "Yes."

"You can say no. Tell me to stop."

"I know, but I want you to keep going. I'm just... nervous."

My heart swells with that, and I pulled away from her neck to press a comforting kiss to her forehead before delicately turning her away from me to face the laces of her stays. Nerves I could manage.

"Alright, nervous. Are you feeling anything else?" I whispered in her ear while sliding her hair back over her shoulder, pressing a kiss to her nape.

"My heart. It skips when you do that."

"Do what?"

"The kiss. I like it."

"So more of this..."

I demonstrated with tongue and gentle teeth while sliding

a hand gently down her spine, catching on the lacing of her stays.

Her "yes" was more of a moan than a word and it burned low in my stomach.

"When you draw your hand down my back, I can almost feel the path you're taking before you get there, anticipate it."

That sparked an idea. I pressed a kiss higher up, just beneath her hairline at the top of her spine before moving to the next vertebra. By the third, she was shivering in my arms. The fourth elicited a whimper.

"How is that? Do you like that?"

There was a slight movement beneath her shift, her thighs rubbing together. I couldn't suppress a groan at the sight.

"So much..."

"What are you feeling now?"

Far from trying to draw her from her nerves, I was just desperate for the answer now, to hear confirmations of her desires.

"I... That place, between my legs. Every time you touch me I feel it there, even though you're not touching me there."

"Arousal?" I was desperate for a yes.

"I don't think that word is sufficient, but it's the best I have."

I reached the place where her shift met her spine now.

"That's good. That is how I want you. Too desperate for words."

She whimpered.

"Still nervous?"

Her negative was definitive this time. I was confident to begin my work on the lacings under my fingers. In my eagerness, I loosened it in mere seconds and slid the straps from her shoulders. I traced one finger down her spine, only separated from warm skin by the thin fabric of her chemise. This time my finger tapped down the bumps of her spine instead of the lacing.

"How are you feeling about the chemise. Should it stay or go?"

"Off, please."

"So polite," I teased before edging the thin fabric up and over her thighs, her waist, her breasts, her curls. Her whimper was barely audible under my groan. The sight of her, clad in only stockings and slippers, wrenched the sound from me. "So beautiful..."

I took only a moment to enjoy the sight before returning to the newly bared skin I was intently tracing with my lips and tongue, kneeling to reach the lower divots at the base.

"How are you feeling now?" I whispered against her.

"So good..." She seemed unsteady on her feet, the thought that it was due to my ministrations was heady.

I drew both hands up as I slowly stood before cupping her breasts, offering her ample time to stop me. Her answering "*Michael*" had a potent effect in my breeches. I turned her to face me, and she followed willingly, all previous hints of apprehension seem to have abandoned her. I was left with a flushed, warm woman.

She dragged me, hand fisted in my hair, pulling my lips down to hers. My bare chest met hers, pebbled nipples dragging against my skin. The feeling wrenched an inelegant, desperate grunt from deep inside me. Needing to be closer still, I lifted her by her thighs onto the table behind her. The very same one she hid under all those months ago. This was a much better use for it—crowding against her bare center, hidden only by dark curls.

Delicacy abandoned me in my urgency, and the best I could hope for was something short of brute. Tilting her jaw with my fingers to open her lips to mine, I thrust my tongue deep to slide against hers with an accompanying grind of my hips against her damp mound. She clutched at my shoulders, her small nails branding my flesh. All the while, she breathed quiet desperate noises into my mouth for me to taste. She cried out when I abandoned her lips for the miles of flushed skin that was bared for me to savor. I didn't have the patience to tease her further. Her tight nipples capping heavy breasts called to me, and I covered one with my mouth and sucked less gently than I ought, pinching the other between two fingers. Her hands fisted in my hair, pulling me impossibly closer.

I switch my attentions to her other breast. I couldn't neglect it. She curled one of her stocking-clad legs around my hip to pull my arousal against hers. Our matching groans echoed in the empty library. I could sense her wetness through the thick fabric of my breeches and felt myself harden even more desperately.

I wrenched myself from her skin. "Jules. I want to taste you. Can I taste you?"

"Anything..." She tried to drag my mouth back to her breasts. Briefly, the fog of arousal cleared enough for me to realize that she might not have grasped my meaning.

I slipped a hand from her chest down, brushing it against her damp curls. "I want to taste you here."

Her moan might have been my name. It was difficult to determine, but she nodded enthusiastically and pulled my lips back to meet hers.

She tragically broke away to whisper, "Anything, anywhere you want. I'm yours."

I couldn't help but thrust my still-clothed erection against her cleft in response. I reluctantly pulled my hips away, working my way down in damp kisses and nips. I paused to appreciate her breasts once more, to nibble on a rib, swirl my tongue in her navel, and press a fervent kiss just above her mound. I urged her to lie back before settling to my knees before her. Her shyness peaked once more, but she followed my lead, her thighs pressed closed against my scrutiny.

Her eyes met mine over the curving lines of her body, gaze still sensual, the heat in them slightly dampened.

"Yes?" I offered her one more opportunity to decline my advances. Her nod was still sure.

Instead of pressing my lips straight to her center, I decided to ease her into the idea. I grasped one slipper-clad foot in my hand, sliding it off her foot. Once free of its confines, I glided my hands up to grasp the top of her stockings, held up by a simple fold, and guided it down her leg. Lips followed silk with only the slightest of detours to the back of her knee. She gave me a whimper for my efforts. I repeated the process with her other leg.

She was finally completely bare before me. Rubbing her outer thighs comfortingly, I pressed another kiss above her center before gently parting her legs, sliding first one, then the other over my shoulder.

For a moment, I breathed in the sight of her, slick pink center spread for my perusal. It was a rush to realize my breath brushing across her slit increased her arousal. I didn't recognize it until her needy pants met my own. When I could hold back no longer, I covered her with my mouth, lips and tongue more enthusiastic than skilled. Her eyes held mine as I tasted her for the first time. She was even sweeter here, but also earthier. It was intoxicating, and I never wanted to leave. I was distracted as I tongued her nub and entrance in equal measure, finally settling into a rhythm. Working her pearl with my tongue and lips, I thrusted a finger in time. When I curled the finger up on the exit, her hand fisted tightly in my hair, her hips lifting desperately from the table, seeking. Her grip on my hair was just shy of painful and all the more arousing for it.

Now that I'd discovered what she liked, I stayed with that, only pausing to add a second finger. All too soon, she was clenching around my fingers. I strengthened my thrusts and pressed harder against her with my tongue before fixing my lips around her bud and sucking. All at once, a half scream half groan burst from her and her channel tightened rhythmically against my probing fingers. I froze, keeping the pressure constant, and she worked around me. One by one, her muscles unclenched, and I pulled my lips away reluctantly. I slipped my fingers free from her but kept a gentle palm pressed against her arousal. I didn't want her to come too far down; I wasn't finished with her yet.

Thirty

GRAYSON HOUSE, LONDON - JULY 1, 1814

JULIET

THAT WAS HEAVEN. I had the same thought that day in the rain, that it was the very definition of ecstasy, but this... Words were insufficient. I slowly returned to my body from my visit to the stars. Michael kept a palm pressed against my center, something substantial to thrust against when occasional shudders ran through me. As awareness returned, and I realized I was offering desperate whimpers with each heaving breath. The blood rushing through my ears slowed, I realized he had been whispering to me between gentle kisses to my thighs and stomach. "My sweet Duchess, so passionate for me. How did I get so lucky? So lovely—"

My lips and throat were dry from panting for him, but eventually, I was able to form the letters of his name. I struggled to rise and, once he figured out my intention, he offered his assistance, cradling me to his chest.

"Was that supposed to happen?"

He chuckled. "That was the intention, yes."

"What about you? Can I do that for you?"

"Well, I don't know if it's exactly the same, but yes, something similar."

"Will you show me how?"

His gaze was tender. "I love you."

With that ardent statement he pressed a soft kiss to the spot on my forehead that was rapidly becoming his. "Let me take you to bed first."

He pulled away, and plucked his shirt from the pile before straightening it out. I mourned the loss of his chest before he surprised me by pulling to over my head and settling it around me. His smile was soft as he whispered, "Perfect."

With that, he began to gather the rest of our things. His hands were more than full when he turned to my gown. I watched the internal struggle to add it to the pile already in his arms. With a giggle, I grabbed it and a candlestick before moving about the room, blowing the rest out. I pulled him to trail up the stairs. Faced with the separation between the family and guest rooms at the top I turned back to him with a questioning gaze.

Understanding dawned in his eyes. "The fire will be lit in your room; they weren't expecting me."

Decision made, I led him in the direction of the guest room I occupied.

After following me into the room, he added our clothing to the small pile I had created this evening. He paused, just long enough for me to set the candle down and lay the dress over a chair before he crowded me back against the nearest surface, the door. As soon as my back hit the door, his mouth was on mine, and his hands were everywhere. All of his previous ardor returned in full force. My own hands slid eagerly but uselessly to the buttons of his breeches, unable and unwilling to separate long enough to maneuver the button through its fabric prison. Eventually, he moved his attentions to my neck, pulling his shirt to the side so my entire shoulder fell free. He bent to enjoy the newly uncovered skin.

Frantically I undid the buttons, shoving his breeches and stockings down to catch on his boots. Frustrated at yet another obstacle, his name escaped, more whine than word. He chuckled but assisted me, tugging off his boots and the rest, leaving him naked before me.

He was nothing like I had imagined, and somehow all the more perfect for it. His length was hard and proud rising between us. I wanted to touch him. He seemed to encourage my explorations earlier, but perhaps this was different. I met his gaze, about to voice the question when he answered for me.

"You can touch anywhere you want, but if you keep looking at me like that..." His chuckle was soft. "If you keep looking at me like that, this is going to be over far too soon."

Permission granted, I tentatively wrapped a hand around his length. He met my touch with a curse.

"I don't know what you mean by it being over too soon."

His hips shuddered against my hand. I understood it to be a rhythm he was seeking, similar to the one he offered me earlier, and I strived to match it. Glancing up, I sought to determine my success from his expression. His attention was on my hand, working between us, before his head fell all the way back. His eyes were pressed tight, his lip caught between his teeth. Slickness was building between my palm, and his member and his hips met my every pump. With a reluctant groan, he pulled away from me, and I couldn't restrain the whimper at the loss.

"So good, Duchess. You're so good for me." He was still panting, swallowing between sentences.

"Why did you stop me? I want to make you feel like that too."

He gave me a gentle kiss in answer.

"It's not quite like you, Duchess. Once that happens to

me, it's some time before it can happen again. For you, the only limit is the hours in the day and our stamina." I set that arousing thought to the side for later perusal while I sought for clarification.

"Oh, how long?"

He groaned. "You're going to kill me, Duchess." Before I could apologize, he continued, "I suspect with you, not too terribly long at all. Still, longer than I'd like. Now, I promised you a bed, and we need to talk before pressing forward."

He drew back the bed coverings before sitting and pulling me closer. He tugged at the hem of his shirt, resting in the middle of my thighs before looking to me questioningly. Rather than answer with words, I slipped the shirt over my head, tossing it in the direction of the aforementioned pile.

He groaned. "Shouldn't have done that until after we talked..."

Despite his comment, he backed farther on the bed, pulling me down beside him. I tucked into his side. He rested one arm around my shoulders, the other tugging the covers over us before settling at my waist.

He finally began in a low voice. "What do you know of how children are created?"

"Just that it can happen between a husband and wife."

Then a horrific thought dawned on me, and I sat up with a start.

"Juliet?"

"Oh, Michael. I completely forgot. You'll never forgive me!"

He tried to tug me back down to him, but I couldn't allow it. Not until I told him everything. I could already feel the tears building.

"Jules, Duchess. It can't be so bad as all that. Tell me."

I could not find the words. After a full minute of starting

and aborting the attempt, words abandoned me. Finally, I blurted out, "I'm infertile."

His only response was a slow blink.

"You cannot want to marry me. I cannot provide you with children."

Still unsuccessful in his effort to pull me back to his arms, he sat up with me. When I refused to meet his eyes, he tucked his fist under my chin, gently directing me to look at him. "Why do you think you're infertile?"

"My father said it was likely. My mother was only able to conceive me."

He swallowed, and his head dipped back with his eyes closed, and my heart broke. Right down the middle.

I could not possibly stay in this bed while he rejected me. Struggling to free myself from the covers, he startled.

"Where are you going?"

I could not stop the tears now. "I understand. You don't need to say anything. I'll leave..." He tugged me back, strong arms caging me to his chest.

"Don't you dare leave this bed."

"But you're mad."

"Damn it all, Jules. I'm mad at your father, not you."

"What?"

"I'm mad because it's not always the woman. Men can be infertile, too. Your father had two wives unable to bear children after many years of trying, so the only commonality was him. There's no reason to think you can't have as many children as you wish. That your mother wouldn't have had many children with a different husband.

"But I feel I need to explain. I love *you*, not your ability or inability to offer me children. I will love you just as much if we have ten children or two or none."

It was all I could do to bury my face into my chest as the tears poured out, the relief escaping in the only way it could.

"Now, my beautiful Duchess, I am perfectly content to never think of your father in this or any other bed. Is that acceptable?"

I nodded against his chest, enthusiastic. Gathering myself enough, I pulled free. He wiped the remaining tears with a thumb, and my heart swelled with affection.

Assured of my composure, he settled back against the pillows, and I allowed him to pull me into his embrace.

"Now, where were we before you decided to give me a small fit of apoplexy?"

"The process of making children."

"Ah, yes." He was running his fingers through my hair and it was so comforting. "It doesn't have to happen between a husband and wife. It can happen between unmarried couples as well. If I were to take the part of me that was hard before, and enter the place inside you until I spend, a child could result. There are ways to lessen the chances, but the only way to be sure is for me not to enter you."

"Why is it hard no longer?"

His smile was wry. "I don't find it particularly arousing watching the woman I love try to escape my bed in tears."

"But it will become hard again?"

"Yes, and as charming as your priorities are, I want to be sure you understand the choices before us and the consequences for those decisions." He focused mostly on the canopy above me as he explained the process, his teasing is only mild at my questioning. "I fully intend to apply for a special license in the morn if that impacts your decision in any way."

"You do?"

"As long as you approve. I've spent far too much time without you these last weeks. Also, if I remember correctly, your trousseau should be all but completed by now."

"Mostly. I was given to understand I also need night dresses, but I didn't feel right taking Sophie's."

He rolled himself above me. "Juliet, I can safely promise you have no need of night dresses. However, if you wish them or anything else, I have more than enough that you can purchase everything the modiste has to offer and more."

"You do?"

He pressed a warm kiss to my lips at that question.

"You're certainly not a fortune hunter, are you my Duchess?"

"You have a fortune?"

His chuckle was smooth, silken.

"Quite a vast one. Trading on gentlemen's dishonor is quite lucrative. You'll want for nothing."

"I hope you know that's not why I wish to marry you."

"You've made that quite clear."

"I think I'd quite like to feel you inside me tonight. Is that acceptable?"

He froze for a moment above me before bursting into laughter, tucking his head in my neck.

"I'm going to spend my entire life trying to keep up with you, aren't I?"

"Probably, but you didn't answer my question."

"I've created a monster..."

I was about to press him again, when he took my lips with his, his tongue sweeping inside in that sensual way I felt deep inside my belly.

When he broke away for air I replied, "Was that a yes?"

"Yes, now stop thinking for a few moments. I have work to do here."

"Work?"

"Yes, you're far too coherent."

With his gentle nip on my neck, my retort disappeared from my mind. His newly returned, hardness was brushing against my opening in the cradle of my hips. Just that whisper was enough to reignite the flames that had cooled with our conversation. His lips and tongue on mine mimicked the gentle roll of his hips above me, stoking the fire. Dimly, I became aware that the wistful whines I heard were mine. His attention shifted to my neck, making thorough work of the sensitive flesh there. I had no idea sensations in one part of my being could be felt in entirely different areas, but my throat was directly connected to the pleasure point between my legs.

My hands resumed their post, tangled in his hair. The soft thick waves served as purchase, pinning him in place. When he gave a sharp nip at my shoulder followed by an apologetic kiss, my hand fisted unconsciously in his hair. He let out a groan that was all pleasure, and his gentle thrusts roughened slightly.

An idea sparked with that groan, and I used the hand in his hair to move him to where I was most desperate for touch. His response was a half growl, half purr around my breast where I directed him and a thrust that brought his hardness against that pleasurable button he made sing earlier. He mumbled against my breast about how wonderful I am and how good I taste, and I felt more than comprehended his words.

His free hand slid down my stomach, pausing above the place I was desperate for him to touch once again. He lifted his head with a questioning brow. In answer, I grabbed his hand and moved it to my entrance. He chuckled before moving to my other breast and sliding a finger inside me simultaneously. I felt his grin when I arched off the bed, my hands restless in his hair, on his shoulders, his back. I felt my earlier peak rebuilding, stronger now. My hips met his hand eagerly. In short order, he added a second than a third finger. Slowly, he pulled back. I couldn't restrain my whimper at the loss.

He pressed himself to hover above me, eyes seeking mine. Before he could ask the question, I replied with a fervent

"Yes." Instead of pushing inside as I expected, he hovered over me, an indescribable warmth in his eyes. His fingers brushed damp curls back from my forehead. I responded with the only answer to such tenderness. "I love you." His kiss was gentle but full of feeling. Finally, he pushed forward, and we were joined.

It hurt less than I had expected, but he paused at the hilt, panting against my lips. I gave an experimental wiggle, and his grunt was inelegant but heady. His forehead fell to my shoulder. With another hip roll, he pulled out slightly and thrust back in gently. He somehow hit that spot inside of me that was everything wonderful. My hands found his hips, encouraging him. He seemed to understand my unspoken meaning, finding an unhurried rhythm.

The sensation from before was building once again, each thrust bringing me higher. He was whispering in my ear, words of love, words of lust, and everything in between. Each press of his hips somehow felt *more* than the one before. Mine met his at every opportunity. Then he dropped a hand down between us, to that magical spot at the top of my mound. Without warning the ecstasy from before crashed over me.

By the time I returned once more from the heavens, his movements had become erratic. He thrust once, twice more, burying himself to the hilt with a desperate groan. His breathing against my ear was harsh. I wrapped my arms even tighter around him.

"Oh Michael, that was wonderful!"

He gave me an exhausted chuckle in return before pulling from me and flopping gracelessly onto his back. He yanked me against him once more, curled against his side with my head resting on his shoulder. Our breaths were harsh, the only sound above the crackling fire in my room.

Once in a while, a jolt of residual pleasure shuddered through me. He pulled me even tighter to him in response with a whispered, "Come here." A forehead kiss accompanied the gesture. Eventually, our breathing evened out. His fingers trailed through my hair soothingly. I used the opportunity to further explore the sweat-slicked panes of his chest with wanton fingertips. When he finally spoke, his voice was a rumble from his chest.

"I can't believe you agreed to marry me. That I'll wake up with you in my arms every morning for the rest of my days. Juliet, every time I look at you, I think I couldn't possibly love you more. Then I see you again and I do."

"Michael..." My own voice was thick against the emotions rising in my chest.

"Enough sentimentality. Any second now, I will move. I will move, and I will fetch something to clean us. Just as soon as I can feel my legs."

In response, I started to rise in his stead. He tightened his arm around me in response, trapping me to his chest.

"That was not a suggestion for you to move. You, my darling Duchess, are to remain in this bed, naked and wanting, until an hour or so before our wedding. The only exception is if this house is actually on fire."

With that order he did rise, dipped a cloth in the nearby basin, and returned to see to my intimate areas. He tossed it in the general direction of our clothing pile before returning to my arms. Smoothing the floral bed coverings over us, he shrouded us in a quiet peace. His eyes were closed but his fingers still swirled lazily through my hair. I lay there, tracing patterns through the sparse hair on his chest, wondering if the question at the tip of my tongue was entirely inappropriate.

He preempted my musings. "Ask it."

"What?"

"Whatever question is burning in that beautiful head of yours."

"How did...?"

"When you want to ask something but you're not sure if you should, you open and close your mouth like a fish." I accompanied my denial with a playful swat to his chest. "Then how did I know you wanted to ask something?"

I had no rebuttal to that, so I was forced to ask my question. "When can we do that again?'

His answering laugh brought forth my own.

"In the morning, Duchess. I need rest and possibly food if I'm to keep you satisfied. Now go to sleep."

"You'll show me what to do in the morning?"

"I already showed you what to do."

"But you did all the work."

"You really are going to kill me... I'll show you whatever you want just as soon as I'm rested enough to reliably move my extremities."

He said that with a final forehead kiss before pulling me still closer. I started again before he shushed me. After a moment or so of quiet, his breathing evened out as he fell asleep. My worries of a sleepless night proved to be unfounded, and I joined him in an exhausted but satisfied slumber a few moments later.

Thirty-One

MICHAEL

I AWOKE with a mouthful of hair and a numbness in my arm. My heart stuttered once I recalled the source of both predicaments. When I opened my eyes, it was to a wild mess of tangled curls and little else. The sun, barely beginning to stream through the window, turned some of the chocolate strands to cinnamon. Slowly, so as not to wake her, I brushed the cloud of her hair back.

Arms full of warm, naked Juliet, it was the best morning of my life. My erection made its agreement obvious. I ignored it in favor of observing her in this unguarded state. Her pale skin was scattered with the results of my admiration, and her neck and chest were still reddened with my lovemaking. An entirely inappropriate feeling of pleasure surfaced at the thought that her gown might not hide all of the evidence.

Dawn broke, a ray of light landed across her closed lids, and she gave a sleepy grumble in protest, burying her face against my chest. Just then, blood returned to my arm, and a painful tingling began. I wiggled my fingers, trying to do so without waking her. The drowsy kiss on my chest accompanied by a warm hum was evidence of my failure. I pressed a kiss to her forehead and whispered a greeting.

"Morning," she mumbled in return before rubbing the sleep from her eyes with a shy smile.

"Are you hungry?"

She nodded with an enticing stretch, freeing my arm entirely so I could rise to ring the bell. Task completed, I bundled both of us under the bed coverings.

"How are you feeling?" The question was paired with a hand sliding low on her back, emphasizing my meaning.

"Perfect."

"Not sore?" She looked puzzled at my question for a moment before pressing her thighs together with a slight wince and nod. "I'll ask them to fill a bath once they bring breakfast." I pulled her back to my chest and rubbed her shoulders and back soothingly.

I was surprised when it was not Anna but Mary, looking slightly worse for wear, who knocked on the door with the breakfast tray. There was a great deal of blushing and stammering on both her part and Juliet's. Mary was one for gossip. Juliet may believe she was thoroughly ruined last night, but I needed to head off the household rumors.

"Mary, can you have a note sent to Augie? I need him to set up a meeting with my solicitor and a visit to the Doctors Commons. Lady Juliet did me the great honor of agreeing to be my wife yesterday." At least the gossip downstairs would be accurate now.

"Oh, that is wonderful news! Congratulations to both of you." Her countenance was much improved with the acquisition of gossip. "I'll just go fetch a second tray and have a note sent to Augie."

"No need on the tray, Mary. But thank you."

She disappeared out the door with a quick half-bob, half-curtsy.

"That will be all over downstairs in the next five minutes. I hope you haven't changed your mind." I strived for a casual tone as I spread the jam on her toast and handed it over to her before filling the cup with tea from the pot.

She took a prim bite of her toast with an equally studied air. "I suppose I shall have to accept my fate." Trading toast for tea she took a sip before continuing. "Such a terrible fate, too. To marry a kind, handsome, intelligent man who professes to love me and sets my entire world aflame. I can think of nothing worse."

I enjoyed a sip from her abandoned teacup to hide my relieved smile.

"Well, I hear you're quite famous for throwing over fiancés, if it's truly such a terrible future." I stole a bite from her toast before peeking under the cloche to see what else Mary had brought.

She sat up to face me fully before responding. "Michael, I can think of no better fate than to be your wife."

Quest for sustenance forgotten, I marveled at her ability to say exactly what I most needed to hear, even before I understood its necessity. She pulled the tray from my lap and set it on the side table before settling a gentle hand against my jaw.

"Now, dearest fiancé, I believe you promised me a lesson this morning..."

It was all I could do to provide a very insincere chastisement for her insatiability before delving into a very thorough, hands-on lesson.

～

SOMETIME LATER, with all appetites temporarily satisfied, her delicious curves were pressed against my side once more.

"Jules, I need to discuss a few things with you before I

meet with my solicitor." She offered little more than a contented hum of acknowledgment. "Do you have any thoughts about the wedding? We could likely wait until Kate can be summoned from Lincolnshire if you desire it. Or, if you wish, more time to prepare."

"I had assumed we would wed as soon as possible. Is that not what you desire?"

"Oh, it's very much what I desire, but I did not wish to rush you."

"I am available at your leisure, sir." She pressed a sweet kiss to my chest just above where my heart skipped at her words.

"Monday then." She nodded in agreement with her chin pressed to my chest, head bobbing in a manner that warmed my chest. "About our future situation, I was thinking I might give up day-to-day management of Wayland's and just retain an ownership stake." She tried to sit up, but I tightened my hold to keep her in my arms where she belonged.

"But why?"

"I haven't been managing it since I met you, not really. You're far too distracting. Augie has done a wonderful job in my absence, and he would hold up to the responsibility well. If I continued managing it, we would be forced to remain in London for the majority of the year. That's the other thing I wanted to discuss with you. What would you say to us letting a country estate?"

"You're serious?"

"Yes. Unless you object."

"I have no objection, of course. I adored every moment we spent in the country together. But Wayland's is your life's work. I can't ask you to give that up."

"My life's work of a few years. I'd quite like your happiness to be my life's work going forward. And you're not asking; I'm offering. I wouldn't give it up entirely. I'd still have income from it and some say in decisions."

"If you're certain. I believe I would be happier in the country, yes."

"I have one last, slightly less pleasant question to put to you. I intend to transfer your father's debts to my personal funds when I meet with my solicitor. I can have his debts forgiven, and he will be released from prison. Does that meet with your agreement?"

The tentative bite of her lip was unexpected. "Did Augie tell you?"

"Tell me what?"

"He purchased the additional debts my father worked up at some less reputable gaming hells. Including the deed to the house. They amounted to thousands. I asked him not to, but he insisted." Her refusal to remove her face from my chest and her guilty tone caused my heart to give a little lurch.

"Duchess, Augie doesn't have to clear expenses with me. I told you I was vastly wealthy, money no concern. I put up £5,000 a night at the club, sometimes more." She peered up from my chest now, eyes round with shock. I couldn't resist the urge to boast further. "I opened Wayland's with £100,000 I got off three gentlemen playing hazard in a single day." That resulted in a slow blink before she burst into laughter. Not the reaction I was expecting.

Between peals of laughter she struggled to explain. "You have £100,000?" The question was accompanied by an undignified snort. It was rather charming. I chose not to correct her by telling her I now had vastly more. "My father has been telling me for the last ten years at least that he would never be able to make me an advantageous match." Infectious giggles escaped between every word. "But he was quite inadvertently successful, wasn't he? He led me right to the richest man in the country!"

"Not quite the richest, Duchess." That pulled even more laughter from her, and she wiped tears from her eyes.

"It's just, the irony…" She struggled for composure, and after several failed attempts she seemed to pull herself together. "I suppose we should have him released since it seems the effort will not put you in the gaol as well. Perhaps after the wedding, though?"

"You wish to wait?"

"He deserves to feel the weight of his choices for a bit longer, I think. Given that he was quite willing to allow me to live with the consequences of his actions for the rest of my life."

I rewarded her vindictiveness with a nip to the neck. I had no idea I found such pettiness so alluring. I was plotting to entice her to another vow anticipation. Unfortunately, there was a knock on the door from the sitting room. I retrieved the bedclothes from the floor where they were tossed earlier, and covered us both before Juliet offered entry. This time it was Anna who poked her head in.

"I thought you might like a bath, Lady Juliet. Before we work on your hair. I have it prepared in the sitting room."

Juliet's hand flew to her head. Feeling the state of her curls, she groaned. If I was honest, I was quite pleased with the mess I'd created, but I decided to keep that to myself. I was also hoping to have the honor of righting them.

I would have to leave this bed at some point if I was to meet with my solicitor and the archbishop. I had a feeling he would require some financial convincing of the sanctity of my word before he was compelled to issue the license. However, the thought of Juliet in the bath was much more tempting than my responsibilities, no matter how important.

"Thank you, Anna, I can take over from here."

She just laughed in response, before leaving us to our own ends.

I helped a blushing Juliet into the warm water before settling beside the tub.

"Can you bring my comb over? It's on that table there." She gestured toward the window, and I fetched it while she dipped her head under the water, surfacing just as I returned. She tried to take the comb from me, but I was stubborn.

"Tell me what to do."

"Start from the ends, one lock at a time."

"Lean forward."

Her expression was one of surprised delight when I slid behind her in the copper tub. She settled herself comfortably against me, and I took a moment to press a kiss to the delightful freckle on the side of her neck, the one I have claimed as my own. Her hum of appreciation was enticing, but I had a task to complete. I started with one damp curl and followed her instructions, working from the end up. Slowly it succumbed to my efforts, leaving behind a perfect ringlet. One by one, I tamed them until her hair was returned to some semblance of order. In the meantime, she made a luxurious display of soaping every tantalizing inch of herself during my work.

"Did you really join me just to comb my hair?"

My reply was a teasing, "Of course. Did you have some other activity in mind?"

"You know I did."

I brushed her righted curls over one shoulder, returning to my freckle once more. "Tell me?"

"Michael..." It was more whine than word at this point.

"You know I like to hear you say it, Duchess."

Her abrupt turn startled me; I had anticipated another whine of my name. She faced me, pressing her lips fervently against my own. When she pulled away, bright eyes meeting mine, she whispered, "I love you," in a tone of absolute sincerity. In that moment, I vowed to spend the rest of my days returning her love as she deserved.

Epilogue

REVELLO HOUSE, KENT - AUGUST 24, 1814

JULIET

My husband guided me over the uneven terrain. My sight was missing, defeated by the fabric of his cravat. I felt his every touch more acutely and I set that thought aside for a later time, following the lead of his hand at the small of my back.

"Just a bit farther."

"I should hope so," I complained with mock annoyance. In response to my impertinence, the hand on my back slipped farther down to give a gentle smack to my bottom—something else for further consideration.

"Behave, or you won't receive your present."

That was a lie, and we both knew it. In the near two months since we had wed, we had discussions of his new-found penchant for gift-giving. I knew the desire stemmed from his own insecurities, but they were entirely unnecessary. My love for him was not contingent on his pocketbook. I suspected only time would ease his worry. Time and the unending affection I was eager to bestow. Though our wedding had eased my own nerves somewhat, I still found myself scolded for my far too frequent, unnecessary apologies. These worries, too, would only fade with time and his love.

Just to be difficult, I stopped abruptly. He crashed gently into me. In his hand must have been some sort of basket because it bumped into my hip when his free hand wrapped around my stomach to steady me. My mischief ensured his front was pressed firmly along my back. I pressed even more firmly against him, teasing him further still. His only response was a low grumble against my ear, somewhere between a purr and a growl.

"Was that my fault?"

"You're lucky we're almost there." His voice had gone low, just as it did in our bed. I felt it at the base of my spine and couldn't suppress a shiver of desire. That earned me a chuckle before he resumed his leading.

We had gone no more than another hundred paces when he guided me to a stop. I could hear the gentle burble of slowly running water. The birdsong was familiar, but I could not place it. I inhaled deeply. Underneath the prominent scent of vanilla and citrus, the scent of Michael, I detected an indefinable bouquet of wildflowers and some sort of fruit. Another breath and I recognized the scent of overripe raspberries. A smile bloomed when the pieces slipped into place.

"Now?"

His fingers tugged at the knot, working it gently from between the curls that claimed it for their own. Finally, free of my bindings, he whispered, "Yes," pulling the cravat away. My guess was slightly off. We were at our bridge but from the opposite bank. That explained the stronger scent of raspberries. I turned to him with a question in my eyes.

"You did say you wanted to live in the country."

A delighted laugh bubbled up from within, and I turned to wrap my arms around his neck.

"I let Revello House. Does it meet with your approval?"

"How could it not?"

"You haven't seen the house yet."

"It's perfect. Everything I could want is right here."

He met my grin with a kiss, and his smile formed to match mine.

He pulled away after a moment, pressing a kiss to my forehead. "Come, I've packed a picnic. I think it's well past time for you to teach me to embroider."

His plan had merit, but I had one of my own. I took one of his hands in mine, pulling him along with me as I crossed the bridge. He slowed in the middle, assuming I would stop here, but he allowed me to tug him farther, even in his confusion. Once we reached the other side, I led him farther, under the dogwood tree. His crooked smile widened when I took the basket from him and set it at our feet. Wrapping both hands around his neck, I pulled him down to me, my back hitting the bark.

"Perhaps later. I have a better idea."

His answering laughter was bright and warm, and my own joined his.

The End

≈

The *Most Imprudent Matches* series will continue with Augie and Anna's story:
The Baker and the Bookmaker.

To stay with Michael and Juliet on their bridge a little longer, you can find an extended bonus epilogue at
https://www.allyhudson.com/bonus-scenes.

Support the author, leave a review on Amazon!

Acknowledgments

I wanted to take this opportunity to thank my mother. Mom, you shared your unmatched love of reading. Also, the fact that I could always find a Regency to borrow before you got home explains a lot about my genre preferences. Your suggestions are wonderful, as always.

Martha, thank you for listening to me complain about this process far too often. Thank you for instilling a lifelong love of Mr. Darcy. Also, thank you for all the suggestions of books that are not romances. I will not read them, but I appreciate it nonetheless.

Thank you to Bryton, for keeping me alive and more or less sane in the last few years.

Thanks to Mariah, for actually reading my awful, unedited first drafts and pretending they're good.

Ali, thank you for encouraging me to be my pettiest self.

Thank you to Rebecca Sanchez at Once Upon an Editor and Ann Leslie Tuttle for helping me edit this into something great. I couldn't have done it without you.

Holly Perret at The Swoonies Romance art, my cover is so beautiful it makes me cry.

And finally, thank you to all the authors who came before me and those who will come after. Your work is an inspiration.

About the Author

Ally Hudson was raised in Hudson, Ohio. Currently, she resides in Fort Wayne, Indiana, with a very sassy dog. *Courting Scandal*, her debut novel, is the first in the *Most Imprudent Matches* series. She writes of cinnamon-bun heroes, snarky friendships, and true love. Her other hobbies include reading, embroidery, and re-watching television shows she has seen ten times already.

Printed in Great Britain
by Amazon

51971543R00150